THE GREAT GATSBY

F. SCOTT FITZGERALD

The Great Gatsby

With an Introduction and
Contemporary Criticism

Edited by STEPHEN MIRARCHI

Ignatius Critical Editions Editor
JOSEPH PEARCE

IGNATIUS PRESS SAN FRANCISCO

This book is a work of fiction. Any references to historical events, real people, or real places are used fictitiously. Other names, characters, places, and events are products of the author's imagination, and any resemblance to actual events or places or persons, living or dead, is entirely coincidental.

Cover art: Original cover art for the first edition of *The Great Gatsby* (Celestial Eyes) by Francis Cugat, 1925.
Public domain, collection of Princeton University.

Cover design by John Herreid

ISBN 978-1-62164-683-9 (PB)
ISBN 978-1-64229-300-5 (eBook)
Library of Congress Control Number 2023945042
Printed in India ♾

Dedicated once again to Zelda

Then wear the gold hat, if that will move her;
  If you can bounce high, bounce for her too,
Till she cry "Lover, gold-hatted, high-bouncing lover,
  I must have you!"

—Thomas Parke D'Invilliers

Thomas Parke D'Invilliers: fictional character from Fitzgerald's novel *This Side of Paradise*.

Tradition is the extension of Democracy through time; it is the proxy of the dead and the enfranchisement of the unborn.

Tradition may be defined as the extension of the franchise. Tradition means giving votes to the most obscure of all classes, our ancestors. It is the democracy of the dead. Tradition refuses to submit to the small and arrogant oligarchy of those who merely happen to be walking about. All democrats object to men being disqualified by the accident of birth; tradition objects to their being disqualified by the accident of death. Democracy tells us not to neglect a good man's opinion, even if he is our groom; tradition asks us not to neglect a good man's opinion, even if he is our father. I, at any rate, cannot separate the two ideas of democracy and tradition.

—G.K. Chesterton

Ignatius Critical Editions—Tradition-Oriented Criticism for a new generation

CONTENTS

INTRODUCTION

Stephen Mirarchi

I. The Critics on Fitzgerald and Catholicism

F. Scott Fitzgerald must have been fond of writing letters, considering not only how many survive but how many exhibit his obviously pleasurable exercise of an incisive intellect, contrasted just as often with the more than few that outpour his frank, cathartic confessions. On June 20, 1922, Fitzgerald wrote what he likely considered a routine letter to his editor, Maxwell Perkins. As sometimes happens in the history of lettered men, that epistle—and particularly one phrase or sentence of it—has become one of the most cited of all his works, especially for readers intrigued by the religious theme in *The Great Gatsby*:

> When I send on this last bunch of stories I may start my novel and I may not. Its locale will be the middle west and New York of 1885 I think. It will concern less superlative beauties that I run to usually + will be centered on a smaller period of time. It will have a catholic element. I'm not quite sure whether I'm ready to start it quite yet or not.[1]

The editors note at this point that "*The Great Gatsby* developed from Fitzgerald's projected novel, but no manuscript material from 1922 survives."[2] For readers familiar with both

[1] Matthew J. Bruccoli with Judith S. Baughman, eds., *The Sons of Maxwell Perkins: Letters of F. Scott Fitzgerald, Ernest Hemingway, Thomas Wolfe, and Their Editor* (Columbia: University of South Carolina Press, 2004), pp. 15–16.

[2] Ibid., p. 17, note 8.

the novel and Catholicism in general, the obvious question arises: What happened to that "catholic element"? May we simply take Fitzgerald's word that he eliminated it, since he admitted to librarian and writer John Jamieson[3] that "a story of mine, called 'Absolution' ... was intended to be a picture of [Gatsby's] early life, but that I cut it [from the novel] because I preferred to preserve the sense of mystery"?[4] And what then do we make of this same Fitzgerald who defended G.K. Chesterton—whose writings bear his faith as proudly as his witticisms—as one of the top British novelists?[5]

Lest we presume the classic status of the novel, perhaps an assessment of its place among critics and scholars should be established first. James Wood—widely regarded as one of the most perceptive and widely read literary critics of recent times—gives Gatsby, the character, as a prime example of a "large, round, towering" hero who is "vivid ... rich, and ... sustaining".[6] Academic giant Harold Bloom likewise includes Fitzgerald in an elite list of "major" American novelists, from Melville and Twain to Faulkner and Hemingway. Adapting a phrase of Ralph Waldo Emerson's, however, Bloom bemoans how this sequence of "imaginative literature ... gives us as yet neither a terrible nor a beautiful condensation of our national character ... [these authors] tend to keep their distance from the Orphic and Gnostic abysses of the national self."[7]

[3] For a detailed examination of Fitzgerald's education and book knowledge, see John Kuehl, "Scott Fitzgerald's Reading", *The Princeton University Library Chronicle* 22, no. 2 (Winter 1961): 58–89.

[4] F. Scott Fitzgerald, letter to John Jamieson, April 15, 1934, in *The Letters of F. Scott Fitzgerald*, ed. Andrew Turnbull (New York: Dell, 1963), p. 529.

[5] He considered only H.G. Wells to be better: "I read Mrs. Gerould's *British Novelists Limited* and think she underestimates [H.G.] Wells but is right in putting Mackenzie at the head of his school. She seems to disregard [J.M.] Barrie and Chesterton whom I should put above Bennett or in fact anyone except Wells." F. Scott Fitzgerald, letter to Edmund Wilson, Fall 1917, in Turnbull, *Letters*, p. 344.

[6] James Wood, *How Fiction Works*, Tenth Anniversary Edition (New York: Picador, 2018), p. 93. Note, however, that Wood uses Gatsby as a contrast to minor characters who, in the right hands, can produce similar effects.

[7] Harold Bloom, *The American Religion: The Emergence of the Post-Christian Nation* (New York: Touchstone, 1992), p. 16.

More specifically in terms of religion, a typical view of Fitzgerald's place in American letters vis-à-vis his Catholicism is expressed by theologian Chester Gillis: "From the beginning of the [twentieth] century ... Catholics could boast at least one prominent writer in every literary generation. Though many, like Kate Chopin, F. Scott Fitzgerald, and Jack Kerouac, were more Catholic by birth than practice, others consciously worked at creating a distinctly Catholic identity."[8] In his book-length study of Catholic engagement in mid-nineteenth- to early twentieth-century American literary culture, James Emmett Ryan similarly concludes that "writers both faithful and ambivalent participated in the 'dreamwork' of religious literary culture."[9] Ryan includes Fitzgerald in a select list of authors who "have all attempted to address Roman Catholic culture in their work" but admits that most of them, Fitzgerald included, held "beliefs [that] are difficult to summarize."[10]

Even within a few years of Fitzgerald's death, critics knew that *Gatsby* held special appeal. In a perceptive essay in a 1951 collection of critical essays on the American novel, edited and introduced by none other than the great Jesuit literary critic Harold Gardiner, Riley Hughes surveys Fitzgerald's novels, dubbing him "the unrivaled poet of the thousand dollar bill" but laments that "few of his writings, it would seem, other than *The Great Gatsby* and a handful of the short stories, will be remembered as anything more than period pieces."[11] As for the novel at hand, "Jay Gatsby's tragedy escapes triviality and sordidness through its allegorical power.... It is 'metaphysical' in the modern sense."[12]

[8]Chester Gillis, *Roman Catholicism in America* (New York: Columbia University Press, 1999), p. 235.

[9]James Emmett Ryan, *Faithful Passages: American Catholicism in Literary Culture, 1844–1931* (Madison: University of Wisconsin Press, 2013), p. 187.

[10]Ibid., pp. 186–87.

[11]Riley Hughes, "F. Scott Fitzgerald: The Touch of Disaster", in *Fifty Years of the American Novel: A Christian Appraisal*, ed. Harold C. Gardiner, S.J. (New York: Scribner's, 1951), p. 148.

[12]Ibid., pp. 141–42.

Up-and-coming Catholic novelists were looking to Fitzgerald's literary legacy, too. In his academic book *The Catholic Imagination in American Literature*, Ross Labrie implies that none other than Walker Percy learned how to write "American dream symbolism" from "Fitzgerald's descriptions of garish mansions in *The Great Gatsby*."[13] Labrie also credits Fitzgerald with inspiring the main religious conflict of J. F. Powers' great novel *Morte D'Urban*—specifically, from the setting and situational setup of "Winter Dreams", one of Fitzgerald's most important preparatory short stories for the writing of *The Great Gatsby*.[14]

Some writers, however, have begged to differ. A major study of Christianity and literature by an academic Evangelical press relegated *The Great Gatsby* to a single sentence: "Nihilistic skepticism figures strongly in the novels of American writers such as F. Scott Fitzgerald, whose *The Great Gatsby* chronicles a sad cycle of adultery, suicide and murder amid the supposedly light-hearted atmosphere of the Roaring Twenties."[15] Fitzgerald faced such evaluations throughout his career. Una Cadegan notes that, though Catholic literary criticism in the early twentieth century on the whole tended to exhibit a "variegated but clear, surprisingly flexible aesthetic philosophy", certain assessments "do not hold up very well, as in *America's* 1925 dismissal of *The Great Gatsby* as 'an inferior novel, considered from any angle whatsoever ... feeble in theme, in portraiture and even in expression.'"[16]

Many scholarly articles from the mid-twentieth century onward feature a variety of approaches to the novel; I will mention only two well-known ones here and point studious

[13] Ross Labrie, *The Catholic Imagination in American Literature* (Columbia: University of Missouri Press, 1997), p. 144.

[14] Ibid., p. 183.

[15] David Lyle Jeffrey and Gregory Maillet, *Christianity and Literature: Philosophical Foundations and Critical Practice* (Downers Grove, IL: IVP Academic, 2011), p. 273.

[16] Una Cadegan, *All Good Books Are Catholic Books: Print Culture, Censorship, and Modernity in Twentieth-Century America* (Ithaca: Cornell University Press, 2013), p. 25.

readers to the extensive bibliographies printed in the texts in Section III of this introduction. In "Fitzgerald's Catholicism Revisited: The Eucharistic Element in *The Beautiful and the Damned*", Steven Frye argues that "Fitzgerald's fiction often portrays the interpenetration of physical and material realms implicit in the concept of the Eucharist, since physical objects and people become in part mystical in nature."[17] Though Frye focuses much of his attention on *The Beautiful and the Damned*, he does note that "*The Great Gatsby* is the most comprehensive and successful characterization of this aspect of Fitzgerald's consciousness."[18] Taking a very different tack, Tracy Fessenden writes in "F. Scott Fitzgerald's Catholic Closet" that "what Fitzgerald identified as the particularly American difficulty of writing something other than pious tracts while still engaging Catholicism as a living issue would seem to be the difficulty of sustaining an alternative to an observant Catholic vision of America that would not disappear into an unmarked, Protestant vision of America."[19] Fessenden develops this alternative vision using postcolonialism, gender studies, and other critical theory approaches, specifying that her "concern ... is in how affective possibilities, fantasies, and dilemmas that exceed the bounds of a normative heterosexuality find in Catholicism a resource for their forbidden representation".[20] Published as a chapter in Fessenden's 2007 book on American literature's intersection with theology, the article reflects, I would argue, academia's attempt to wrestle with the Catholic Church in America as rocked by the scandals revealed in early 2002.

On the whole, critics and scholars tend to agree that *The Great Gatsby* represents a high point in American literature but

[17] Steven Frye, "Fitzgerald's Catholicism Revisited: The Eucharistic Element in *The Beautiful and the Damned*", in *F. Scott Fitzgerald: New Perspectives*, ed. Jackson R. Bryer et al. (Athens: University of Georgia Press, 2000), p. 64.

[18] Ibid.

[19] Tracy Fessenden, "F. Scott Fitzgerald's Catholic Closet", in *Culture and Redemption: Religion, the Secular, and American Literature* (Princeton: Princeton University Press, 2007), p. 192.

[20] Ibid., p. 196.

that Fitzgerald's Catholicism, and its inscrutable presence in the text, clouds the novel's reception. Paul Giles' voluminous study *American Catholic Arts and Fictions*, still cited by contemporary scholars, mentions Fitzgerald's works throughout and features an entire chapter dedicated to them. About *Gatsby* in particular, Giles argues that it represents "Fitzgerald's most profound yet, at the same time, most enigmatic meditation upon the mythologies of Catholicism".[21] Intriguingly, Giles also posits that Fitzgerald was concerned that Catholicism might have an "inclination toward becoming a parody of the American Dream".[22]

The first book-length treatment of the question of Fitzgerald's Catholicism and its wider implications, *Candles and Carnival Lights: The Catholic Sensibility of F. Scott Fitzgerald*, was published by Joan M. Allen in 1978.[23] Allen's book draws heavily from Fitzgerald's letters—which, at that time, Allen herself consulted in hard copy at the Princeton library—and exhaustively corrects many of the half-truths repeated by scholars of the day. To take two prominent examples, the myth of Fitzgerald's books being banned by the Church is readily contradicted by the fact that they never appeared in the *Index* and that Archbishop Curley "never took any official action";[24] and the supposedly scandalous affair of Fitzgerald's non-Catholic burial is effaced by the fact that Fitzgerald himself had formally abandoned the faith "almost twenty years before" and was by any recognized standard definitively *not* in the state of grace necessary to a Catholic burial at the time.[25] Still, notes Allen, more than three decades later Fitzgerald's daughter petitioned William Cardinal Baum of Washington, D.C., to have both her parents reinterred in a Catholic

[21] Paul Giles, *American Catholic Arts and Fictions: Culture, Ideology, Aesthetics* (Cambridge: Cambridge University Press, 1992), p. 176.

[22] Ibid.

[23] Joan M. Allen, *Candles and Carnival Lights: The Catholic Sensibility of F. Scott Fitzgerald* (New York: New York University Press, 1978).

[24] Ibid., p. 143.

[25] Ibid., p. 142.

cemetery, and Cardinal Baum not only granted it but delivered a statement including a line that could have come straight out of a Georges Bernanos novel: "[Fitzgerald] also experienced in his own life the mystery of suffering and, we hope, the power of God's grace."[26]

Of *The Great Gatsby* itself, Allen argues that although the book does not contain the explicit, visible Catholicism of Fitzgerald's earlier stories such as "Benediction", or even his novel *This Side of Paradise*, it presents morality in supernatural terms: "Allegiance to an earthly vision rather than a heavenly one will pull one down into the heat and sweat of damnation."[27] Allen demonstrates this idea in action with, for instance, the many direct correlations between Gatsby's death and Christ's, which Fitzgerald carefully wrote into his scenes; Gatsby's "worship of materialism ... is an ironic analogue to God's purpose for his son."[28]

I would add to Allen's analysis that Fitzgerald's irony functions as a *via negativa* diagnosis: by showing us what a martyr or so-called Christ figure cannot be, Fitzgerald judges such characters in the overly pious literature of his time as little more than plaster. When Gatsby spends the night watching over the Buchanans' house, hoping that Daisy will give some sign that she does indeed plan to leave Tom and return to Gatsby's arms, Fitzgerald has Nick call this activity a "vigil"—one marked by "sacredness".[29] But Daisy gives no sign; Gatsby's quasi-liturgical overnight observance among the Buchanans' shrubbery becomes a sterile Agony in the Garden, with no descending angel to strengthen him.

Such an absence, however, does not deter Gatsby from keeping the phone by his side during his afternoon use of the

[26] Ibid., p. 145. Cardinal Baum's statement of November 7, 1975, was sent in hard copy to Allen (see her note 31).

[27] Ibid., p. 102.

[28] Ibid., p. 109.

[29] F. Scott Fitzgerald, *The Great Gatsby*, ed. Stephen Mirarchi, Ignatius Critical Editions, ed. Joseph Pearce (San Francisco: Ignatius Press, 2025), p. 139. All subsequent citations are from this edition and will be cited in the text.

pool—to hear, finally, from Daisy, of course, but also to attend to his business. On his way to the pool, Gatsby bears a "pneumatic" mattress (see p. 153)—an odd, uncommon word choice for the commonly attested inflatable mattress. Why does Fitzgerald have Nick use the strange adjective? As devotees of any charismatic movement well know, "pneuma" refers to the life-breath, the Spirit; a particularly Christian study of the Holy Spirit may be termed "pneumatology". William Gilmore Simms, once regarded as one of the top writers and critics in America, uses the word at the beginning of his masterful ghost story "Grayling", which none other than Edgar Allan Poe praised as exemplary.[30] By using "pneumatic" instead of "blow-up" or "inflatable", Fitzgerald gains two additional senses beyond the literal mechanics of the mattress: he asks the reader to think of pneuma, or pneumatology—has Gatsby convinced himself that he is acting in line with the Spirit?—and, more ominously, is Gatsby himself about to become a spirit, a ghost?

As Allen points out, Gatsby is killed at about three post meridiem—the Hour of Divine Mercy—and is innocent of the crime charged against him. We know, however, that Gatsby took the blame for Daisy's accidental killing of Myrtle, though Fitzgerald's multilayered irony shines through since one might too easily imagine Daisy's doing so intentionally to get rid of Tom's mistress. Wilson, too, has the wrong man: Tom told him who owned the car that ran down his wife but neglected to tell him who was driving (and Nick believes that Tom knew, as he describes the last witnessed conversation between Daisy and Tom as their "conspiring together" [see p. 139]). The reader notices grimly, too, that Fitzgerald's depiction of Gatsby's sacrifice shows his blood going literally down the drain. To add ironic insult, the conspicuous absence of nearly everybody at the funeral exhibits the vacuum of his achievement. This

[30] For background on this interaction between Poe and Simms, see Stephen Mirarchi, "Edgar Allan Poe's and William Gilmore Simms's Principled Objections to New England Transcendentalism and Their Sympathy for Roman Catholics", *Simms Review* 24, nos. 1–2 (Summer/Winter 2016): 77–96.

self-made martyr has no apostles (not even Nick, who primly announces that he "disapproved of [Gatsby] from beginning to end" [see p. 146]).

Fitzgerald has accomplished an aesthetically complex and spiritually provocative diagnosis *via negativa*: Gatsby cannot be a Christ figure, and the imitation of Gatsby leads to an accidental, insubstantial death. Disordered hope disappoints—a lesson in aesthetics to the overly sentimental religious authors of Fitzgerald's time, and instruction in virtue to those who would direct their hope to ends that cannot fulfill it.

If Fitzgerald provides an accurate diagnosis, where might one look for a remedy? Allow me to suggest one enduring answer. Only three years after the publication of *The Great Gatsby*, a Catholic writer who had graduated at the top of his class from Boston College and edited one of the most important Catholic journals of the time—the Knights of Columbus' *Columbia*—released what is generally seen as a rejoinder to Fitzgerald's novel. Not an angry retort, mind you, but a joyful "what if" story of a young Saint Francis of Assisi figure who gives away everything in order to serve the poorest of the poor in Boston by actually becoming one of them. The little 1928 novel *Mr. Blue* by Myles Connolly did not sell at first and was roundly panned by Catholic critics, largely because no one knew what to do with it: the book could not be dismissed as pietistic, nor could it be held up as a modern, realistic plunge into the occult depravity of the human heart. Not until Peter Maurin and Dorothy Day became known for their heroic work among the poor in New York City did Connolly's novel gain attention; by the mid-1950s, over half a million copies of *Mr. Blue* were in print. As I have argued elsewhere, "Faithful and patriotic as he was, Connolly would not stand by and let Fitzgerald pronounce both the American dream and Catholicism dead in the water."[31] Readers interested in seeing how one faithfully Catholic author crafted an aesthetically accomplished novel

[31] Stephen Mirarchi, introduction to *Mr. Blue*, by Myles Connolly, ed. Stephen Mirarchi (Tacoma, WA: Cluny Media, 2015), p. xxiii.

that champions a faithful solution to Fitzgerald's diagnosis would do well to consult it.

II. Fitzgerald's Intricate Patterns

One of the sometimes overlooked yet most inspiring aspects of *The Great Gatsby* is its playful yet meticulous construction. Fitzgerald himself acknowledged this overtly aesthetic approach in a letter to Perkins in mid-July 1922:

> I want to write something *new*—something extraordinary and beautiful and simple + intricately patterned.[32]

The editors comment that this letter "anticipates the structural achievement of the novel that became *The Great Gatsby*".[33] We might think of "structural" in terms of the book as a whole; certainly its movement from the present in the opening chapter, to the events of two years past occupying the central part of the book, to a finish just prior to the present moment, creates a formidable and dizzying temporal effect on the reader. Even more so, each section of the novel presents its own misleading memories—some intentional deceptions, others mere accidents—told straight-faced and then later corrected, and the cumulative effect has come to represent a hallmark of Modernistic literature's ability to exhibit in itself a work of art, a work that must be studied, taken in, examined, contemplated, debated, and then left for others to do the same.

Fitzgerald knew he was writing a detective story of sorts—a novel in which the reader must do some work to figure out if Gatsby is who he claims to be, and to what extent. In a forceful letter to Perkins, Fitzgerald implored:

> Be sure not to give away *any* of my plot in the blurb. Don't give away that Gatsby *dies* or is a *parvenu* or *crook* or anything. It's

[32] Bruccoli and Baughman, *Sons of Maxwell Perkins*, p. 17. The editors reprint a facsimile of the original letter.

[33] Ibid.

> a part of the suspense of the book that all these things are in doubt until the end.[34]

Lest we forget, "parvenu" is a derogatory term for "a person from a humble background who has rapidly gained wealth or an influential social position; a nouveau riche; an upstart, a social climber ... generally used with the implication that the person concerned is unsuited to the new social position, esp. through lacking the necessary manners or accomplishments" (*Oxford English Dictionary*). To put it another way, Fitzgerald has constructed the novel such that readers should only by the end of the novel see clearly through the illusion of Gatsby—that is, Nick's description of him as a "rough-neck" is frighteningly apt (see p. 47).

I would like, however, to focus on "structural" in terms of much smaller choices that Fitzgerald made—choices that nonetheless produce an outsized effect. Take Fitzgerald's uses of "colossal" (see pp. 7, 90, 92, 141). Contextually, the word had rich connotations in late nineteenth- and early twentieth-century America, thanks to two interrelated events: the gift of the Statue of Liberty, dedicated in 1886, and the fundraising that preceded it, famously punctuated by Emma Lazarus's poem "The New Colossus", a copy of which was enshrined inside the statue's pedestal in 1903. The word "colossal", in Fitzgerald's and many Americans' minds, had come to stand in some spectacular way for the American promise itself. However, since Fitzgerald has a tragic story to tell in that regard, he uses the word four times with three different meanings, each use showing a distinct facet of the American promise as lived by Gatsby.

The first "colossal" describes Gatsby's mansion, and Nick emphasizes the world-leading size of the estate with the phrase "by any standard" (see p. 7). As Nick speaks of a city hall-style building in France in the next sentence, the reader begins to

[34] F. Scott Fitzgerald, letter to Maxwell Perkins, January 24, 1925, in Turnbull, *Letters*, p. 196.

think globally of the house, Gatsby, and perhaps the ancient Colossus of Rhodes itself.

If the first use has not provoked that image, the second surely will. Nick describes the disappearance of the mystique of the green light for Gatsby; with Daisy now literally in his arms, he may embrace the actual object of his desire and no longer needs the symbol. "The colossal significance of that light had now vanished forever" (see p. 90), Nick notes, pointing out in the next few sentences the locale of their former separation: the dock, and, as the reader has noted, the bay between East Egg and West Egg. And now readers can revel in the explicitly unstated but implicitly hinted image: Gatsby himself is the New Colossus, one foot on either Egg, astride the bay separating them, a giant in his own right and of two minds—one in the past, one desperately in the present.

Fitzgerald's third use, however, gives the reader pause—grave pause. Observing some doubts or confusions creeping into Gatsby's facial expressions, even as Gatsby beholds the actual Daisy, Nick wisely concludes that the spirit of Daisy—rather, the invented Daisy that Gatsby had invested with "a creative passion"—was outshining the person herself. Why? "Because of the colossal vitality of his illusion" (see p. 92). The figuratively gargantuan life Gatsby had given that imaginative creation was interfering with Gatsby's ability to accept the incarnate Daisy—an obstacle that would eventually lead to Daisy's frustrated cry that he wants "too much" (see p. 127).

The fourth and final use hammers home the sense of foreboding now accompanying the word. Nick speaks with Gatsby after the latter kept vigil over the Buchanans' house, and Nick proceeds to relate the final supposedly true pieces of Gatsby's past. In so doing, Nick ascribes a motivation to Gatsby's absolute pursuit of Daisy: "He knew that he was in Daisy's house by a colossal accident" (see p. 141). This distinct meaning of "colossal"—a strong intensifier for an action gone horribly wrong—colors every other use of the word *in reverse*, precisely because Fitzgerald has left it until the beginning, that is, chronologically, the beginning of Gatsby's adulterated quest for Daisy. Fitzgerald has, in some sense, strung readers along, allowing them to consider the grand accomplishment and symbology of the Colossus and Gatsby's self-appointed role as its progeny, allowing them to hope with Gatsby that his ship will indeed come to port. But the statue without a proper pedestal will crumble; far from substantiated, the Gatsby-Colossus meets the fate of the accidental.

Fitzgerald weaves many such word-threads throughout the novel: only two moments of the word "hulking" (see pp. 13, 89), which surprisingly and emotionally bind two seemingly disparate events; a gag both amusing and tragic about how cordials—which should not be present in Prohibition-era America—can make an introvert suddenly cordial; a running joke about poor butlers made to do poor work that ends up ruining a body part such as a thumb or nose; and a confidential aside to the reader—a most intimate revelation of dramatic irony—when Nick discloses a wayward yet hilarious thought about "the rubies" (see p. 90). Even longtime readers can miss these correspondences, as many of them are separated by several chapters; in this edition I have strived to annotate the major ones, though no doubt others remain to be discovered. Not as intimidating as a first experience of Eliot's *The Wasteland* or Pound's *The Cantos*, Fitzgerald's wordsmithing brings the themes of the whole novel into greater relief, all with the joyful crafting of an artist at play with the tragic.

III. Further Resources

As *The Great Gatsby* became a schoolroom warhorse, academic essays and informational material about every aspect of it proliferated; it can be difficult, therefore, to vet reliable resources. In addition to the sources present in the footnotes of this introduction, I also recommend the following two books for their scholarly expertise and their ability to point researchers to equally dependable, area-specific studies.

Bruccoli, Matthew J., ed. *F. Scott Fitzgerald's* The Great Gatsby*: A Literary Reference*. New York: Carroll and Graf, 2000. The best single-volume resource for readers new to the novel, the time period, or any combination thereof, this oversize book was edited by Matthew Bruccoli, the preeminent Fitzgerald scholar since the designation has existed. The *Literary Reference* contains finely selected materials on the novel's historical background, Fitzgerald's writing process, early reviews of the book, its legacy, and excerpts from influential critical essays. The eleven-page bibliography alone is worth the price of admission, not to mention the numerous facsimiles, illustrations, and photographs reprinted throughout.

West, James L. W., III, ed. *The Great Gatsby: A Variorum Edition.* Cambridge: Cambridge University Press, 2019. The long-awaited eighteenth volume in the Cambridge Edition of the Works of F. Scott Fitzgerald, this version features all the textual variations that appear throughout the various published texts and their sources footnoted on each page. An extensive introductory essay by West explains in great detail the editor's own processes, the reliability of the various manuscripts, curious features such as Fitzgerald's space breaks, and an illuminating publishing history of the novel. It also includes explanatory notes, a list of variants among the editions, illustrations, and Fitzgerald's own introduction to the 1934 Modern Library edition.

TEXTUAL NOTE

In the Ignatius Critical Edition of *The Great Gatsby*, we are presenting the original 1925 (now public domain) text with all its oddities and variations, with only a few changes as indicated in the the footnotes.

The Text of

THE GREAT GATSBY

CHAPTER I

In my younger and more vulnerable years my father gave me some advice that I've been turning over in my mind ever since.

"Whenever you feel like criticizing anyone," he told me, "just remember that all the people in this world haven't had the advantages that you've had."

He didn't say any more, but we've always been unusually communicative in a reserved way, and I understood that he meant a great deal more than that. In consequence, I'm inclined to reserve all judgments, a habit that has opened up many curious natures to me and also made me the victim of not a few veteran bores. The abnormal mind is quick to detect and attach itself to this quality when it appears in a normal person, and so it came about that in college I was unjustly accused of being a politician, because I was privy[1] to the secret griefs of wild, unknown men. Most of the confidences were unsought—frequently I have feigned sleep, preoccupation, or a hostile levity[2] when I realized by some unmistakable sign that an intimate revelation was quivering on the horizon; for the intimate revelations of young men, or at least the terms in which they express them, are usually plagiaristic and marred by obvious suppressions. Reserving judgments is a matter of infinite hope. I am still a little afraid of missing something if I forget that, as my father snobbishly suggested, and I snobbishly repeat, a sense of the fundamental decencies is parcelled out unequally at birth.

And, after boasting this way of my tolerance, I come to the admission that it has a limit. Conduct may be founded on

[1] *privy*: sharing in secret knowledge; also, pun on the noun "privy", outhouse or toilet.

[2] *levity*: lack of seriousness.

the hard rock or the wet marshes, but after a certain point I don't care what it's founded on. When I came back from the East last autumn I felt that I wanted the world to be in uniform and at a sort of moral attention forever; I wanted no more riotous[3] excursions with privileged glimpses into the human heart. Only Gatsby,[4] the man who gives his name to this book, was exempt from my reaction—Gatsby, who represented everything for which I have an unaffected[5] scorn. If personality is an unbroken series of successful gestures, then there was something gorgeous about him, some heightened sensitivity to the promises of life, as if he were related to one of those intricate machines that register earthquakes ten thousand miles away. This responsiveness had nothing to do with that flabby impressionability which is dignified under the name of the "creative temperament"—it was an extraordinary gift for hope, a romantic readiness such as I have never found in any other person and which it is not likely I shall ever find again. No—Gatsby turned out all right at the end; it is what preyed on Gatsby, what foul dust floated in the wake of his dreams that temporarily closed out my interest in the abortive[6] sorrows and short-winded elations of men.

* * * * *

My family have been prominent, well-to-do people in this Middle Western city for three generations. The Carraways are something of a clan, and we have a tradition that we're descended from the Dukes of Buccleuch,[7] but the actual founder of my line was my grandfather's brother, who came

[3] *riotous*: unrestrained; excessive; wild.

[4] *Gatsby*: That mobsters carried "gats" or guns was common, popular usage. To get a modern sense, imagine the title *The Great Smith & Wesson*, or *The Great Glocksby*.

[5] *unaffected*: free from affectation; sincere.

[6] *abortive*: fruitless; unsuccessful.

[7] *Dukes of Buccleuch*: Scottish hereditary line of the Scott clan, established in 1663 (pronounced bə-KLOO).

here in fifty-one, sent a substitute to the Civil War,[8] and started the wholesale hardware business that my father carries on today.

I never saw this great-uncle, but I'm supposed to look like him—with special reference to the rather hard-boiled[9] painting that hangs in father's office. I graduated from New Haven in 1915, just a quarter of a century after my father, and a little later I participated in that delayed Teutonic migration[10] known as the Great War. I enjoyed the counter-raid so thoroughly that I came back restless. Instead of being the warm center of the world, the Middle West now seemed like the ragged edge of the universe—so I decided to go East and learn the bond business.[11] Everybody I knew was in the bond business, so I supposed it could support one more single man. All my aunts and uncles talked it over as if they were choosing a prep school for me, and finally said, "Why—ye-es," with very grave, hesitant faces. Father agreed to finance me for a year, and after various delays I came East, permanently, I thought, in the spring of twenty-two.

The practical thing was to find rooms in the city, but it was a warm season, and I had just left a country of wide lawns and friendly trees, so when a young man at the office suggested that we take a house together in a commuting town, it sounded like a great idea. He found the house, a weatherbeaten cardboard bungalow[12] at eighty a month, but at the last minute the firm ordered him to Washington, and I went out to the country alone. I had a dog—at least I had him for a few days until he

[8] *sent ... Civil War*: perfectly legal, if one had the funds to hire a substitute or pay a fee that very few could afford.

[9] *hard-boiled*: of a person, hardened or tough.

[10] *Teutonic migration*: Nick refers to the ancient Germanic peoples, Teutons, who warred with Rome at the end of the second century B.C., ostensibly because of their migrations.

[11] *bond business*: buying and selling of fixed-income debts—a multibillion-dollar industry in 1920s America. E.g., see J. Fred Rippy, "A Bond-Selling Extravaganza of the 1920's", *Journal of Business of the University of Chicago* 23, no. 4 (October 1950): 238–47.

[12] *cardboard bungalow*: flimsy single-story house.

ran away—and an old Dodge and a Finnish woman, who made my bed and cooked breakfast and muttered Finnish wisdom to herself over the electric stove.

It was lonely for a day or so until one morning some man, more recently arrived than I, stopped me on the road.

"How do you get to West Egg Village?" he asked helplessly.

I told him. And as I walked on I was lonely no longer. I was a guide, a pathfinder, an original settler. He had casually conferred on me the freedom of the neighborhood.

And so with the sunshine and the great bursts of leaves growing on the trees, just as things grow in fast movies, I had that familiar conviction that life was beginning over again with the summer.

There was so much to read, for one thing, and so much fine health to be pulled down out of the young breath-giving air. I bought a dozen volumes on banking and credit and investment securities, and they stood on my shelf in red and gold like new money from the mint, promising to unfold the shining secrets that only Midas[13] and Morgan[14] and Maecenas[15] knew. And I had the high intention of reading many other books besides. I was rather literary in college—one year I wrote a series of very solemn and obvious editorials for the *Yale News*—and now I was going to bring back all such things into my life and become again that most limited of all specialists, the "well-rounded man." This isn't just an epigram[16]—life is much more successfully looked at from a single window, after all.

It was a matter of chance that I should have rented a house in one of the strangest communities in North America. It was on that slender riotous island which extends itself due east of New York—and where there are, among other natural curiosities, two unusual formations of land.[17] Twenty miles from the

[13] *Midas*: mythological king with "the golden touch".

[14] *Morgan*: J. P. Morgan, railroad magnate and financial genius; one of the richest men in the world at the time.

[15] *Maecenas*: first-century B.C. Roman patron of artists such as Virgil.

[16] *epigram*: clever saying.

[17] *two unusual formations of land*: Nick refers to modern-day Great Neck and Kings Point (West Egg) versus Manhasset (East Egg).

city a pair of enormous eggs, identical in contour and separated only by a courtesy bay, jut out into the most domesticated body of salt water in the Western hemisphere, the great wet barnyard of Long Island Sound. They are not perfect ovals—like the egg in the Columbus story, they are both crushed flat at the contact end—but their physical resemblance must be a source of perpetual confusion to the gulls that fly overhead. To the wingless a more arresting phenomenon is their dissimilarity in every particular except shape and size.

I lived at West Egg, the—well, the less fashionable of the two, though this is a most superficial tag to express the bizarre and not a little sinister contrast between them. My house was at the very tip of the egg, only fifty yards from the Sound, and squeezed between two huge places that rented for twelve or fifteen thousand a season. The one on my right was a colossal affair by any standard—it was a factual imitation of some Hôtel de Ville[18] in Normandy, with a tower on one side, spanking new under a thin beard of raw ivy, and a marble swimming pool, and more than forty acres of lawn and garden. It was Gatsby's mansion. Or, rather, as I didn't know Mr. Gatsby, it was a mansion inhabited by a gentleman of that name. My own house was an eyesore, but it was a small eyesore, and it had been overlooked, so I had a view of the water, a partial view of my neighbor's lawn, and the consoling proximity of millionaires—all for eighty dollars a month.

Across the courtesy bay the white palaces of fashionable East Egg glittered along the water, and the history of the summer really begins on the evening I drove over there to have dinner with the Tom Buchanans. Daisy was my second cousin once removed, and I'd known Tom in college. And just after the war I spent two days with them in Chicago.

Her husband, among various physical accomplishments, had been one of the most powerful ends that ever played football at New Haven—a national figure in a way, one of those men who reach such an acute limited excellence at twenty-one that everything afterward savors of anticlimax. His family were

[18] *Hôtel de Ville*: not a hotel, but a city hall or town hall for governance.

enormously wealthy—even in college his freedom with money was a matter for reproach[19]—but now he'd left Chicago and come East in a fashion that rather took your breath away; for instance, he'd brought down a string of polo ponies from Lake Forest.[20] It was hard to realize that a man in my own generation was wealthy enough to do that.

Why they came East I don't know. They had spent a year in France for no particular reason, and then drifted here and there unrestfully wherever people played polo and were rich together. This was a permanent move, said Daisy over the telephone, but I didn't believe it—I had no sight into Daisy's heart, but I felt that Tom would drift on forever seeking, a little wistfully,[21] for the dramatic turbulence of some irrecoverable football game.

And so it happened that on a warm windy evening I drove over to East Egg to see two old friends whom I scarcely knew at all. Their house was even more elaborate than I expected, a cheerful red-and-white Georgian Colonial[22] mansion, overlooking the bay. The lawn started at the beach and ran toward the front door for a quarter of a mile, jumping over sundials and brick walks and burning gardens—finally when it reached the house drifting up the side in bright vines as though from the momentum of its run. The front was broken by a line of French windows, glowing now with reflected gold and wide open to the warm windy afternoon, and Tom Buchanan in riding clothes was standing with his legs apart on the front porch.

He had changed since his New Haven years. Now he was a sturdy straw-haired man of thirty with a rather hard mouth and a supercilious[23] manner. Two shining arrogant eyes had established dominance over his face and gave him the appearance of always leaning aggressively forward. Not even the effeminate

[19] *reproach*: disapproval. Given Fitzgerald's extensive Catholic background, note also that Reproaches are the traditional Good Friday litany of God's lamentations over his people.

[20] *Lake Forest*: well-to-do city just north of Chicago.

[21] *wistfully*: with longing and regret for the unobtainable or the past.

[22] *Georgian Colonial*: after the British kings of that name, a formal and stately architectural style nostalgically revived in the early twentieth century.

[23] *supercilious*: with a superior air; haughty.

swank of his riding clothes could hide the enormous power of that body—he seemed to fill those glistening boots until he strained the top lacing, and you could see a great pack of muscle shifting when his shoulder moved under his thin coat. It was a body capable of enormous leverage—a cruel body.

His speaking voice, a gruff husky tenor, added to the impression of fractiousness[24] he conveyed. There was a touch of paternal contempt in it, even toward people he liked—and there were men at New Haven who had hated his guts.

"Now, don't think my opinion on these matters is final," he seemed to say, "just because I'm stronger and more of a man than you are." We were in the same senior society,[25] and while we were never intimate I always had the impression that he approved of me and wanted me to like him with some harsh, defiant wistfulness of his own.

We talked for a few minutes on the sunny porch.

"I've got a nice place here," he said, his eyes flashing about restlessly.

Turning me around by one arm, he moved a broad flat hand along the front vista, including in its sweep a sunken Italian garden, a half acre of deep, pungent roses, and a snub-nosed motor-boat that bumped the tide offshore.

"It belonged to Demaine,[26] the oil man." He turned me around again, politely and abruptly. "We'll go inside."

We walked through a high hallway into a bright rosy-colored space, fragilely bound into the house by French windows at either end. The windows were ajar and gleaming white against the fresh grass outside that seemed to grow a little way into the house. A breeze blew through the room, blew curtains

[24] *fractiousness*: unruly; easily annoyed; stubborn; used especially of children.

[25] *senior society*: restricted entry club at a college, often secretive and exclusive; members would generally keep their associations with the society the rest of their lives.

[26] *Demaine*: fictional as a name, but Fitzgerald is likely punning on "demesne", sometimes spelled "demaine", which means a manor or estate held by the landowner (*Oxford English Dictionary*; hereafter, *OED*). The oil reference may be to the Teapot Dome scandal of the early 1920s, in which presidential cabinet member Albert B. Fall would be convicted of accepting oil company bribes.

in at one end and out the other like pale flags, twisting them up toward the frosted wedding-cake of the ceiling, and then rippled over the wine-colored rug, making a shadow on it as wind does on the sea.

The only completely stationary object in the room was an enormous couch on which two young women were buoyed up as though upon an anchored balloon. They were both in white, and their dresses were rippling and fluttering as if they had just been blown back in after a short flight around the house. I must have stood for a few moments listening to the whip and snap of the curtains and the groan of a picture on the wall. Then there was a boom as Tom Buchanan shut the rear windows and the caught wind died out about the room, and the curtains and the rugs and the two young women ballooned slowly to the floor.

The younger of the two was a stranger to me. She was extended full length at her end of the divan, completely motionless, and with her chin raised a little, as if she were balancing something on it which was quite likely to fall. If she saw me out of the corner of her eyes she gave no hint of it—indeed, I was almost surprised into murmuring an apology for having disturbed her by coming in.

The other girl, Daisy, made an attempt to rise—she leaned slightly forward with a conscientious expression—then she laughed, an absurd, charming little laugh, and I laughed too and came forward into the room.

"I'm p-paralyzed with happiness."

She laughed again, as if she said something very witty, and held my hand for a moment, looking up into my face, promising that there was no one in the world she so much wanted to see. That was a way she had. She hinted in a murmur that the surname of the balancing girl was Baker. (I've heard it said that Daisy's murmur was only to make people lean toward her; an irrelevant criticism that made it no less charming.)

At any rate, Miss Baker's lips fluttered, she nodded at me almost imperceptibly, and then quickly tipped her head back again—the object she was balancing had obviously tottered a little and given her something of a fright. Again a sort of apology arose to my lips. Almost any exhibition of complete self-sufficiency draws a stunned tribute from me.

I looked back at my cousin, who began to ask me questions in her low, thrilling voice. It was the kind of voice that the ear follows up and down, as if each speech is an arrangement of notes that will never be played again. Her face was sad and lovely with bright things in it, bright eyes and a bright passionate mouth, but there was an excitement in her voice that men who had cared for her found difficult to forget: a singing compulsion, a whispered "Listen," a promise that she had done gay, exciting things just a while since and that there were gay, exciting things hovering in the next hour.

I told her how I had stopped off in Chicago for a day on my way East, and how a dozen people had sent their love through me.

"Do they miss me?" she cried ecstatically.

"The whole town is desolate. All the cars have the left rear wheel painted black[27] as a mourning wreath, and there's a persistent wail all night along the north shore."

"How gorgeous! Let's go back, Tom. Tomorrow!" Then she added irrelevantly: "You ought to see the baby."

"I'd like to."

"She's asleep. She's three years old. Haven't you ever seen her?"

"Never."

"Well, you ought to see her. She's—"

Tom Buchanan, who had been hovering restlessly about the room, stopped and rested his hand on my shoulder.

"What you doing, Nick?"

"I'm a bond man."

"Who with?"

I told him.

"Never heard of them," he remarked decisively.

[27] *rear wheel painted black*: Nick's joke makes sense because many tires after 1910 had white walls; a single all-black tire would be immediately noticeable.

This annoyed me.

"You will," I answered shortly. "You will if you stay in the East."

"Oh, I'll stay in the East, don't you worry," he said, glancing at Daisy and then back at me, as if he were alert for something more. "I'd be a God damned fool to live anywhere else."

At this point Miss Baker said: "Absolutely!" with such suddenness that I started—it was the first word she had uttered since I came into the room. Evidently it surprised her as much as it did me, for she yawned and with a series of rapid, deft[28] movements stood up into the room.

"I'm stiff," she complained. "I've been lying on that sofa for as long as I can remember."

"Don't look at me," Daisy retorted. "I've been trying to get you to New York all afternoon."

"No, thanks," said Miss Baker to the four cocktails just in from the pantry. "I'm absolutely in training."

Her host looked at her incredulously.

"You are!" He took down his drink as if it were a drop in the bottom of a glass. "How you ever get anything done is beyond me."

I looked at Miss Baker, wondering what it was she "got done." I enjoyed looking at her. She was a slender, small-breasted girl, with an erect carriage, which she accentuated by throwing her body backward at the shoulders like a young cadet. Her gray sun-strained eyes looked back at me with polite reciprocal curiosity out of a wan,[29] charming, discontented face. It occurred to me now that I had seen her, or a picture of her, somewhere before.

"You live in West Egg," she remarked contemptuously. "I know somebody there."

"I don't know a single——"

"You must know Gatsby."

"Gatsby?" demanded Daisy. "What Gatsby?"

[28] *deft*: not only dexterous, but "neat and pretty".

[29] *wan*: especially pale.

Before I could reply that he was my neighbor dinner was announced; wedging his tense arm imperatively under mine, Tom Buchanan compelled me from the room as though he were moving a checker to another square.

Slenderly, languidly,[30] their hands set lightly on their hips, the two young women preceded us out onto a rosy-colored porch, open toward the sunset, where four candles flickered on the table in the diminished wind.

"Why *candles?*" objected Daisy, frowning. She snapped them out with her fingers. "In two weeks it'll be the longest day in the year." She looked at us all radiantly. "Do you always watch for the longest day of the year and then miss it? I always watch for the longest day in the year and then miss it."

"We ought to plan something," yawned Miss Baker, sitting down at the table as if she were getting into bed.

"All right," said Daisy. "What'll we plan?" She turned to me helplessly: "What do people plan?"

Before I could answer her eyes fastened with an awed expression on her little finger.

"Look!" she complained; "I hurt it."

We all looked—the knuckle was black and blue.

"You did it, Tom," she said accusingly. "I know you didn't mean to, but you *did* do it. That's what I get for marrying a brute of a man, a great, big, hulking physical specimen of a——"

"I hate that word hulking," objected Tom crossly,[31] "even in kidding."

"Hulking," insisted Daisy.

Sometimes she and Miss Baker talked at once, unobtrusively and with a bantering inconsequence that was never quite chatter, that was as cool as their white dresses and their impersonal eyes in the absence of all desire. They were here, and they accepted Tom and me, making only a polite pleasant effort to entertain or to be entertained. They knew that presently dinner would be over and a little later the evening too would

[30] *languidly*: not just slowly but affectedly so.

[31] *crossly*: irritably; in a bad temper.

be over and casually put away. It was sharply different from the West, where an evening was hurried from phase to phase toward its close, in a continually disappointed anticipation or else in sheer nervous dread of the moment itself.

"You make me feel uncivilized, Daisy," I confessed on my second glass of corky[32] but rather impressive claret.[33] "Can't you talk about crops or something?"

I meant nothing in particular by this remark, but it was taken up in an unexpected way.

"Civilization's going to pieces," broke out Tom violently. "I've gotten to be a terrible pessimist about things. Have you read 'The Rise of the Coloured Empires' by this man Goddard?"[34]

"Why, no," I answered, rather surprised by his tone.

"Well, it's a fine book, and everybody ought to read it. The idea is if we don't look out the white race will be—will be utterly submerged. It's all scientific stuff; it's been proved."

"Tom's getting very profound," said Daisy, with an expression of unthoughtful sadness. "He reads deep books with long words in them. What was that word we——"

"Well, these books are all scientific," insisted Tom, glancing at her impatiently. "This fellow has worked out the whole thing. It's up to us, who are the dominant race, to watch out or these other races will have control of things."

"We've got to beat them down," whispered Daisy, winking ferociously toward the fervent[35] sun.

"You ought to live in California—" began Miss Baker, but Tom interrupted her by shifting heavily in his chair.

"This idea is that we're Nordics.[36] I am, and you are, and you are, and—" After an infinitesimal hesitation he included Daisy with a slight nod, and she winked at me again. "—And we've

[32] *corky*: tainted by a chemical that can form if natural cork is contaminated.

[33] *claret*: a fine red wine blend, at this time ordinarily a Bordeaux.

[34] *'The Rise … Goddard*: Fitzgerald alludes to *The Rising Tide of Color against White World-Supremacy* by Lothrop Stoddard, released in 1920 by the same publisher as *Gatsby*. Stoddard was a eugenicist, racist, and Nazi supporter.

[35] *fervent*: radiant or burning.

[36] *Nordics*: Stoddard follows conservationist and eugenicist Madison Grant in positing three divisions of the white race: Nordic, Alpine, and Mediterranean.

produced all the things that go to make civilization—oh, science and art, and all that. Do you see?"

There was something pathetic in his concentration, as if his complacency,[37] more acute than of old, was not enough to him any more. When, almost immediately, the telephone rang inside and the butler left the porch Daisy seized upon the momentary interruption and leaned toward me.

"I'll tell you a family secret," she whispered enthusiastically. "It's about the butler's nose.[38] Do you want to hear about the butler's nose?"

"That's why I came over tonight."

"Well, he wasn't always a butler; he used to be the silver polisher for some people in New York that had a silver service for two hundred people. He had to polish it from morning till night, until finally it began to affect his nose——"

"Things went from bad to worse," suggested Miss Baker.

"Yes. Things went from bad to worse, until finally he had to give up his position."

For a moment the last sunshine fell with romantic affection[39] upon her glowing face; her voice compelled me forward breathlessly as I listened—then the glow faded, each light deserting her with lingering regret, like children leaving a pleasant street at dusk.

The butler came back and murmured something close to Tom's ear, whereupon Tom frowned, pushed back his chair, and without a word went inside. As if his absence quickened[40] something within her, Daisy leaned forward again, her voice glowing and singing.

"I love to see you at my table, Nick. You remind me of a—of a rose, an absolute rose. Doesn't he?" She turned to Miss Baker for confirmation: "An absolute rose?"

This was untrue. I am not even faintly like a rose. She was only extemporizing,[41] but a stirring warmth flowed from her,

[37] *complacency*: being self-satisfied.

[38] *butler's nose*: first entry in the running gag of butlers' overused body parts.

[39] *romantic affection*: i.e., fanciful goodwill or imagined fondness.

[40] *quickened*: to bring to life; to revive.

[41] *extemporizing*: to speak offhandedly; to improvise.

as if her heart was trying to come out to you concealed in one of those breathless, thrilling words. Then suddenly she threw her napkin on the table and excused herself and went into the house.

Miss Baker and I exchanged a short glance consciously devoid of meaning. I was about to speak when she sat up alertly and said "*Sh!*" in a warning voice. A subdued impassioned murmur was audible in the room beyond, and Miss Baker leaned forward unashamed, trying to hear. The murmur trembled on the verge of coherence, sank down, mounted excitedly, and then ceased altogether.

"This Mr. Gatsby you spoke of is my neighbor—" I said.

"Don't talk. I want to hear what happens."

"Is something happening?" I inquired innocently.

"You mean to say you don't know?" said Miss Baker, honestly surprised. "I thought everybody knew."

"I don't."

"Why—" she said hesitantly, "Tom's got some woman in New York."

"Got some woman?" I repeated blankly.

Miss Baker nodded.

"She might have the decency not to telephone him at dinner time. Don't you think?"

Almost before I had grasped her meaning there was the flutter of a dress and the crunch of leather boots, and Tom and Daisy were back at the table.

"It couldn't be helped!" cried Daisy with tense gayety.

She sat down, glanced searchingly at Miss Baker and then at me, and continued: "I looked outdoors for a minute, and it's very romantic outdoors. There's a bird on the lawn that I think must be a nightingale come over on the Cunard or White Star Line.[42] He's singing away—" Her voice sang: "It's romantic, isn't it, Tom?"

"Very romantic," he said, and then miserably to me: "If it's light enough after dinner, I want to take you down to the stables."

[42] *Cunard ... Line*: competitive transatlantic shipping lines.

The telephone rang inside, startlingly, and as Daisy shook her head decisively at Tom the subject of the stables, in fact all subjects, vanished into air. Among the broken fragments of the last five minutes at table I remember the candles being lit again, pointlessly, and I was conscious of wanting to look squarely at everyone, and yet to avoid all eyes. I couldn't guess what Daisy and Tom were thinking, but I doubt if even Miss Baker, who seemed to have mastered a certain hardy skepticism, was able utterly to put this fifth guest's shrill metallic urgency out of mind. To a certain temperament the situation might have seemed intriguing—my own instinct was to telephone immediately for the police.

The horses, needless to say, were not mentioned again. Tom and Miss Baker, with several feet of twilight between them, strolled back into the library, as if to a vigil[43] beside a perfectly tangible body, while, trying to look pleasantly interested and a little deaf, I followed Daisy around a chain of connecting verandas to the porch in front. In its deep gloom we sat down side by side on a wicker settee.[44]

Daisy took her face in her hands as if feeling its lovely shape, and her eyes moved gradually out into the velvet dusk. I saw that turbulent emotions possessed her, so I asked what I thought would be some sedative questions about her little girl.

"We don't know each other very well, Nick," she said suddenly. "Even if we are cousins. You didn't come to my wedding."

"I wasn't back from the war."

"That's true." She hesitated. "Well, I've had a very bad time, Nick, and I'm pretty cynical about everything."

Evidently she had reason to be. I waited but she didn't say any more, and after a moment I returned rather feebly to the subject of her daughter.

"I suppose she talks, and—eats, and everything."

[43] *vigil*: nocturnal watch or religious service for the dead. In Catholicism, a vigil is the eve of a holy day (e.g., the Easter Vigil) and formerly the early morning Liturgy of the Hours (which in many cases is subsumed into Matins).

[44] *settee*: long bench with a back, often ornate.

"Oh, yes." She looked at me absently. "Listen, Nick; let me tell you what I said when she was born. Would you like to hear?"

"Very much."

"It'll show you how I've gotten to feel about—things. Well, she was less than an hour old and Tom was God knows where. I woke up out of the ether[45] with an utterly abandoned feeling, and asked the nurse right away if it was a boy or a girl. She told me it was a girl, and so I turned my head away and wept. 'All right,' I said, 'I'm glad it's a girl. And I hope she'll be a fool—that's the best thing a girl can be in this world, a beautiful little fool.'

"You see I think everything's terrible anyhow," she went on in a convinced way. "Everybody thinks so—the most advanced people. And I *know*. I've been everywhere and seen everything and done everything." Her eyes flashed around her in a defiant way, rather like Tom's, and she laughed with thrilling scorn. "Sophisticated—God, I'm sophisticated!"

The instant her voice broke off, ceasing to compel my attention, my belief, I felt the basic insincerity of what she had said. It made me uneasy, as though the whole evening had been a trick of some sort to exact a contributary emotion from me. I waited, and sure enough, in a moment she looked at me with an absolute smirk on her lovely face, as if she had asserted her membership in a rather distinguished secret society to which she and Tom belonged.

* * * * *

Inside, the crimson room bloomed with light. Tom and Miss Baker sat at either end of the long couch and she read aloud to him from *The Saturday Evening Post*[46]—the words, murmurous and uninflected, running together in a soothing tune. The lamp-light, bright on his boots and dull on the autumn-leaf

[45] *ether*: chemical used for anesthetic; also likely an allusion to T. S. Eliot's famous line from 1915's *Prufrock*: "Like a patient etherized upon a table."

[46] Saturday Evening Post: one of the most popular literary and general interest magazines; Fitzgerald would publish many stories in its pages.

yellow of her hair, glinted along the paper as she turned a page with a flutter of slender muscles in her arms.

When we came in she held us silent for a moment with a lifted hand.

"To be continued," she said, tossing the magazine on the table, "in our very next issue."

Her body asserted itself with a restless movement of her knee, and she stood up.

"Ten o'clock," she remarked, apparently finding the time on the ceiling. "Time for this good girl to go to bed."

"Jordan's going to play in the tournament tomorrow," explained Daisy, "over at Westchester."

"Oh—you're *Jor*dan Baker."

I knew now why her face was familiar—its pleasing contemptuous expression had looked out at me from many rotogravure[47] pictures of the sporting life at Asheville and Hot Springs and Palm Beach.[48] I had heard some story of her too, a critical, unpleasant story, but what it was I had forgotten long ago.

"Good night," she said softly. "Wake me at eight, won't you."

"If you'll get up."

"I will. Good night, Mr. Carraway. See you anon."[49]

"Of course you will," confirmed Daisy. "In fact I think I'll arrange a marriage. Come over often, Nick, and I'll sort of—oh—fling you together. You know—lock you up accidentally in linen closets and push you out to sea in a boat, and all that sort of thing——"

"Good night," called Miss Baker from the stairs. "I haven't heard a word."

"She's a nice girl," said Tom after a moment. "They oughtn't to let her run around the country this way."

[47] *rotogravure*: still somewhat new at this time, a process for printing illustrations or photos in newspapers or magazines, often in their own sections or supplements.

[48] *Asheville ... Palm Beach*: sites of famous golf tournaments. Women formally played amateur golf in the United States from the 1890s in New York and New Jersey, and by 1917 the Women's Tournament Committee of the USGA had formed.

[49] *anon*: soon; in a little while.

"Who oughtn't to?" inquired Daisy coldly.

"Her family."

"Her family is one aunt about a thousand years old. Besides, Nick's going to look after her, aren't you, Nick? She's going to spend lots of weekends out here this summer. I think the home influence will be very good for her."

Daisy and Tom looked at each other for a moment in silence.

"Is she from New York?" I asked quickly.

"From Louisville. Our white girlhood was passed together there. Our beautiful white——"

"Did you give Nick a little heart-to-heart talk on the veranda?" demanded Tom suddenly.

"Did I?" She looked at me. "I can't seem to remember, but I think we talked about the Nordic race. Yes, I'm sure we did. It sort of crept up on us and first thing you know——"

"Don't believe everything you hear, Nick," he advised me.

I said lightly that I had heard nothing at all, and a few minutes later I got up to go home. They came to the door with me and stood side by side in a cheerful square of light. As I started my motor Daisy peremptorily[50] called: "Wait!"

"I forgot to ask you something, and it's important. We heard you were engaged to a girl out West."

"That's right," corroborated Tom kindly. "We heard that you were engaged."

"It's a libel.[51] I'm too poor."

"But we heard it," insisted Daisy, surprising me by opening up again in a flower-like way. "We heard it from three people, so it must be true."

Of course I knew what they were referring to, but I wasn't even vaguely engaged. The fact that gossip had published the banns[52] was one of the reasons I had come East. You can't stop going with an old friend on account of rumors, and on the other hand I had no intention of being rumored into marriage.

[50] *peremptorily*: in the imperative; as a command; also, to settle a question.
[51] *libel*: not necessarily written, but a false statement.
[52] *banns*: public notices of impending marriages, usually posted in churches.

Their interest rather touched me and made them less remotely rich—nevertheless, I was confused and a little disgusted as I drove away. It seemed to me that the thing for Daisy to do was to rush out of the house, child in arms—but apparently there were no such intentions in her head. As for Tom, the fact that he "had some woman in New York" was really less surprising than that he had been depressed by a book. Something was making him nibble at the edge of stale ideas as if his sturdy physical egotism no longer nourished his peremptory[53] heart.

Already it was deep summer on roadhouse[54] roofs and in front of wayside garages,[55] where new red gas-pumps sat out in pools of light, and when I reached my estate at West Egg I ran the car under its shed and sat for a while on an abandoned grass roller[56] in the yard. The wind had blown off, leaving a loud, bright night, with wings beating in the trees and a persistent organ sound as the full bellows of the earth blew the frogs full of life. The silhouette of a moving cat wavered across the moonlight, and turning my head to watch it, I saw that I was not alone—fifty feet away a figure had emerged from the shadow of my neighbor's mansion and was standing with his hands in his pockets regarding the silver pepper of the stars. Something in his leisurely movements and the secure position of his feet upon the lawn suggested that it was Mr. Gatsby himself, come out to determine what share was his of our local heavens.

I decided to call to him. Miss Baker had mentioned him at dinner, and that would do for an introduction. But I didn't call to him, for he gave a sudden intimation[57] that he was content to be alone—he stretched out his arms toward the dark

[53] *peremptory*: decisive; absolute; overconfident.

[54] *roadhouse*: roadside establishments just outside of town for the "three Ds": dining, dancing, and drinking.

[55] *garages*: In the early to mid-twentieth century, the standard places to stop for gas and oil ordinarily had multiple bays for repairs.

[56] *grass roller*: large cylinder used for flattening or evening out turf or grass.

[57] *intimation*: suggestion; symbolic expression.

water in a curious way, and, far as I was from him, I could have sworn he was trembling. Involuntarily I glanced seaward—and distinguished nothing except a single green light, minute and far away, that might have been at the end of a dock. When I looked once more for Gatsby he had vanished, and I was alone again in the unquiet darkness.

CHAPTER II

ABOUT HALF-WAY between West Egg and New York the motor road hastily joins the railroad and runs beside it for a quarter of a mile, so as to shrink away from a certain desolate area of land. This is a valley of ashes[1]—a fantastic[2] farm where ashes grow like wheat into ridges and hills and grotesque[3] gardens; where ashes take the forms of houses and chimneys and rising smoke and, finally, with a transcendent effort, of men who move dimly and already crumbling through the powdery air. Occasionally a line of gray cars crawls along an invisible track, gives out a ghastly creak, and comes to rest, and immediately the ash-gray men swarm up with leaden spades and stir up an impenetrable cloud, which screens their obscure operations from your sight.

But above the gray land and the spasms of bleak dust which drift endlessly over it, you perceive, after a moment, the eyes of Doctor T. J. Eckleburg. The eyes of Doctor T. J. Eckleburg are blue and gigantic—their retinas[4] are one yard high. They look out of no face, but, instead, from a pair of enormous yellow spectacles which pass over a non-existent nose. Evidently some wild wag of an oculist[5] set them there to fatten his practice in the borough of Queens, and then sank down himself into eternal blindness, or forgot them and moved away. But

[1] *valley of ashes*: The Corona Ash Dump or Mount Corona in the Corona neighborhood of Queens received tons of furnace ash and other debris from around the area. The city cleared it for the 1939 New York World's Fair.

[2] *fantastic*: imaginary; fanciful.

[3] *grotesque*: distorted, exaggerated; absurd.

[4] *retinas*: backs of the eyeballs, where light triggers rods and cones. Some scholars believe Fitzgerald mistook retina for "iris", the front membrane of the eye, but an established literary precedent allows "retina" to represent the whole, e.g., an impression or sight "on the retina".

[5] *wag . . . oculist*: joking or playfully mischievous optician or ophthalmologist.

his eyes, dimmed a little by many paintless days under sun and rain, brood on over the solemn dumping ground.

The valley of ashes is bounded on one side by a small foul river, and, when the drawbridge is up to let barges through, the passengers on waiting trains can stare at the dismal scene for as long as half an hour. There is always a halt there of at least a minute, and it was because of this that I first met Tom Buchanan's mistress.[6]

The fact that he had one was insisted upon wherever he was known. His acquaintances resented the fact that he turned up in popular restaurants with her and, leaving her at a table, sauntered about, chatting with whomsoever he knew. Though I was curious to see her, I had no desire to meet her—but I did. I went up to New York with Tom on the train one afternoon, and when we stopped by the ashheaps he jumped to his feet and, taking hold of my elbow, literally forced me from the car.

"We're getting off," he insisted. "I want you to meet my girl."

I think he'd tanked up[7] a good deal at luncheon, and his determination to have my company bordered on violence. The supercilious assumption was that on Sunday afternoon I had nothing better to do.

I followed him over a low whitewashed railroad fence, and we walked back a hundred yards along the road under Doctor Eckleburg's persistent stare. The only building in sight was a small block of yellow brick sitting on the edge of the waste land,[8] a sort of compact Main Street ministering[9] to it, and contiguous[10] to absolutely nothing. One of the three shops it contained was for rent and another was an all-night restaurant, approached by a trail of ashes; the third was a garage—*Repairs*. GEORGE B. WILSON. *Cars bought and sold.*—and I followed Tom inside.

[6] *mistress*: woman not one's wife with whom one is having a sexual (and necessarily adulterous) relationship.

[7] *tanked up*: slang for heavy consumption of alcohol.

[8] *the waste land*: reference to "The Waste Land", T. S. Eliot's famous poem published in late 1922.

[9] *ministering*: to be of service, especially to one in need, and often with religious function.

[10] *contiguous*: touching, bordering, or neighboring.

The interior was unprosperous and bare; the only car visible was the dust-covered wreck of a Ford which crouched in a dim corner. It had occurred to me that this shadow of a garage must be a blind,[11] and that sumptuous[12] and romantic apartments were concealed overhead, when the proprietor himself appeared in the door of an office, wiping his hands on a piece of waste. He was a blond, spiritless man, anaemic,[13] and faintly handsome. When he saw us a damp gleam of hope sprang into his light blue eyes.

"Hello, Wilson, old man," said Tom, slapping him jovially on the shoulder. "How's business?"

"I can't complain," answered Wilson unconvincingly. "When are you going to sell me that car?"

"Next week; I've got my man working on it now."

"Works pretty slow, don't he?"

"No, he doesn't," said Tom coldly. "And if you feel that way about it, maybe I'd better sell it somewhere else after all."

"I don't mean that," explained Wilson quickly. "I just meant——"

His voice faded off and Tom glanced impatiently around the garage. Then I heard footsteps on a stairs, and in a moment the thickish figure of a woman blocked out the light from the office door. She was in the middle thirties, and faintly stout, but she carried her surplus flesh sensuously as some women can. Her face, above a spotted dress of dark blue crêpe-de-chine,[14] contained no facet or gleam of beauty, but there was an immediately perceptible vitality about her as if the nerves of her body were continually smouldering.[15] She smiled slowly and, walking through her husband as if he were a ghost, shook hands with Tom, looking him flush in the eye. Then she wet her lips, and without turning around spoke to her husband in a soft, coarse voice:

[11] *blind*: lawful business hiding a criminal one; a front.
[12] *sumptuous*: costly; luxurious.
[13] *anaemic*: overly pale from a lack of blood; lacking strength.
[14] *crêpe-de-chine*: fine, light fabric ordinarily made of silk.
[15] *smouldering*: burning or smoking without flame.

"Get some chairs, why don't you, so somebody can sit down."

"Oh, sure," agreed Wilson hurriedly, and went toward the little office, mingling immediately with the cement color of the walls. A white ashen dust veiled his dark suit and his pale hair as it veiled everything in the vicinity—except his wife, who moved close to Tom.

"I want to see you," said Tom intently. "Get on the next train."

"All right."

"I'll meet you by the newsstand on the lower level."

She nodded and moved away from him just as George Wilson emerged with two chairs from his office door.

We waited for her down the road and out of sight. It was a few days before the Fourth of July, and a gray, scrawny Italian child was setting torpedoes[16] in a row along the railroad track.

"Terrible place, isn't it," said Tom, exchanging a frown with Doctor Eckleburg.

"Awful."

"It does her good to get away."

"Doesn't her husband object?"

"Wilson? He thinks she goes to see her sister in New York. He's so dumb he doesn't know he's alive."

So Tom Buchanan and his girl and I went up together to New York—or not quite together, for Mrs. Wilson sat discreetly in another car. Tom deferred that much to the sensibilities of those East Eggers who might be on the train.

She had changed her dress to a brown figured muslin,[17] which stretched tight over her rather wide hips as Tom helped her to the platform in New York. At the newsstand she bought a copy of *Town Tattle*[18] and a moving-picture magazine, and in

[16] *torpedoes*: A torpedo is "a toy consisting of fulminating powder and fine gravel wrapped in thin paper, which explodes when thrown on a hard surface" (*OED*).

[17] *muslin*: lightweight, plain fabric usually made of cotton.

[18] Town Tattle: parody of the real *Town Topics* and other such gossip magazines. See Sharon Hamilton, "The New York Gossip Magazine in 'The Great Gatsby'", *F. Scott Fitzgerald Review* 8 (2010): 34–56.

the station drugstore some cold cream and a small flask of perfume. Upstairs, in the solemn echoing drive she let four taxicabs drive away before she selected a new one, lavender-colored with gray upholstery, and in this we slid out from the mass of the station into the glowing sunshine. But immediately she turned sharply from the window and, leaning forward, tapped on the front glass.

"I want to get one of those dogs," she said earnestly. "I want to get one for the apartment. They're nice to have—a dog."

We backed up to a gray old man who bore an absurd resemblance to John D. Rockefeller.[19] In a basket swung from his neck cowered a dozen very recent puppies of an indeterminate breed.

"What kind are they?" asked Mrs. Wilson eagerly, as he came to the taxi-window.

"All kinds. What kind do you want, lady?"

"I'd like to get one of those police dogs; I don't suppose you got that kind?"

The man peered doubtfully into the basket, plunged in his hand and drew one up, wriggling, by the back of the neck.

"That's no police dog," said Tom.

"No, it's not exactly a police dog," said the man with disappointment in his voice. "It's more of an Airedale."[20] He passed his hand over the brown washrag of a back. "Look at that coat. Some coat. That's a dog that'll never bother you with catching cold."

"I think it's cute," said Mrs. Wilson enthusiastically. "How much is it?"

"That dog?" He looked at it admiringly. "That dog will cost you ten dollars."[21]

[19] *John D. Rockefeller*: oil magnate and philanthropist; one of the richest men in the world.

[20] *Airedale*: large, intelligent terriers that saw police duty in Britain in the 1910s.

[21] *ten dollars*: To estimate current value (from 1925 to 2024), multiply by 18.10 (via the Consumer Price Index). E.g., Tom gives the street vendor the modern equivalent of about $181.

The Airedale—undoubtedly there was an Airedale concerned in it somewhere, though its feet were startlingly white—changed hands and settled down into Mrs. Wilson's lap, where she fondled the weatherproof coat with rapture.

"Is it a boy or a girl?" she asked delicately.

"That dog? That dog's a boy."

"It's a bitch,"[22] said Tom decisively. "Here's your money. Go and buy ten more dogs with it."

We drove over to Fifth Avenue, so warm and soft, almost pastoral,[23] on the summer Sunday afternoon that I wouldn't have been surprised to see a great flock of white sheep turn the corner.

"Hold on," I said. "I have to leave you here."

"No, you don't," interposed Tom quickly. "Myrtle'll be hurt if you don't come up to the apartment. Won't you, Myrtle?"

"Come on," she urged. "I'll telephone my sister Catherine. She's said to be very beautiful by people who ought to know."

"Well, I'd like to, but——"

We went on, cutting back again over the Park[24] toward the West Hundreds. At 158th Street the cab stopped at one slice in a long white cake of apartment-houses. Throwing a regal homecoming glance around the neighborhood, Mrs. Wilson gathered up her dog and her other purchases, and went haughtily in.

"I'm going to have the McKees come up," she announced as we rose in the elevator. "And, of course, I got to call up my sister, too."

The apartment was on the top floor—a small living-room, a small dining-room, a small bedroom, and a bath. The living-room was crowded to the doors with a set of tapestried furniture entirely too large for it, so that to move about was to stumble continually over scenes of ladies swinging in the gardens of

[22] *bitch*: female dog. Because it is difficult to imagine the street vendor misidentifying the dog's gender (which would be easily visible), scholars generally see Tom's statement as applying to Myrtle; that is, he buys her presents in return for her supplying him with sexual favors.

[23] *pastoral*: bucolic; romantically rural.

[24] *the Park*: Central Park.

Versailles. The only picture was an over-enlarged photograph, apparently a hen sitting on a blurred rock. Looked at from a distance, however, the hen resolved itself into a bonnet, and the countenance of a stout old lady beamed down into the room. Several old copies of *Town Tattle* lay on the table together with a copy of *Simon Called Peter*,[25] and some of the small scandal magazines of Broadway. Mrs. Wilson was first concerned with the dog. A reluctant elevator boy went for a box full of straw and some milk, to which he added on his own initiative a tin of large, hard dog-biscuits—one of which decomposed apathetically in the saucer of milk all afternoon. Meanwhile Tom brought out a bottle of whiskey from a locked bureau door.

I have been drunk just twice in my life, and the second time was that afternoon; so everything that happened has a dim, hazy cast over it, although until after eight o'clock the apartment was full of cheerful sun. Sitting on Tom's lap Mrs. Wilson called up several people on the telephone; then there were no cigarettes, and I went out to buy some at the drugstore on the corner. When I came back they had disappeared, so I sat down discreetly in the living-room and read a chapter of *Simon Called Peter*—either it was terrible stuff or the whiskey distorted things, because it didn't make any sense to me.

Just as Tom and Myrtle (after the first drink Mrs. Wilson and I called each other by our first names) reappeared, company commenced to arrive at the apartment-door.

The sister, Catherine, was a slender, worldly girl of about thirty, with a solid, sticky bob[26] of red hair, and a complexion powdered milky white. Her eyebrows had been plucked and then drawn on again at a more rakish[27] angle, but the efforts of nature toward the restoration of the old alignment gave a blurred air to her face. When she moved about there was an incessant clicking as innumerable pottery bracelets jingled up

[25] Simon Called Peter: bestselling novel by Robert Keable published by E. P. Dutton in 1921; its protagonist Catholic priest carries on a sexual affair with a nurse.

[26] *bob*: short, even women's haircut. See also Fitzgerald's mid-1920 short story "Bernice Bobs Her Hair".

[27] *rakish*: jaunty; slanting.

and down upon her arms. She came in with such a proprietary[28] haste, and looked around so possessively at the furniture that I wondered if she lived here. But when I asked her she laughed immoderately, repeated my question aloud, and told me she lived with a girl friend[29] at a hotel.

Mr. McKee was a pale, feminine man from the flat[30] below. He had just shaved, for there was a white spot of lather on his cheekbone, and he was most respectful in his greeting to everyone in the room. He informed me that he was in the "artistic game," and I gathered later that he was a photographer and had made the dim enlargement of Mrs. Wilson's mother which hovered like an ectoplasm[31] on the wall. His wife was shrill, languid, handsome,[32] and horrible. She told me with pride that her husband had photographed her a hundred and twenty-seven times since they had been married.

Mrs. Wilson had changed her costume[33] some time before, and was now attired in an elaborate afternoon dress of cream-colored chiffon,[34] which gave out a continual rustle as she swept about the room. With the influence of the dress her personality had also undergone a change. The intense vitality that had been so remarkable in the garage was converted into impressive hauteur.[35] Her laughter, her gestures, her assertions became more violently affected moment by moment, and as she expanded the room grew smaller around her, until she seemed to be revolving on a noisy, creaking pivot through the smoky air.

[28] *proprietary*: as if she were the proprietor or owner.

[29] *girl friend*: that is, a roommate, assumedly platonic.

[30] *flat*: set of rooms on one floor; uncommon in American English.

[31] *ectoplasm*: Fitzgerald draws here on the horror genre and the occult practice of spiritualism, in which ectoplasm is what oozes from a medium and takes human form. The other famous use of the word in American literature is the masterpiece opening of Ralph Ellison's 1952 *Invisible Man*: "No, I am not a spook like those who haunted Edgar Allan Poe; nor am I one of your Hollywood-movie ectoplasms."

[32] *handsome*: even in the early twentieth century, commonly used of women as noble and dignified instead of pretty.

[33] *costume*: Fitzgerald's choice here emphasizes the clothing as being worn to act a certain part or role.

[34] *chiffon*: translucent fabric, often made of silk.

[35] *hauteur*: haughtiness; being lofty.

"My dear," she told her sister in a high, mincing[36] shout, "most of these fellas will cheat you every time. All they think of is money. I had a woman up here last week to look at my feet, and when she gave me the bill you'd of thought she had my appendicitis[37] out."

"What was the name of the woman?" asked Mrs. McKee.

"Mrs. Eberhardt. She goes around looking at people's feet in their own homes."

"I like your dress," remarked Mrs. McKee, "I think it's adorable."

Mrs. Wilson rejected the compliment by raising her eyebrow in disdain.

"It's just a crazy old thing," she said. "I just slip it on sometimes when I don't care what I look like."

"But it looks wonderful on you, if you know what I mean," pursued Mrs. McKee. "If Chester could only get you in that pose I think he could make something of it."

We all looked in silence at Mrs. Wilson, who removed a strand of hair from over her eyes and looked back at us with a brilliant smile. Mr. McKee regarded her intently with his head on one side, and then moved his hand back and forth slowly in front of his face.

"I should change the light," he said after a moment. "I'd like to bring out the modelling of the features. And I'd try to get hold of all the back hair."

"I wouldn't think of changing the light," cried Mrs. McKee, "I think it's——"

Her husband said "*Sh!*" and we all looked at the subject again, where upon Tom Buchanan yawned audibly and got to his feet.

"You McKees have something to drink," he said. "Get some more ice and mineral water,[38] Myrtle, before everybody goes to sleep."

[36] *mincing*: affectedly refined or elegant.

[37] *appendicitis*: Myrtle confuses her actual appendix with the condition, appendicitis, that occasions its removal.

[38] *mineral water*: Touted for its health benefits, mineral water could also be used in mixed drinks. See John J. Riley, *A History of the American Soft Drink Industry* (New York: Arno Press, 1972).

"I told that boy about the ice." Myrtle raised her eyebrows in despair at the shiftlessness[39] of the lower orders. "These people! You have to keep after them all the time."

She looked at me and laughed pointlessly. Then she flounced[40] over to the dog, kissed it with ecstasy, and swept into the kitchen, implying that a dozen chefs awaited her orders there.

"I've done some nice things out on Long Island," asserted Mr. McKee.

Tom looked at him blankly.

"Two of them we have framed downstairs."

"Two what?" demanded Tom.

"Two studies. One of them I call *Montauk Point*[41]*—The Gulls*, and the other I call *Montauk Point—The Sea*."

The sister Catherine sat down beside me on the couch.

"Do you live down on Long Island, too?" she inquired.

"I live at West Egg."

"Really? I was down there at a party about a month ago. At a man named Gatsby's. Do you know him?"

"I live next door to him."

"Well, they say he's a nephew or a cousin of Kaiser Wilhelm's.[42] That's where all his money comes from."

"Really?"

She nodded.

"I'm scared of him. I'd hate to have him get anything on me."

This absorbing information about my neighbor was interrupted by Mrs. McKee's pointing suddenly at Catherine:

"Chester, I think you could do something with *her*," she broke out, but Mr. McKee only nodded in a bored way, and turned his attention to Tom.

"I'd like to do more work on Long Island, if I could get the entry. All I ask is that they should give me a start."

[39] *shiftlessness*: laziness; lacking resourcefulness or work ethic.

[40] *flounced*: "to go with agitated, clumsy, or violent motion; to dash, flop, plunge, rush" (*OED*).

[41] Montauk Point: very end of Long Island, and the easternmost point of New York.

[42] *Kaiser Wilhelm's*: reference to William II, who was the last emperor of Germany and a well-known public figure.

"Ask Myrtle," said Tom, breaking into a short shout of laughter as Mrs. Wilson entered with a tray. "She'll give you a letter of introduction,[43] won't you, Myrtle?"

"Do what?" she asked, startled.

"You'll give McKee a letter of introduction to your husband, so he can do some studies of him." His lips moved silently for a moment as he invented. "'*George B. Wilson at the Gasoline Pump*,' or something like that."

Catherine leaned close to me and whispered in my ear:

"Neither of them can stand the person they're married to."

"Can't they?"

"Can't *stand* them." She looked at Myrtle and then at Tom. "What I say is, why go on living with them if they can't stand them? If I was them I'd get a divorce and get married to each other right away."

"Doesn't she like Wilson either?"

The answer to this was unexpected. It came from Myrtle, who had overheard the question, and it was violent and obscene.

"You see," cried Catherine triumphantly. She lowered her voice again. "It's really his wife that's keeping them apart. She's a Catholic, and they don't believe in divorce."[44]

Daisy was not a Catholic, and I was a little shocked at the elaborateness of the lie.

"When they do get married," continued Catherine, "they're going West to live for a while until it blows over."

"It'd be more discreet to go to Europe."

"Oh, do you like Europe?" she exclaimed surprisingly. "I just got back from Monte Carlo."[45]

"Really."

"Just last year. I went over there with another girl."

"Stay long?"

[43] *letter of introduction*: A formal letter detailing and approving the talents of someone outside the social circles of the addressee was often the only way for that person to gain access to high society.

[44] *Catholic ... divorce*: Catherine is correct that a declaration of nullity (an annulment) would have to be pursued to demonstrate that the marriage was never valid.

[45] *Monte Carlo*: district in the city-state of Monaco with a world-famous casino; also, the site of the first Women's Olympiad in 1921.

"No, we just went to Monte Carlo and back. We went by way of Marseilles. We had over twelve hundred dollars when we started, but we got gypped[46] out of it all in two days in the private rooms.[47] We had an awful time getting back, I can tell you. God, how I hated that town!"

The late afternoon sky bloomed in the window for a moment like the blue honey of the Mediterranean—then the shrill voice of Mrs. McKee called me back into the room.

"I almost made a mistake, too," she declared vigorously. "I almost married a little kike[48] who'd been after me for years. I knew he was below me. Everybody kept saying to me: 'Lucille, that man's way below you!' But if I hadn't met Chester, he'd of got me sure."

"Yes, but listen," said Myrtle Wilson, nodding her head up and down. "At least you didn't marry him."

"I know I didn't."

"Well, I married him," said Myrtle, ambiguously.[49] "And that's the difference between your case and mine."

"Why did you, Myrtle?" demanded Catherine. "Nobody forced you to."

Myrtle considered.

"I married him because I thought he was a gentleman," she said finally. "I thought he knew something about breeding, but he wasn't fit to lick my shoe."

"You were crazy about him for a while," said Catherine.

"Crazy about him!" cried Myrtle incredulously. "Who said I was crazy about him? I never was any more crazy about him than I was about that man there."

She pointed suddenly at me, and everyone looked at me accusingly. I tried to show by my expression that I had played no part in her past.

[46] *gypped*: to be cheated out of money.

[47] *private rooms*: in a casino, betting tables and games in restricted areas by invitation only.

[48] *kike*: "derogatory and offensive [term for] a Jewish person" (*OED*).

[49] *ambiguously*: with ambivalence or mixed feelings.

"The only *crazy* I was was when I married him. I knew right away I made a mistake. He borrowed somebody's best suit to get married in, and never even told me about it, and the man came after it one day when he was out: 'Oh, is that your suit?' I said. 'This is the first I ever heard about it.' But I gave it to him and then I lay down and cried to beat the band[50] all afternoon."

"She really ought to get away from him," resumed Catherine to me. "They've been living over that garage for eleven years. And Tom's the first sweetie[51] she ever had."

The bottle of whiskey—a second one—was now in constant demand by all present, excepting Catherine, who "felt just as good on nothing at all." Tom rang for the janitor[52] and sent him for some celebrated sandwiches, which were a complete supper in themselves. I wanted to get out and walk eastward toward the Park through the soft twilight, but each time I tried to go I became entangled in some wild, strident argument which pulled me back, as if with ropes, into my chair. Yet high over the city our line of yellow windows must have contributed their share of human secrecy to the casual watcher in the darkening streets, and I was him too, looking up and wondering. I was within and without, simultaneously enchanted and repelled by the inexhaustible variety of life.

Myrtle pulled her chair close to mine, and suddenly her warm breath poured over me the story of her first meeting with Tom.

"It was on the two little seats facing each other that are always the last ones left on the train. I was going up to New York to see my sister and spend the night. He had on a dress suit and patent leather shoes, and I couldn't keep my eyes off him, but every time he looked at me I had to pretend to be looking at the advertisement over his head. When we came into the station he was next to me, and his white shirt-front

[50] *beat the band*: "so as to drown the noise made by the band; hence, to exceed, surpass, or beat everything" (*OED*).

[51] *sweetie*: American colloquialism for a lover in an endearing sense.

[52] *janitor*: not merely a cleaning man but "a caretaker of a building" (*OED*).

pressed against my arm, and so I told him I'd have to call a policeman, but he knew I lied. I was so excited that when I got into a taxi with him I didn't hardly know I wasn't getting into a subway train. All I kept thinking about, over and over, was 'You can't live forever; you can't live forever.'"

She turned to Mrs. McKee and the room rang full of her artificial laughter.

"My dear," she cried, "I'm going to give you this dress as soon as I'm through with it. I've got to get another one tomorrow. I'm going to make a list of all the things I've got to get. A massage and a wave,[53] and a collar for the dog, and one of those cute little ash-trays where you touch a spring, and a wreath with a black silk bow for mother's grave that'll last all summer. I got to write down a list so I won't forget all the things I got to do."

It was nine o'clock—almost immediately afterward I looked at my watch and found it was ten. Mr. McKee was asleep on a chair with his fists clenched in his lap, like a photograph of a man of action. Taking out my handkerchief I wiped from his cheek the remains of the spot of dried lather that had worried me all the afternoon.

The little dog was sitting on the table looking with blind eyes through the smoke, and from time to time groaning faintly. People disappeared, reappeared, made plans to go somewhere, and then lost each other, searched for each other, found each other a few feet away. Some time toward midnight Tom Buchanan and Mrs. Wilson stood face to face discussing, in impassioned voices, whether Mrs. Wilson had any right to mention Daisy's name.

"Daisy! Daisy! Daisy!" shouted Mrs. Wilson. "I'll say it whenever I want to! Daisy! Dai——"

Making a short deft movement, Tom Buchanan broke her nose with his open hand.

Then there were bloody towels upon the bathroom floor, and women's voices scolding, and high over the confusion a

[53] *wave*: popular 1920s women's hairstyle, often referred to as "finger waves" or "Marcel waves".

long broken wail of pain. Mr. McKee awoke from his doze and started in a daze toward the door. When he had gone half-way he turned around and stared at the scene—his wife and Catherine scolding and consoling as they stumbled here and there among the crowded furniture with articles of aid, and the despairing figure on the couch, bleeding fluently,[54] and trying to spread a copy of *Town Tattle* over the tapestry scenes of Versailles. Then Mr. McKee turned and continued on out the door. Taking my hat from the chandelier,[55] I followed.

"Come to lunch some day," he suggested, as we groaned down in the elevator.

"Where?"

"Anywhere."

"Keep your hands off the lever," snapped the elevator boy.

"I beg your pardon," said Mr. McKee with dignity. "I didn't know I was touching it."

"All right," I agreed, "I'll be glad to."

... I was standing beside his bed and he was sitting up between the sheets, clad in his underwear, with a great portfolio in his hands.

"Beauty and the Beast ... Loneliness ... Old Grocery Horse ... Brook'n Bridge...."

Then I was lying half-asleep in the cold lower level of the Pennsylvania Station,[56] staring at the morning *Tribune*,[57] and waiting for the four o'clock train.

[54] *fluently*: readily, with ease.

[55] *hat ... chandelier*: This joke enhances the frivolity and wildness of the party, as the hat would normally be placed on a hat rack (a standard at this time), and one wonders how the hat made it high up to the luxurious light fixture.

[56] *Pennsylvania Station*: Opened in 1910, Penn Station continues to be the busiest railway station in America.

[57] Tribune: The *New-York Tribune*, established in 1841, was one of the most reputable daily newspapers in the country. It would become the *New York Herald Tribune* in 1924.

CHAPTER III

THERE WAS MUSIC from my neighbor's house through the summer nights. In his blue gardens men and girls came and went like moths among the whisperings and the champagne and the stars. At high tide in the afternoon I watched his guests diving from the tower of his raft, or taking the sun on the hot sand of his beach while his two motor-boats slit the waters of the Sound, drawing aquaplanes[1] over cataracts[2] of foam. On weekends his Rolls-Royce became an omnibus, bearing parties to and from the city between nine in the morning and long past midnight, while his station wagon scampered like a brisk yellow bug to meet all trains. And on Mondays eight servants, including an extra gardener, toiled all day with mops and scrubbing-brushes and hammers and garden-shears, repairing the ravages of the night before.

Every Friday five crates of oranges and lemons arrived from a fruiterer in New York—every Monday these same oranges and lemons left his back door in a pyramid of pulpless halves. There was a machine in the kitchen which could extract the juice of two hundred oranges in half an hour if a little button was pressed two hundred times by a butler's thumb.[3]

At least once a fortnight a corps of caterers came down with several hundred feet of canvas and enough colored lights to make a Christmas tree of Gatsby's enormous garden. On buffet tables, garnished with glistening hors d'oeuvre, spiced baked hams crowded against salads of harlequin[4] designs and pastry

[1] *aquaplanes*: An aquaplane is "a board which rides on the surface of the water when towed with its rider by a speedboat" (*OED*).

[2] *cataracts*: A cataract is "a violent downpour or rush of water" (*OED*).

[3] *butler's thumb*: second entry in the running gag of butlers' overtaxed body parts.

[4] *harlequin*: i.e., like the typical harlequin costume: red, white, and black diamond patterns, for instance.

pigs and turkeys bewitched to a dark gold. In the main hall a bar with a real brass rail was set up, and stocked with gins and liquors and with cordials so long forgotten that most of his female guests were too young to know one from another.

By seven o'clock the orchestra has arrived, no thin five-piece affair, but a whole pitful of oboes and trombones and saxophones and viols and cornets and piccolos, and low and high drums. The last swimmers have come in from the beach now and are dressing upstairs; the cars from New York are parked five deep in the drive, and already the halls and salons and verandas are gaudy with primary colors, and hair shorn in strange new ways, and shawls beyond the dreams of Castile.[5] The bar is in full swing, and floating rounds of cocktails permeate the garden outside, until the air is alive with chatter and laughter, and casual innuendo and introductions forgotten on the spot, and enthusiastic meetings between women who never knew each other's names.

The lights grow brighter as the earth lurches away from the sun, and now the orchestra is playing yellow cocktail music, and the opera of voices pitches a key higher. Laughter is easier minute by minute, spilled with prodigality,[6] tipped out at a cheerful word. The groups change more swiftly, swell with new arrivals, dissolve and form in the same breath; already there are wanderers, confident girls who weave here and there among the stouter and more stable, become for a sharp, joyous moment the center of a group, and then, excited with triumph, glide on through the sea-change of faces and voices and color under the constantly changing light.

Suddenly one of these gypsies, in trembling opal, seizes a cocktail out of the air, dumps it down for courage and, moving her hands like Frisco,[7] dances out alone on the canvas platform. A momentary hush; the orchestra leader varies his

[5] *Castile*: region in Spain where traditional women's dress often included an elaborate shawl or mantilla.

[6] *prodigality*: abundance; lavishly.

[7] *Frisco*: Joe Frisco, hugely popular jazz dancer and comedian, who debuted on Broadway in 1918 in a production of the *Ziegfeld Follies* (see next note).

rhythm obligingly for her, and there is a burst of chatter as the erroneous news goes around that she is Gilda Gray's understudy from the Follies.[8] The party has begun.

I believe that on the first night I went to Gatsby's house I was one of the few guests who had actually been invited. People were not invited—they went there. They got into automobiles which bore them out to Long Island, and somehow they ended up at Gatsby's door. Once there they were introduced by somebody who knew Gatsby, and after that they conducted themselves according to the rules of behavior associated with an amusement park. Sometimes they came and went without having met Gatsby at all, came for the party with a simplicity of heart that was its own ticket of admission.

I had been actually invited. A chauffeur in a uniform of robin's-egg blue crossed my lawn early that Saturday morning with a surprisingly formal note from his employer: the honor would be entirely Gatsby's, it said, if I would attend his "little party" that night. He had seen me several times, and had intended to call on[9] me long before, but a peculiar combination of circumstances had prevented it—signed Jay Gatsby, in a majestic hand.

Dressed up in white flannels I went over to his lawn a little after seven, and wandered around rather ill at ease among swirls and eddies[10] of people I didn't know—though here and there was a face I had noticed on the commuting train. I was immediately struck by the number of young Englishmen dotted about; all well dressed, all looking a little hungry, and all talking in low, earnest voices to solid and prosperous Americans. I was sure that they were selling something: bonds or insurance or automobiles. They were at least agonizingly aware of the easy money in the vicinity and convinced that it was theirs for a few words in the right key.

[8] *Gilda Gray's … Follies*: Gilda Gray was a popular actress and dancer who popularized the somewhat scandalous "shimmy" dance move. The *Zeigfeld Follies* was a long-running, extravagant Broadway revue show; Gray starred in 1922.

[9] *call on*: make a formal introduction, for which purpose "calling cards" were printed, carried, and offered.

[10] *eddies*: small whirlpools—and the pun on the name "Eddie" is obvious.

As soon as I arrived I made an attempt to find my host, but the two or three people of whom I asked his whereabouts stared at me in such an amazed way, and denied so vehemently[11] any knowledge of his movements, that I slunk off in the direction of the cocktail table—the only place in the garden where a single man could linger without looking purposeless and alone.

I was on my way to get roaring drunk from sheer embarrassment when Jordan Baker came out of the house and stood at the head of the marble steps, leaning a little backward and looking with contemptuous interest down into the garden.

Welcome or not, I found it necessary to attach myself to someone before I should begin to address cordial remarks to the passers-by.

"Hello!" I roared, advancing toward her. My voice seemed unnaturally loud across the garden.

"I thought you might be here," she responded absently as I came up. "I remembered you lived next door to——"

She held my hand impersonally, as a promise that she'd take care of me in a minute, and gave ear to two girls in twin yellow dresses, who stopped at the foot of the steps.

"Hello!" they cried together. "Sorry you didn't win."

That was for the golf tournament. She had lost in the finals the week before.

"You don't know who we are," said one of the girls in yellow, "but we met you here about a month ago."

"You've dyed your hair since then," remarked Jordan, and I started, but the girls had moved casually on and her remark was addressed to the premature moon,[12] produced like the supper, no doubt, out of a caterer's basket. With Jordan's slender golden arm resting in mine, we descended the steps and sauntered about the garden. A tray of cocktails floated at us through the twilight, and we sat down at a table with the two

[11] *vehemently*: forcefully; with anxiety.

[12] *premature moon*: perhaps a literal paper moon, a romanticized decoration at odds with the actual phase of the moon. For an analysis of Fitzgerald's imagistic patterning here, see Sister M. Bettina, "The Artifact in Imagery", *Twentieth Century Literature* 9, no. 3 (October 1963): 140–42.

girls in yellow and three men, each one introduced to us as Mr. Mumble.

"Do you come to these parties often?" inquired Jordan of the girl beside her.

"The last one was the one I met you at," answered the girl, in an alert confident voice. She turned to her companion: "Wasn't it for you, Lucille?"

It was for Lucille, too.

"I like to come," Lucille said. "I never care what I do, so I always have a good time. When I was here last I tore my gown on a chair, and he asked me my name and address—inside of a week I got a package from Croirier's[13] with a new evening gown in it."

"Did you keep it?" asked Jordan.

"Sure I did. I was going to wear it tonight, but it was too big in the bust and had to be altered. It was gas blue with lavender beads. Two hundred and sixty-five dollars."

"There's something funny about a fellow that'll do a thing like that," said the other girl eagerly. "He doesn't want any trouble with *any*body."

"Who doesn't?" I inquired.

"Gatsby. Somebody told me——"

The two girls and Jordan leaned together confidentially.

"Somebody told me they thought he killed a man once."

A thrill passed over all of us. The three Mr. Mumbles bent forward and listened eagerly.

"I don't think it's so much *that*," argued Lucille skeptically; "it's more that he was a German spy during the war."

One of the men nodded in confirmation.

"I heard that from a man who knew all about him, grew up with him in Germany," he assured us positively.

"Oh, no," said the first girl, "it couldn't be that, because he was in the American army during the war." As our credulity

[13] *Croirier's*: Matthew Bruccoli suggests, as no such business existed, that Fitzgerald was echoing "Poiret's" after Paul Poiret (1879–1944), a master French fashion designer of the time. F. Scott Fitzgerald, *The Great Gatsby*, ed. Matthew Bruccoli (New York: Cambridge University Press, 1991), p. 187.

switched back to her she leaned forward with enthusiasm. "You look at him sometime when he thinks nobody's looking at him. I'll bet he killed a man."

She narrowed her eyes and shivered. Lucille shivered. We all turned and looked around for Gatsby. It was testimony to the romantic[14] speculation he inspired that there were whispers about him from those who had found little that it was necessary to whisper about in this world.

The first supper—there would be another one after midnight—was now being served, and Jordan invited me to join her own party, who were spread around a table on the other side of the garden. There were three married couples and Jordan's escort, a persistent undergraduate given to violent innuendo, and obviously under the impression that sooner or later Jordan was going to yield him up her person to a greater or lesser degree. Instead of rambling this party had preserved a dignified homogeneity,[15] and assumed to itself the function of representing the staid[16] nobility of the countryside—East Egg condescending to West Egg, and carefully on guard against its spectroscopic[17] gayety.

"Let's get out," whispered Jordan, after a somehow wasteful and inappropriate half-hour; "this is much too polite for me."

We got up, and she explained that we were going to find the host: I had never met him, she said, and it was making me uneasy. The undergraduate nodded in a cynical, melancholy way.

The bar, where we glanced first, was crowded, but Gatsby was not there. She couldn't find him from the top of the steps, and he wasn't on the veranda. On a chance we tried an important-looking door, and walked into a high Gothic library, panelled

[14] *romantic*: imaginary; fanciful.

[15] *homogeneity*: of the same character; of uniform composition.

[16] *staid*: steady; dignified.

[17] *spectroscopic*: A rare word outside of physics and astronomy, it refers to the observation of spectra or a spectrum, such as the rainbow of light emitted by a prism. With the use of "retinas" in the previous chapter, Fitzgerald may have had in mind the idea of a spectrum as "the image retained for a time on the retina of the eye when turned away after gazing fixedly for some time at a bright colored object" (*OED*).

with carved English oak, and probably transported complete from some ruin overseas.

A stout, middle-aged man, with enormous owl-eyed spectacles, was sitting somewhat drunk on the edge of a great table, staring with unsteady concentration at the shelves of books. As we entered he wheeled excitedly around and examined Jordan from head to foot.

"What do you think?" he demanded impetuously.[18]

"About what?"

He waved his hand toward the bookshelves.

"About that. As a matter of fact you needn't bother to ascertain. I ascertained. They're real."

"The books?"

He nodded.

"Absolutely real—have pages and everything. I thought they'd be a nice durable cardboard. Matter of fact, they're absolutely real. Pages and—Here! Lemme show you."

Taking our skepticism for granted, he rushed to the bookcases and returned with Volume One of the "Stoddard[19] Lectures."

"See!" he cried triumphantly. "It's a bona-fide piece of printed matter. It fooled me. This fella's a regular Belasco.[20] It's a triumph. What thoroughness! What realism! Knew when to stop, too—didn't cut the pages.[21] But what do you want? What do you expect?"

He snatched the book from me and replaced it hastily on its shelf, muttering that if one brick was removed the whole library was liable to collapse.

[18] *impetuously*: with sudden force or energy.

[19] *Stoddard*: John L. Stoddard (1850–1931) popularized the travel genre through his widely attended lectures featuring an early version of a slide projector, the stereopticon. Also, John L. Stoddard was the father of Lothrop Stoddard (see note 34 in chapter 1).

[20] *Belasco*: David Belasco (1853–1931), theater producer whose lavish and fastidious sets made him a household name. He was often dressed in a clerical collar or a cassock, thus his nickname was the "bishop of Broadway".

[21] *cut the pages*: Some books of the time would be published without the edges trimmed; readers would need to use a penknife or something similar to cut and open each page in succession. A book with uncut pages, therefore, has not been read.

"Who brought you?" he demanded. "Or did you just come? I was brought. Most people were brought."

Jordan looked at him alertly, cheerfully, without answering.

"I was brought by a woman named Roosevelt," he continued. "Mrs. Claud Roosevelt. Do you know her? I met her somewhere last night. I've been drunk for about a week now, and I thought it might sober me up to sit in a library."

"Has it?"

"A little bit, I think. I can't tell yet. I've only been here an hour. Did I tell you about the books? They're real. They're——"

"You told us."

We shook hands with him gravely and went back outdoors.

There was dancing now on the canvas in the garden; old men pushing young girls backward in eternal graceless circles, superior couples holding each other tortuously,[22] fashionably, and keeping in the corners—and a great number of single girls dancing individualistically or relieving the orchestra for a moment of the burden of the banjo or the traps.[23] By midnight the hilarity had increased. A celebrated tenor had sung in Italian, and a notorious contralto had sung in jazz, and between the numbers people were doing "stunts" all over the garden, while happy, vacuous[24] bursts of laughter rose toward the summer sky. A pair of stage twins, who turned out to be the girls in yellow, did a baby act in costume, and champagne was served in glasses bigger than finger-bowls.[25] The moon had risen higher, and floating in the Sound was a triangle of silver scales,[26] trembling a little to the stiff, tinny drip of the banjoes on the lawn.

I was still with Jordan Baker. We were sitting at a table with a man of about my age and a rowdy little girl, who gave way

[22] *tortuously*: i.e., dancing with many twists and turns.

[23] *traps*: "in a jazz or dance band, percussion instruments or devices [e.g., wood-blocks, whistles] used to produce a variety of special effects" (*OED*).

[24] *vacuous*: unintelligent; mentally empty.

[25] *finger-bowls*: traditional, small bowls for rinsing or cleaning one's fingers. Champagne is customarily served in stemmed glasses about the same size.

[26] *scales*: i.e., scale-like reflections of the moon on the waters.

upon the slightest provocation to uncontrollable laughter. I was enjoying myself now. I had taken two finger-bowls of champagne, and the scene had changed before my eyes into something significant, elemental,[27] and profound.

At a lull in the entertainment the man looked at me and smiled.

"Your face is familiar," he said, politely. "Weren't you in the Third Division[28] during the war?"

"Why, yes. I was in the ninth machine-gun battalion."[29]

"I was in the Seventh Infantry until June nineteen-eighteen.[30] I knew I'd seen you somewhere before."

We talked for a moment about some wet, gray little villages in France. Evidently he lived in this vicinity, for he told me that he had just bought a hydroplane,[31] and was going to try it out in the morning.

"Want to go with me, old sport? Just near the shore along the Sound."

"What time?"

"Any time that suits you best."

It was on the tip of my tongue to ask his name when Jordan looked around and smiled.

"Having a gay time now?" she inquired.

"Much better." I turned again to my new acquaintance. "This is an unusual party for me. I haven't even seen the host.

[27] *elemental*: like a force of nature.

[28] *Third Division*: Third Infantry Division of the U.S. Army, which earned the nickname "Rock of the Marne" for its repeated repulsions of Germans at the Marne River just outside Paris.

[29] *ninth ... battalion*: Fitzgerald originally had Nick serving in the "Twenty-eighth Infantry" and Gatsby in the "Sixteenth", neither of which were in the Third Division. Fitzgerald's revisions, as represented in this text, are correct for the Third Division and allow for them to have glimpsed each other.

[30] *June nineteen-eighteen*: June 1918 was a very specific, important date; the famous Second Battle of the Marne occurred from July 15 to July 18, which means Gatsby either missed it or, as Bruccoli argues, "was transferred ... in time for the Argonne Forest battle." F. Scott Fitzgerald, *The Great Gatsby*, The Authorized Text, preface and notes by Matthew J. Bruccoli (New York: Scribner, 1995).

[31] *hydroplane*: fast, sleek racing motorboat designed to skim the water; or, a seaplane, which can take off and alight on water. Gatsby later tells Nick "we're going up" in the hydroplane, so the latter meaning is the case.

I live over there—" I waved my hand at the invisible hedge in the distance, "and this man Gatsby sent over his chauffeur with an invitation."

For a moment he looked at me as if he failed to understand.

"I'm Gatsby," he said suddenly.

"What!" I exclaimed. "Oh, I beg your pardon."

"I thought you knew, old sport. I'm afraid I'm not a very good host."

He smiled understandingly—much more than understandingly. It was one of those rare smiles with a quality of eternal reassurance in it, that you may come across four or five times in life. It faced—or seemed to face—the whole external world for an instant, and then concentrated on *you* with an irresistible prejudice[32] in your favor. It understood you just so far as you wanted to be understood, believed in you as you would like to believe in yourself, and assured you that it had precisely the impression of you that, at your best, you hoped to convey. Precisely at that point it vanished—and I was looking at an elegant young rough-neck,[33] a year or two over thirty, whose elaborate formality of speech just missed being absurd. Sometime before he introduced himself I'd got a strong impression that he was picking his words with care.

Almost at the moment when Mr. Gatsby identified himself, a butler hurried toward him with the information that Chicago was calling him on the wire. He excused himself with a small bow that included each of us in turn.

"If you want anything just ask for it, old sport," he urged me. "Excuse me. I will rejoin you later."

When he was gone I turned immediately to Jordan—constrained[34] to assure her of my surprise. I had expected that Mr. Gatsby would be a florid[35] and corpulent person in his middle years.

[32] *prejudice*: i.e., favorable preference.

[33] *rough-neck*: "person with rough manners; an uncultivated or uneducated person" (*OED*).

[34] *constrained*: compelled; obligated.

[35] *florid*: ruddy-cheeked in appearance; showy in manner; ornate in language.

"Who is he?" I demanded. "Do you know?"

"He's just a man named Gatsby."

"Where is he from, I mean? And what does he do?"

"Now *you*'re started on the subject," she answered with a wan smile. "Well, he told me once he was an Oxford man."

A dim background started to take shape behind him, but at her next remark it faded away.

"However, I don't believe it."

"Why not?"

"I don't know," she insisted. "I just don't think he went there."

Something in her tone reminded me of the other girl's "I think he killed a man," and had the effect of stimulating my curiosity. I would have accepted without question the information that Gatsby sprang from the swamps of Louisiana or from the Lower East Side of New York. That was comprehensible. But young men didn't—at least in my provincial inexperience I believed they didn't—drift coolly out of nowhere and buy a palace on Long Island Sound.

"Anyhow, he gives large parties," said Jordan, changing the subject with an urban[36] distaste for the concrete. "And I like large parties. They're so intimate.[37] At small parties there isn't any privacy."

There was the boom of a bass drum, and the voice of the orchestra leader rang out suddenly above the echolalia[38] of the garden.

"Ladies and gentlemen," he cried. "At the request of Mr. Gatsby we are going to play for you Mr. Vladimir Tostoff's[39]

[36] *urban*: both "of the city", emphasizing the anonymity that accompanies large urban centers, and a play on "urbane", having the sophistication and elegance to avoid rumor-mongering.

[37] *intimate*: Jordan's use of this word makes sense in light of the popular theater productions mentioned in this chapter. The word can be used in reference to "a theatrical performance, esp. a revue: that aims at establishing familiar and friendly relations with the audience" (*OED*).

[38] *echolalia*: repetition of similar sounds or words.

[39] *Vladimir Tostoff's*: Jeffrey Meyers suggests that Fitzgerald adapted this name from Toby Tostoff, the character in James Joyce's *Ulysses*. See Jeffrey Meyers, "The Literary Lineage of Names in *The Great Gatsby*", *Notes on Contemporary Literature* 43, no. 3 (May 2013): 2–4.

latest work, which attracted so much attention at Carnegie Hall last May. If you read the papers you know there was a big sensation." He smiled with jovial condescension, and added: "Some sensation!" Whereupon everybody laughed.

"The piece is known," he concluded lustily,[40] "as 'Vladimir Tostoff's Jazz History of the World.'"[41]

The nature of Mr. Tostoff's composition eluded me, because just as it began my eyes fell on Gatsby, standing alone on the marble steps and looking from one group to another with approving eyes. His tanned skin was drawn attractively tight on his face and his short hair looked as though it were trimmed every day. I could see nothing sinister about him. I wondered if the fact that he was not drinking helped to set him off from his guests, for it seemed to me that he grew more correct as the fraternal hilarity increased. When the "Jazz History of the World" was over, girls were putting their heads on men's shoulders in a puppyish, convivial way, girls were swooning backward playfully into men's arms, even into groups, knowing that someone would arrest their falls—but no one swooned backward on Gatsby, and no French bob touched Gatsby's shoulder, and no singing quartets were formed with Gatsby's head for one link.

"I beg your pardon."

Gatsby's butler was suddenly standing beside us.

"Miss Baker?" he inquired. "I beg your pardon, but Mr. Gatsby would like to speak to you alone."

"With me?" she exclaimed in surprise.

"Yes, madame."

She got up slowly, raising her eyebrows at me in astonishment, and followed the butler toward the house. I noticed that she wore her evening-dress, all her dresses, like sports clothes—there was a jauntiness[42] about her movements as if she had first learned to walk upon golf courses on clean, crisp mornings.

[40] *lustily*: i.e., with cheer and vigor.

[41] *Jazz ... World*: No such piece exists. For an examination of this title in relation to jazz history and race relations, see David Artis, "Swing, Judy Garland and All That Jazz", *Black Scholar* 21, no. 4 (Fall 1991): 30–34.

[42] *jauntiness*: "having or affecting well-bred or easy sprightliness; affecting airy self-satisfaction or unconcern" (*OED*).

I was alone and it was almost two. For some time confused and intriguing sounds had issued from a long, many-windowed room which overhung the terrace. Eluding Jordan's undergraduate, who was now engaged in an obstetrical[43] conversation with two chorus girls, and who implored me to join him, I went inside.

The large room was full of people. One of the girls in yellow was playing the piano, and beside her stood a tall, red-haired young lady from a famous chorus, engaged in song. She had drunk a quantity of champagne, and during the course of her song she had decided, ineptly, that everything was very, very sad—she was not only singing, she was weeping too. Whenever there was a pause in the song she filled it with gasping, broken sobs, and then took up the lyric again in a quavering soprano. The tears coursed down her cheeks—not freely, however, for when they came into contact with her heavily beaded eyelashes they assumed an inky color, and pursued the rest of their way in slow black rivulets. A humorous suggestion was made that she sing the notes on her face, whereupon she threw up her hands, sank into a chair, and went off into a deep vinous[44] sleep.

"She had a fight with a man who says he's her husband," explained a girl at my elbow.

I looked around. Most of the remaining women were now having fights with men said to be their husbands. Even Jordan's party, the quartet from East Egg, were rent asunder by dissension. One of the men was talking with curious intensity to a young actress, and his wife, after attempting to laugh at the situation in a dignified and indifferent way, broke down entirely and resorted to flank attacks—at intervals she appeared suddenly at his side like an angry diamond, and hissed: "You promised!" into his ear.

The reluctance to go home was not confined to wayward[45] men. The hall was at present occupied by two deplorably[46]

[43] *obstetrical*: relating to childbirth—or, more specifically in this case, the making of babies.

[44] *vinous*: i.e., wine-induced.

[45] *wayward*: going against proper behavior; perverse.

[46] *deplorably*: i.e., miserable because they are not intoxicated.

sober men and their highly indignant wives. The wives were sympathizing with each other in slightly raised voices.

"Whenever he sees I'm having a good time he wants to go home."

"Never heard anything so selfish in my life."

"We're always the first ones to leave."

"So are we."

"Well, we're almost the last tonight," said one of the men sheepishly. "The orchestra left half an hour ago."

In spite of the wives' agreement that such malevolence was beyond credibility, the dispute ended in a short struggle, and both wives were lifted, kicking, into the night.

As I waited for my hat in the hall the door of the library opened and Jordan Baker and Gatsby came out together. He was saying some last word to her, but the eagerness in his manner tightened abruptly into formality as several people approached him to say good-bye.

Jordan's party were calling impatiently to her from the porch, but she lingered for a moment to shake hands.

"I've just heard the most amazing thing," she whispered. "How long were we in there?"

"Why, about an hour."

"It was ... simply amazing," she repeated abstractedly. "But I swore I wouldn't tell it and here I am tantalizing you." She yawned gracefully in my face. "Please come and see me.... Phone book.... Under the name of Mrs. Sigourney Howard.... My aunt...." She was hurrying off as she talked—her brown hand waved a jaunty salute as she melted into her party at the door.

Rather ashamed that on my first appearance I had stayed so late, I joined the last of Gatsby's guests, who were clustered around him. I wanted to explain that I'd hunted for him early in the evening and to apologize for not having known him in the garden.

"Don't mention it," he enjoined me eagerly. "Don't give it another thought, old sport." The familiar expression held no more familiarity than the hand which reassuringly brushed my shoulder. "And don't forget we're going up in the hydroplane tomorrow morning, at nine o'clock."

Then the butler, behind his shoulder:

"Philadelphia wants you on the phone, sir."

"All right, in a minute. Tell them I'll be right there.... Good night."

"Good night."

"Good night." He smiled—and suddenly there seemed to be a pleasant significance in having been among the last to go, as if he had desired it all the time. "Good night, old sport.... Good night."

But as I walked down the steps I saw that the evening was not quite over. Fifty feet from the door a dozen headlights illuminated a bizarre and tumultuous[47] scene. In the ditch beside the road, right side up, but violently shorn of one wheel, rested a new coupé[48] which had left Gatsby's drive not two minutes before. The sharp jut of a wall accounted for the detachment of the wheel, which was now getting considerable attention from half a dozen curious chauffeurs. However, as they had left their cars blocking the road, a harsh, discordant din from those in the rear had been audible for some time, and added to the already violent confusion of the scene.

A man in a long duster[49] had dismounted from the wreck and now stood in the middle of the road, looking from the car to the tire and from the tire to the observers in a pleasant, puzzled way.

"See!" he explained. "It went in the ditch."

The fact was infinitely astonishing to him, and I recognized first the unusual quality of wonder, and then the man—it was the late patron of Gatsby's library.

"How'd it happen?"

He shrugged his shoulders.

"I know nothing whatever about mechanics," he said decisively.

"But how did it happen? Did you run into the wall?"

[47] *tumultuous*: "marked by confusion and uproar; disorderly and noisy; violent and clamorous" (*OED*).

[48] *coupé*: two-door car ordinarily with only two seats.

[49] *duster*: cloak.

"Don't ask me," said Owl Eyes, washing his hands of the whole matter. "I know very little about driving—next to nothing. It happened, and that's all I know."

"Well, if you're a poor driver you oughtn't to try driving at night."

"But I wasn't even trying," he explained indignantly. "I wasn't even trying."

An awed hush fell upon the bystanders.

"Do you want to commit suicide?"

"You're lucky it was just a wheel! A bad driver and not even *trying*!"

"You don't understand," explained the criminal. "I wasn't driving. There's another man in the car."

The shock that followed this declaration found voice in a sustained "Ah-h-h!" as the door of the coupé swung slowly open. The crowd—it was now a crowd—stepped back involuntarily, and when the door had opened wide there was a ghostly pause. Then, very gradually, part by part, a pale, dangling individual stepped out of the wreck, pawing tentatively at the ground with a large uncertain dancing shoe.

Blinded by the glare of the headlights and confused by the incessant groaning of the horns, the apparition stood swaying for a moment before he perceived the man in the duster.

"Wha's matter?" he inquired calmly. "Did we run outa gas?"

"Look!"

Half a dozen fingers pointed at the amputated wheel—he stared at it for a moment, and then looked upward as though he suspected that it had dropped from the sky.

"It came off," someone explained.

He nodded.

"At first I din' notice we'd stopped."

A pause. Then, taking a long breath and straightening his shoulders, he remarked in a determined voice:

"Wonder'ff tell me where there's a gas'line station?"

At least a dozen men, some of them little better off than he was, explained to him that wheel and car were no longer joined by any physical bond.

"Back out," he suggested after a moment. "Put her in reverse."

"But the *wheel's* off!"

He hesitated.

"No harm in trying," he said.

The caterwauling[50] horns had reached a crescendo and I turned away and cut across the lawn toward home. I glanced back once. A wafer of a moon was shining over Gatsby's house, making the night fine as before, and surviving the laughter and the sound of his still glowing garden. A sudden emptiness seemed to flow now from the windows and the great doors, endowing with complete isolation the figure of the host, who stood on the porch, his hand up in a formal gesture of farewell.

* * * * *

Reading over what I have written so far, I see I have given the impression that the events of three nights several weeks apart were all that absorbed me. On the contrary, they were merely casual events in a crowded summer, and, until much later, they absorbed me infinitely less than my personal affairs.

Most of the time I worked. In the early morning the sun threw my shadow westward as I hurried down the white chasms[51] of lower New York to the Probity Trust. I knew the other clerks and young bond-salesmen by their first names, and lunched with them in dark, crowded restaurants on little pig sausages and mashed potatoes and coffee. I even had a short affair with a girl who lived in Jersey City and worked in the accounting department, but her brother began throwing mean looks in my direction, so when she went on her vacation in July I let it blow quietly away.

I took dinner usually at the Yale Club—for some reason it was the gloomiest event of my day—and then I went upstairs to the library and studied investments and securities

[50] *caterwauling*: making cacophonous howls like cats in heat. Given the multiple descriptions of sexuality in this chapter, note also caterwauling as "the action of actively seeking sexual partners; lecherous actions or behavior" (*OED*).

[51] *chasms*: i.e., being surrounded by skyscrapers makes one feel in a chasm.

for a conscientious hour. There were generally a few rioters[52] around, but they never came into the library, so it was a good place to work. After that, if the night was mellow, I strolled down Madison Avenue past the old Murray Hill Hotel,[53] and over Thirty-third Street to the Pennsylvania Station.

I began to like New York, the racy, adventurous feel of it at night, and the satisfaction that the constant flicker of men and women and machines gives to the restless eye. I liked to walk up Fifth Avenue and pick out romantic women from the crowd and imagine that in a few minutes I was going to enter into their lives, and no one would ever know or disapprove. Sometimes, in my mind, I followed them to their apartments on the corners of hidden streets, and they turned and smiled back at me before they faded through a door into warm darkness. At the enchanted metropolitan twilight I felt a haunting loneliness sometimes, and felt it in others—poor young clerks who loitered in front of windows waiting until it was time for a solitary restaurant dinner—young clerks in the dusk, wasting the most poignant moments of night and life.

Again at eight o'clock, when the dark lanes of the Forties were five deep with throbbing taxicabs, bound for the theatre district, I felt a sinking in my heart. Forms leaned together in the taxis as they waited, and voices sang, and there was laughter from unheard jokes, and lighted cigarettes outlined unintelligible gestures inside. Imagining that I, too, was hurrying toward gayety and sharing their intimate excitement, I wished them well.

For a while I lost sight of Jordan Baker, and then in midsummer I found her again. At first I was flattered to go places with her, because she was a golf champion, and everyone knew her name. Then it was something more. I wasn't actually in love, but I felt a sort of tender curiosity. The bored haughty face that she turned to the world concealed something—most

[52] *rioters*: merrymakers; revelers, especially with alcohol.

[53] *Murray Hill Hotel*: six-hundred room hotel near Grand Central station; one of the owners was a member of the New York Stock Exchange. It was demolished in 1947.

affectations conceal something eventually, even though they don't in the beginning—and one day I found what it was. When we were on a house-party together up in Warwick, she left a borrowed car out in the rain with the top down,[54] and then lied about it—and suddenly I remembered the story about her that had eluded me that night at Daisy's. At her first big golf tournament there was a row[55] that nearly reached the newspapers—a suggestion that she had moved her ball from a bad lie[56] in the semi-final round. The thing approached the proportions of a scandal—then died away. A caddy retracted his statement, and the only other witness admitted that he might have been mistaken. The incident and the name had remained together in my mind.

Jordan Baker instinctively avoided clever, shrewd men, and now I saw that this was because she felt safer on a plane where any divergence from a code would be thought impossible. She was incurably dishonest. She wasn't able to endure being at a disadvantage and, given this unwillingness, I suppose she had begun dealing in subterfuges when she was very young in order to keep that cool, insolent[57] smile turned to the world and yet satisfy the demands of her hard, jaunty body.

It made no difference to me. Dishonesty in a woman is a thing you never blame deeply—I was casually sorry, and then I forgot. It was on that same house-party that we had a curious conversation about driving a car. It started because she passed so close to some workmen that our fender flicked a button on one man's coat.

"You're a rotten[58] driver," I protested. "Either you ought to be more careful, or you oughtn't to drive at all."

[54] *top down*: A car with a convertible top left down (i.e., folded down; not up) would expose the interior to the elements, likely causing extensive damage.

[55] *row*: nasty argument or bitter controversy.

[56] *ball … lie*: i.e., where the ball lay. Very rare conditions excepted (e.g., dangerous animal situation), moving one's ball is prohibited and would accrue a penalty as well as the obligation to replace the ball where it was.

[57] *insolent*: "contemptuous of rightful authority … those who treat superiors or equals with offensive familiarity or disrespect" (*OED*).

[58] *rotten*: incompetent; lacking the necessary skills.

"I am careful."

"No, you're not."

"Well, other people are," she said lightly.

"What's that got to do with it?"

"They'll keep out of my way," she insisted. "It takes two to make an accident."

"Suppose you met somebody just as careless as yourself."

"I hope I never will," she answered. "I hate careless people. That's why I like you."

Her gray, sun-strained eyes stared straight ahead, but she had deliberately shifted our relations, and for a moment I thought I loved her. But I am slow-thinking and full of interior rules that act as brakes on my desires, and I knew that first I had to get myself definitely out of that tangle[59] back home. I'd been writing letters once a week and signing them: "Love, Nick," and all I could think of was how, when that certain girl played tennis, a faint mustache of perspiration appeared on her upper lip. Nevertheless there was a vague understanding that had to be tactfully broken off before I was free.

Everyone suspects himself of at least one of the cardinal virtues,[60] and this is mine: I am one of the few honest people that I have ever known.

[59] *tangle*: complicated, perplexing situation.

[60] *cardinal virtues*: At least as old as Socratic philosophy, and clearly systematized by Aquinas, the four cardinal virtues are prudence, justice, temperance, and fortitude.

CHAPTER IV

ON SUNDAY MORNING while church bells rang in the villages alongshore, the world and its mistress[1] returned to Gatsby's house and twinkled hilariously[2] on his lawn.

"He's a bootlegger,"[3] said the young ladies, moving somewhere between his cocktails and his flowers. "One time he killed a man who had found out that he was nephew to Von Hindenburg[4] and second cousin to the devil. Reach me a rose, honey, and pour me a last drop into that there crystal glass."

Once I wrote down on the empty spaces of a timetable[5] the names of those who came to Gatsby's house that summer. It is an old timetable now, disintegrating at its folds, and headed "This schedule in effect July 5th, 1922." But I can still read the gray names, and they will give you a better impression than my generalities of those who accepted Gatsby's hospitality and paid him the subtle tribute of knowing nothing whatever about him.

From East Egg, then, came the Chester Beckers[6] and the Leeches, and a man named Bunsen, whom I knew at Yale, and Doctor Webster Civet, who was drowned last summer up in Maine. And the Hornbeams and the Willie Voltaires, and a whole clan named Blackbuck, who always gathered in a corner and flipped up their noses like goats at whosoever came near.

[1] *mistress*: in this context, "a woman having control or authority" (*OED*).

[2] *hilariously*: cheerfully; merrily.

[3] *bootlegger*: someone who sells alcohol or liquor illegally.

[4] *Von Hindenburg*: Paul von Hindenburg (1847–1934), field marshal for Germany in WWI. About a month after *Gatsby* was first published, von Hindenburg became president of Germany (1925–1934).

[5] *timetable*: detailed schedule showing the exact times of train arrivals and departures.

[6] *Beckers*: Many scholars have discussed the list of names in this passage, with its entries both humorous and enlightening; animal and human; literary and prosaic; and so forth. E.g., see Peter Lisca, "Nick Carraway and the Imagery of Disorder", *Twentieth Century Literature* 13, no. 1 (April 1967): 18–28.

And the Ismays and the Chrysties (or rather Hubert Auerbach and Mr. Chrystie's wife), and Edgar Beaver, whose hair, they say, turned cotton-white one winter afternoon for no good reason at all.

Clarence Endive was from East Egg, as I remember. He came only once, in white knickerbockers,[7] and had a fight with a bum named Etty in the garden. From farther out on the Island came the Cheadles and the O. R. P. Schraeders, and the Stonewall Jackson Abrams of Georgia, and the Fishguards and the Ripley Snells. Snell was there three days before he went to the penitentiary, so drunk out on the gravel drive that Mrs. Ulysses Swett's automobile ran over his right hand. The Dancies came, too, and S. B. Whitebait, who was well over sixty, and Maurice A. Flink, and the Hammerheads, and Beluga the tobacco importer, and Beluga's girls.

From West Egg came the Poles and the Mulreadys and Cecil Roebuck and Cecil Schoen and Gulick the State senator and Newton Orchid, who controlled Films Par Excellence, and Eckhaust and Clyde Cohen and Don S. Schwartze (the son) and Arthur McCarty, all connected with the movies in one way or another. And the Catlips and the Bembergs and G. Earl Muldoon, brother to that Muldoon who afterward strangled his wife. Da Fontano the promoter came there, and Ed Legros and James B. ("Rot-Gut") Ferret and the De Jongs and Ernest Lilly—they came to gamble, and when Ferret wandered into the garden it meant he was cleaned out[8] and Associated Traction would have to fluctuate profitably next day.

A man named Klipspringer was there so often and so long that he became known as "the boarder"[9]—I doubt if he had any other home. Of theatrical people there were Gus Waize and Horace O'Donavan and Lester Myer and George Duckweed and Francis Bull. Also from New York were the Chromes and the Backhyssons and the Dennickers and Russel Betty

[7] *knickerbockers*: "loose-fitting breeches, gathered in at the knee, and worn by boys, sportsmen, and others who require a freer use of their limbs" (*OED*).

[8] *cleaned out*: i.e., lost all his money gambling.

[9] *boarder*: someone who lives in a room or house in exchange for payment.

and the Corrigans and the Kellehers and the Dewers and the Scullys and S.W. Belcher and the Smirkes and the young Quinns, divorced now, and Henry L. Palmetto, who killed himself by jumping in front of a subway train in Times Square.

Benny McClenahan arrived always with four girls. They were never quite the same ones in physical person, but they were so identical one with another that it inevitably seemed they had been there before. I have forgotten their names—Jaqueline, I think, or else Consuela, or Gloria or Judy or June, and their last names were either the melodious names of flowers and months or the sterner ones of the great American capitalists whose cousins, if pressed, they would confess themselves to be.

In addition to all these I can remember that Faustina O'Brien came there at least once and the Baedeker girls and young Brewer, who had his nose shot off in the war, and Mr. Albrucksburger and Miss Haag, his fiancée, and Ardita Fitz-Peters and Mr. P. Jewett, once head of the American Legion, and Miss Claudia Hip, with a man reputed to be her chauffeur, and a prince of something, whom we called Duke, and whose name, if I ever knew it, I have forgotten.

All these people came to Gatsby's house in the summer.

* * * * *

At nine o'clock, one morning late in July, Gatsby's gorgeous[10] car lurched up the rocky drive to my door and gave out a burst of melody from its three-noted horn. It was the first time he had called on me, though I had gone to two of his parties, mounted in his hydroplane, and, at his urgent invitation, made frequent use of his beach.

"Good morning, old sport. You're having lunch with me today and I thought we'd ride up together."

He was balancing himself on the dashboard[11] of his car with that resourcefulness of movement that is so peculiarly

[10] *gorgeous*: magnificently showy.

[11] *dashboard*: James L. W. West claims that the word means a running board—a platform on each side of the car running fender to fender—and that the term

American—that comes, I suppose, with the absence of lifting work or rigid sitting in youth and, even more, with the formless grace of our nervous, sporadic games. This quality was continually breaking through his punctilious[12] manner in the shape of restlessness. He was never quite still; there was always a tapping foot somewhere or the impatient opening and closing of a hand.

He saw me looking with admiration at his car.

"It's pretty, isn't it, old sport?" He jumped off to give me a better view. "Haven't you ever seen it before?"

I'd seen it. Everybody had seen it. It was a rich cream color, bright with nickel, swollen here and there in its monstrous length with triumphant hat-boxes and supper-boxes and tool-boxes, and terraced with a labyrinth of wind-shields that mirrored a dozen suns. Sitting down behind many layers of glass in a sort of green leather conservatory,[13] we started to town.

I had talked with him perhaps half a dozen times in the past month and found, to my disappointment, that he had little to say. So my first impression, that he was a person of some undefined consequence, had gradually faded and he had become simply the proprietor of an elaborate road-house next door.

And then came that disconcerting ride. We hadn't reached West Egg Village before Gatsby began leaving his elegant sentences unfinished and slapping himself indecisively on the knee of his caramel-colored suit.

"Look here, old sport," he broke out surprisingly. "What's your opinion of me, anyhow?"

"running board" did not come into use until later (James L. W. West III, ed., *The Great Gatsby: A Variorum Edition* [Cambridge: Cambridge University Press, 2019], p. 236). However, the term "running board" was already in wide use in the 1900s and 1910s (*OED*), as was "dashboard", from which it was distinguished. Gatsby may have been standing on the running board, but he was balancing on the dashboard—presumably with one arm or elbow behind him, to give an impression of reclining back in ease.

[12] *punctilious*: "strictly observant of or insistent on fine points of procedure, etiquette, or conduct; extremely or excessively particular or correct" (*OED*).

[13] *conservatory*: "living room with a glass roof and glass wall panels ... used as a sun lounge" (*OED*).

A little overwhelmed, I began the generalized evasions which that question deserves.

"Well, I'm going to tell you something about my life," he interrupted. "I don't want you to get a wrong idea of me from all these stories you hear."

So he was aware of the bizarre accusations that flavored conversation in his halls.

"I'll tell you God's truth." His right hand suddenly ordered divine retribution to stand by. "I am the son of some wealthy people in the Middle West—all dead now. I was brought up in America but educated at Oxford, because all my ancestors have been educated there for many years. It is a family tradition."

He looked at me sideways—and I knew why Jordan Baker had believed he was lying. He hurried the phrase "educated at Oxford," or swallowed it, or choked on it, as though it had bothered him before. And with this doubt, his whole statement fell to pieces, and I wondered if there wasn't something a little sinister about him, after all.

"What part of the Middle West?" I inquired casually.

"San Francisco."

"I see."

"My family all died and I came into a good deal of money."

His voice was solemn, as if the memory of that sudden extinction of a clan still haunted him. For a moment I suspected that he was pulling my leg,[14] but a glance at him convinced me otherwise.

"After that I lived like a young rajah[15] in all the capitals of Europe—Paris, Venice, Rome—collecting jewels, chiefly rubies,[16] hunting big game, painting a little, things for myself only, and trying to forget something very sad that had happened to me long ago."

With an effort I managed to restrain my incredulous laughter. The very phrases were worn so threadbare that they evoked

[14] *pulling my leg*: playfully lying.

[15] *rajah*: prince or ruler in India.

[16] *rubies*: See Nick's aside to the reader in chapter 5 about this facet of the story.

no image except that of a turbaned "character" leaking sawdust[17] at every pore as he pursued a tiger through the Bois de Boulogne.[18]

"Then came the war, old sport. It was a great relief, and I tried very hard to die, but I seemed to bear an enchanted life. I accepted a commission as first lieutenant when it began. In the Argonne Forest[19] I took two machine-gun detachments so far forward that there was a half-mile gap on either side of us where the infantry couldn't advance. We stayed there two days and two nights, a hundred and thirty men with sixteen Lewis guns,[20] and when the infantry came up at last they found the insignia of three German divisions among the piles of dead. I was promoted to be a major, and every Allied government gave me a decoration—even Montenegro,[21] little Montenegro down on the Adriatic Sea!"

Little Montenegro! He lifted up the words and nodded at them—with his smile. The smile comprehended Montenegro's troubled history and sympathized with the brave struggles of the Montenegrin people. It appreciated fully the chain of national circumstances which had elicited this tribute from Montenegro's warm little heart. My incredulity was submerged in fascination now; it was like skimming hastily through a dozen magazines.

He reached in his pocket, and a piece of metal,[22] slung on a ribbon, fell into my palm.

[17] *leaking sawdust*: "with reference to the use of sawdust for stuffing dolls or puppets" (*OED*).

[18] *Bois de Boulogne*: famous park of more than two thousand acres on the western outskirts of Paris, once hunting grounds and home to an exotic zoo.

[19] *Argonne Forest*: Gatsby refers to what is now called the Meuse-Argonne offensive, which began in late September 1918. Since Gatsby earlier said he served in the Seventh Infantry until June, his story makes sense only if he was transferred to the Eighth Machine Gun Battalion.

[20] *Lewis guns*: light machine guns with a bipod in front, and teams of seven per gun. While the British used them extensively in WWI, Americans ordinarily used Hotchkiss machine guns or the Chauchat light machine gun.

[21] *Montenegro*: The Kingdom of Montenegro surrendered to Austria-Hungary in early 1916 and by late 1918 had effectively been absorbed by the future Yugoslavia. It would not become an independent nation again until 2006.

[22] *piece of metal*: The genuine award is a striking four-armed cross with Cyrillic writing.

"That's the one from Montenegro."

To my astonishment, the thing had an authentic look. "Orderi de Danilo,"[23] ran the circular legend, "Montenegro, Nicolas Rex."[24]

"Turn it."

"Major Jay Gatsby," I read, "For Valour Extraordinary."

"Here's another thing I always carry. A souvenir of Oxford days. It was taken in Trinity Quad[25]—the man on my left is now the Earl of Doncaster."[26]

It was a photograph of half a dozen young men in blazers loafing in an archway through which were visible a host of spires. There was Gatsby, looking a little, not much, younger—with a cricket bat in his hand.

Then it was all true. I saw the skins of tigers flaming in his palace on the Grand Canal;[27] I saw him opening a chest of rubies to ease, with their crimson-lighted depths, the gnawings of his broken heart.

"I'm going to make a big request of you today," he said, pocketing his souvenirs with satisfaction, "so I thought you ought to know something about me. I didn't want you to think I was just some nobody. You see, I usually find myself among strangers because I drift here and there trying to forget the sad thing that happened to me." He hesitated. "You'll hear about it this afternoon."

"At lunch?"

"No, this afternoon. I happened to find out that you're taking Miss Baker to tea."

[23] *Orderi de Danilo*: award bearing the name of Prince Danilo I of Montenegro, given for military or civic accomplishment, in five ranks or classes. Between 1918 and 1922, 123 such medals were awarded to officers, enlisted men, and affiliates by Montenegro. See *Report of the Secretary of War to the President* (Washington, D.C.: Government Printing Office, June 30, 1922), pp. 215–20.

[24] *Nicolas Rex*: King Nicholas I was exiled when Montenegro surrendered in early 1916. Even after Montenegro was absorbed in late 1918, he continued to claim governance from Bordeaux, France, until his death in 1921.

[25] *Trinity Quad*: Trinity is one of Oxford's many colleges. At the time it had three quadrangles, or quads.

[26] *Earl of Doncaster*: subsidiary title of the Duke of Buccleuch (see note 7 in chapter 1).

[27] *Grand Canal*: major internal water corridor of Venice.

"Do you mean you're in love with Miss Baker?"

"No, old sport, I'm not. But Miss Baker has kindly consented to speak to you about this matter."

I hadn't the faintest idea what "this matter" was, but I was more annoyed than interested. I hadn't asked Jordan to tea in order to discuss Mr. Jay Gatsby. I was sure the request would be something utterly fantastic,[28] and for a moment I was sorry I'd ever set foot upon his overpopulated lawn.

He wouldn't say another word. His correctness grew on him as we neared the city. We passed Port Roosevelt,[29] where there was a glimpse of red-belted ocean-going ships, and sped along a cobbled slum lined with the dark, undeserted saloons of the faded-gilt nineteen- hundreds. Then the valley of ashes opened out on both sides of us, and I had a glimpse of Mrs. Wilson straining at the garage pump with panting vitality as we went by.

With fenders spread like wings we scattered light through half Astoria—only half, for as we twisted among the pillars of the elevated[30] I heard the familiar "jug-jug-*spat!*" of a motorcycle, and a frantic policeman rode alongside.

"All right, old sport," called Gatsby. We slowed down. Taking a white card from his wallet, he waved it before the man's eyes.

"Right you are," agreed the policeman, tipping his cap. "Know you next time, Mr. Gatsby. Excuse *me!*"

"What was that?" I inquired. "The picture of Oxford?"

"I was able to do the commissioner a favor once, and he sends me a Christmas card every year."

Over the great bridge, with the sunlight through the girders making a constant flicker upon the moving cars, with the city rising up across the river in white heaps and sugar lumps all built with a wish out of non-olfactory[31] money. The city seen

[28] *fantastic*: "extravagantly fanciful, odd and irrational in behavior" (*OED*).

[29] *Port Roosevelt*: imaginary, but likely near the Flushing Bay area.

[30] *Astoria ... elevated*: Astoria, a neighborhood in northwest Queens, bordered by the East River; "elevated" refers to a commuter train running over the Queensboro Bridge.

[31] *non-olfactory*: rarely used outside of anatomy or scientific texts; it means to be not related to the sense of smell. Fitzgerald's figurative use here points to the ideal of clean money, i.e., not counterfeit or otherwise criminal.

from the Queensboro Bridge is always the city seen for the first time, in its first wild promise of all the mystery and the beauty in the world.

A dead man passed us in a hearse heaped with blooms, followed by two carriages with drawn blinds, and by more cheerful carriages for friends. The friends looked out at us with the tragic eyes and short upper lips of southeastern Europe, and I was glad that the sight of Gatsby's splendid car was included in their somber holiday.[32] As we crossed Blackwell's Island[33] a limousine passed us, driven by a white chauffeur, in which sat three modish[34] negroes, two bucks[35] and a girl. I laughed aloud as the yolks of their eyeballs rolled toward us in haughty rivalry.

"Anything can happen now that we've slid over this bridge," I thought; "anything at all. . . ."

Even Gatsby could happen, without any particular wonder.

* * * * *

Roaring noon. In a well-fanned Forty-second Street cellar I met Gatsby for lunch. Blinking away the brightness of the street outside, my eyes picked him out obscurely in the anteroom,[36] talking to another man.

"Mr. Carraway, this is my friend Mr. Wolfshiem."[37]

A small, flat-nosed Jew raised his large head and regarded me with two fine growths of hair which luxuriated in either nostril. After a moment I discovered his tiny eyes in the half-darkness.

[32] *holiday*: i.e., holy day; day of religious observance.

[33] *Blackwell's Island*: modern-day Roosevelt Island. Significantly, Nick does not use the designated new name adopted in early 1921, Welfare Island, to reflect the hospitals, sanitarium, and prison located there.

[34] *modish*: fashionable; stylish.

[35] *bucks*: Given Nick's propriety and the context, he means the neutral usage: "a confident, high-spirited young man" (*OED*).

[36] *anteroom*: entry space; waiting room.

[37] *Wolfshiem*: Fitzgerald loosely based this character on Arnold Rothstein (1882–1928), lynchpin of the so-called Jewish mafia in New York City. Rothstein's criminal empire, with its façade of gentlemanly elegance, spanned the entire Northeast.

"—So I took one look at him," said Mr. Wolfshiem, shaking my hand earnestly, "and what do you think I did?"

"What?" I inquired politely.

But evidently he was not addressing me, for he dropped my hand and covered Gatsby with his expressive nose.

"I handed the money to Katspaugh and I said: 'All right, Katspaugh, don't pay him a penny till he shuts his mouth.' He shut it then and there."

Gatsby took an arm of each of us and moved forward into the restaurant, whereupon Mr. Wolfshiem swallowed a new sentence he was starting and lapsed into a somnambulatory[38] abstraction.

"Highballs?"[39] asked the head waiter.

"This is a nice restaurant here," said Mr. Wolfshiem, looking at the Presbyterian nymphs[40] on the ceiling. "But I like across the street better!"

"Yes, highballs," agreed Gatsby, and then to Mr. Wolfshiem: "It's too hot over there."

"Hot and small—yes," said Mr. Wolfshiem, "but full of memories."

"What place is that?" I asked.

"The old Metropole,"[41] said Gatsby.

"The old Metropole," brooded Mr. Wolfshiem gloomily. "Filled with faces dead and gone. Filled with friends gone now forever. I can't forget so long as I live the night they shot Rosy Rosenthal[42] there. It was six of us at the table, and Rosy had eat and drunk a lot all evening. When it was almost morning the waiter came up to him with a funny look and says somebody

[38] *somnambulatory*: in the manner of sleepwalking.

[39] *highballs*: originally whiskey and sparkling or soda water in a tall glass with ice.

[40] *Presbyterian nymphs*: Presbyterian here means "strait-laced; frugal; strict" (*OED*); thus, the female nature spirits or nymphs depicted are clothed or modest.

[41] *metropole*: Hotel Metropole on West 43rd Street (now called the Casablanca Hotel).

[42] *Rosy Rosenthal*: Herman Rosenthal, a "bookie" (one who, ordinarily illegally, accepts and pays off bets on established odds), was gunned down outside the Metropole in July 1912. After a long, publicized trial, five men received the death penalty and were executed, including former police lieutenant Charles Becker.

wants to speak to him outside. 'All right,' says Rosy, and begins to get up, and I pulled him down in his chair.

"'Let the bastards come in here if they want you, Rosy, but don't you, so help me, move outside this room.'

"It was four o'clock in the morning then, and if we'd of raised the blinds[43] we'd of seen daylight."

"Did he go?" I asked innocently.

"Sure he went." Mr. Wolfshiem's nose flashed at me indignantly. "He turned around in the door and says: 'Don't let that waiter take away my coffee!' Then he went out on the sidewalk, and they shot him three times in his full belly and drove away."

"Four of them were electrocuted," I said, remembering.

"Five, with Becker." His nostrils turned to me in an interested way. "I understand you're looking for a business gonnegtion."

The juxtaposition[44] of these two remarks was startling. Gatsby answered for me:

"Oh, no," he exclaimed, "this isn't the man."

"No?" Mr. Wolfshiem seemed disappointed.

"This is just a friend. I told you we'd talk about that some other time."

"I beg your pardon," said Mr. Wolfshiem. "I had a wrong man."

A succulent hash arrived, and Mr. Wolfshiem, forgetting the more sentimental atmosphere of the old Metropole, began to eat with ferocious delicacy. His eyes, meanwhile, roved very slowly all around the room—he completed the arc by turning to inspect the people directly behind. I think that, except for my presence, he would have taken one short glance beneath our own table.

"Look here, old sport," said Gatsby leaning toward me, "I'm afraid I made you a little angry this morning in the car."

There was the smile again, but this time I held out against it.

"I don't like mysteries," I answered, "and I don't understand why you won't come out frankly and tell me what you want. Why has it all got to come through Miss Baker?"

[43] *blinds*: window coverings to block out the light; also, pun on "blind" as a front for an illegal business.

[44] *juxtaposition*: unexpected or notable placement of two things together.

"Oh, it's nothing underhand," he assured me. "Miss Baker's a great sportswoman, you know, and she'd never do anything that wasn't all right."

Suddenly he looked at his watch, jumped up, and hurried from the room, leaving me with Mr. Wolfshiem at the table.

"He has to telephone," said Mr. Wolfshiem, following him with his eyes. "Fine fellow, isn't he? Handsome to look at and a perfect gentleman."

"Yes."

"He's an Oggsford man."

"Oh!"

"He went to Oggsford College in England. You know Oggsford College?"

"I've heard of it."

"It's one of the most famous colleges in the world."

"Have you known Gatsby for a long time?" I inquired.

"Several years," he answered in a gratified way. "I made the pleasure of his acquaintance just after the war. But I knew I had discovered a man of fine breeding after I talked with him an hour. I said to myself: 'There's the kind of man you'd like to take home and introduce to your mother and sister.'" He paused. "I see you're looking at my cuff buttons."

I hadn't been looking at them, but I did now. They were composed of oddly familiar pieces of ivory.

"Finest specimens of human molars,"[45] he informed me.

"Well!" I inspected them. "That's a very interesting idea."

"Yeah." He flipped his sleeves up under his coat. "Yeah, Gatsby's very careful about women. He would never so much as look at a friend's wife."

When the subject of this instinctive trust returned to the table and sat down Mr. Wolfshiem drank his coffee with a jerk and got to his feet.

"I have enjoyed my lunch," he said, "and I'm going to run off from you two young men before I outstay my welcome."

[45] *human molars*: Mafia victims would sometimes have their teeth removed; dental records could be the only way of making positive identification of the remains. Cuff buttons or cuff links hold the cuff of a dress shirt securely around the wrist.

"Don't hurry, Meyer," said Gatsby, without enthusiasm. Mr. Wolfshiem raised his hand in a sort of benediction.[46]

"You're very polite, but I belong to another generation," he announced solemnly. "You sit here and discuss your sports and your young ladies and your—" He supplied an imaginary noun with another wave of his hand. "As for me, I am fifty years old, and I won't impose myself on you any longer."

As he shook hands and turned away his tragic nose was trembling. I wondered if I had said anything to offend him.

"He becomes very sentimental sometimes," explained Gatsby. "This is one of his sentimental days. He's quite a character around New York—a denizen of Broadway."

"Who is he, anyhow, an actor?"

"No."

"A dentist?"

"Meyer Wolfshiem? No, he's a gambler." Gatsby hesitated, then added coolly: "He's the man who fixed the World's Series back in 1919."[47]

"Fixed the World's Series?" I repeated.

The idea staggered me. I remembered, of course, that the World's Series had been fixed in 1919, but if I had thought of it at all I would have thought of it as a thing that merely *happened*, the end of some inevitable chain. It never occurred to me that one man could start to play with the faith of fifty million people—with the single-mindedness of a burglar blowing a safe.

"How did he happen to do that?" I asked after a minute.

"He just saw the opportunity."

"Why isn't he in jail?"

"They can't get him, old sport. He's a smart man."

I insisted on paying the check. As the waiter brought my change I caught sight of Tom Buchanan across the crowded room.

[46] *benediction*: blessing—in Catholic practice, after spending time adoring Christ in the Eucharist in a monstrance. See also Fitzgerald's short story "Benediction", first published in early 1920, which involves a Catholic seminary.

[47] *fixed … 1919*: Rothstein apparently did play a role in this sordid affair. See David Pietrusza, *Rothstein: The Life, Times, and Murder of the Criminal Genius Who Fixed the 1919 World Series* (New York: Carroll & Graf, 2003).

"Come along with me for a minute," I said; "I've got to say hello to someone."

When he saw us Tom jumped up and took half a dozen steps in our direction.

"Where've you been?" he demanded eagerly. "Daisy's furious because you haven't called up."

"This is Mr. Gatsby, Mr. Buchanan."

They shook hands briefly, and a strained, unfamiliar look of embarrassment came over Gatsby's face.

"How've you been, anyhow?" demanded Tom of me. "How'd you happen to come up this far to eat?"

"I've been having lunch with Mr. Gatsby."

I turned toward Mr. Gatsby, but he was no longer there.

* * * * *

One October day in nineteen-seventeen—

(said Jordan Baker that afternoon, sitting up very straight on a straight chair in the tea-garden at the Plaza Hotel[48])—I was walking along from one place to another, half on the sidewalks and half on the lawns. I was happier on the lawns because I had on shoes from England with rubber knobs on the soles that bit into the soft ground. I had on a new plaid skirt also that blew a little in the wind, and whenever this happened the red, white, and blue[49] banners in front of all the houses stretched out stiff and said *tut-tut-tut-tut*, in a disapproving way.

The largest of the banners and the largest of the lawns belonged to Daisy Fay's house. She was just eighteen, two years older than me, and by far the most popular of all the young girls in Louisville. She dressed in white, and had a little white roadster, and all day long the telephone rang in her house and excited young officers from Camp Taylor demanded the privilege of monopolizing her that night. "Anyways, for an hour!"

[48] *Plaza Hotel*: Located on Fifth Avenue next to Central Park, the Plaza Hotel was (and continues to be) associated with wealth, luxury, and high-class living.

[49] *red, white, and blue*: Fitzgerald at the last minute wanted to change the title of this novel to *Under the Red, White and Blue*, but his editor wisely and tactfully disallowed it.

When I came opposite her house that morning her white roadster was beside the curb, and she was sitting in it with a lieutenant I had never seen before. They were so engrossed in each other that she didn't see me until I was five feet away.

"Hello, Jordan," she called unexpectedly. "Please come here."

I was flattered that she wanted to speak to me, because of all the older girls I admired her most. She asked me if I was going to the Red Cross and make bandages. I was. Well, then, would I tell them that she couldn't come that day? The officer looked at Daisy while she was speaking, in a way that every young girl wants to be looked at sometime, and because it seemed romantic to me I have remembered the incident ever since. His name was Jay Gatsby, and I didn't lay eyes on him again for over four years—even after I'd met him on Long Island I didn't realize it was the same man.

That was nineteen-seventeen. By the next year I had a few beaux myself, and I began to play in tournaments, so I didn't see Daisy very often. She went with a slightly older crowd—when she went with anyone at all. Wild rumors were circulating about her—how her mother had found her packing her bag one winter night to go to New York and say good-bye to a soldier who was going overseas. She was effectually prevented, but she wasn't on speaking terms with her family for several weeks. After that she didn't play around with the soldiers any more, but only with a few flat-footed,[50] short-sighted young men in town, who couldn't get into the army at all.

By the next autumn she was gay again, gay as ever. She had a début[51] after the armistice,[52] and in February she was presumably engaged to a man from New Orleans. In June she married Tom Buchanan of Chicago, with more pomp and circumstance than Louisville ever knew before. He came down with a hundred people in four private cars, and hired a whole

[50] *flat-footed*: plain; clumsy, awkward.

[51] *début*: formal introduction of a young lady to society, opening the door for suitors for marriage.

[52] *armistice*: ceasefire of November 11, 1918, which effectively ended WWI.

floor of the Seelbach Hotel,[53] and the day before the wedding he gave her a string of pearls valued at three hundred and fifty thousand dollars.

I was a bridesmaid. I came into her room half an hour before the bridal dinner, and found her lying on her bed as lovely as the June night in her flowered dress—and as drunk as a monkey. She had a bottle of Sauterne[54] in one hand and a letter in the other.

"'Gratulate me," she muttered. "Never had a drink before, but oh how I do enjoy it."

"What's the matter, Daisy?"

I was scared, I can tell you; I'd never seen a girl like that before.

"Here, dearies'." She groped around in a waste-basket she had with her on the bed and pulled out the string of pearls. "Take 'em downstairs and give 'em back to whoever they belong to. Tell 'em all Daisy's change' her mine. Say: 'Daisy's change' her mine!'"

She began to cry—she cried and cried. I rushed out and found her mother's maid, and we locked the door and got her into a cold bath. She wouldn't let go of the letter. She took it into the tub with her and squeezed it up into a wet ball, and only let me leave it in the soap-dish when she saw that it was coming to pieces like snow.

But she didn't say another word. We gave her spirits of ammonia[55] and put ice on her forehead and hooked her back into her dress, and half an hour later, when we walked out of the room, the pearls were around her neck and the incident was over. Next day at five o'clock she married Tom Buchanan

[53] *Seelbach Hotel*: luxurious Louisville landmark. Among its famous visitors were presidents Taft and Wilson; notorious gangster Al Capone; and Fitzgerald himself.

[54] *Sauterne [sic]*: rich, complex white Bordeaux dessert wine, highly prized for its uniquely sweet flavor and its ability to mature over decades, even a century or more. Both singular and plural are spelled "Sauternes" after the French region; Fitzgerald's typo has not been corrected in many editions.

[55] *spirits of ammonia*: i.e., smelling salts, to revive someone who has fainted.

without so much as a shiver, and started off on a three months' trip to the South Seas.[56]

I saw them in Santa Barbara when they came back, and I thought I'd never seen a girl so mad about her husband. If he left the room for a minute she'd look around uneasily, and say: "Where's Tom gone?" and wear the most abstracted expression until she saw him coming in the door. She used to sit on the sand with his head in her lap by the hour, rubbing her fingers over his eyes and looking at him with unfathomable delight. It was touching to see them together—it made you laugh in a hushed, fascinated way. That was in August. A week after I left Santa Barbara Tom ran into a wagon on the Ventura road one night, and ripped a front wheel off his car. The girl who was with him got into the papers,[57] too, because her arm was broken—she was one of the chambermaids in the Santa Barbara Hotel.

The next April Daisy had her little girl, and they went to France for a year. I saw them one spring in Cannes, and later in Deauville, and then they came back to Chicago to settle down. Daisy was popular in Chicago, as you know. They moved with a fast crowd, all of them young and rich and wild, but she came out with an absolutely perfect reputation. Perhaps because she doesn't drink. It's a great advantage not to drink among hard-drinking people. You can hold your tongue, and, moreover, you can time any little irregularity of your own so that everybody else is so blind that they don't see or care. Perhaps Daisy never went in for amour[58] at all—and yet there's something in that voice of hers....

Well, about six weeks ago, she heard the name Gatsby for the first time in years. It was when I asked you—do you remember?—if you knew Gatsby in West Egg. After you had

[56] *South Seas*: Polynesia, and more broadly from Hawaii to New Zealand. Robert Louis Stevenson's travel book *In the South Seas* had been published posthumously in 1896.

[57] *got ... papers*: i.e., explicitly mentioned in the newspaper accounts of the incident.

[58] *amour*: "romantic or sexual love; lovemaking" (*OED*). Jordan wonders if Daisy married Tom only for societal, cultural, and financial considerations—not an uncommon arrangement.

gone home she came into my room and woke me up, and said: "What Gatsby?" and when I described him—I was half-asleep—she said in the strangest voice that it must be the man she used to know. It wasn't until then that I connected this Gatsby with the officer in her white car.

* * * * *

When Jordan Baker had finished telling all this we had left the Plaza for half an hour and were driving in a victoria[59] through Central Park. The sun had gone down behind the tall apartments of the movie stars in the West Fifties, and the clear voices of children, already gathered like crickets on the grass, rose through the hot twilight:

"I'm the Sheik of Araby.[60]
Your love belongs to me.
At night when you're asleep
Into your tent I'll creep——"

"It was a strange coincidence," I said.

"But it wasn't a coincidence at all."

"Why not?"

"Gatsby bought that house so that Daisy would be just across the bay."

Then it had not been merely the stars to which he had aspired on that June night. He came alive to me, delivered suddenly from the womb of his purposeless splendor.

"He wants to know," continued Jordan, "if you'll invite Daisy to your house some afternoon and then let him come over."

The modesty of the demand shook me. He had waited five years and bought a mansion where he dispensed starlight to casual moths—so that he could "come over" some afternoon to a stranger's garden.

[59] *victoria*: typically elegant four-wheeled, horsedrawn carriage, with a canopy for privacy.

[60] *Sheik of Araby*: one of the most popular jazz tunes of 1922, likely benefitting from the widespread success of the George Melford film *The Sheik* (1921).

"Did I have to know all this before he could ask such a little thing?"

"He's afraid, he's waited so long. He thought you might be offended. You see, he's a regular tough[61] underneath it all."

Something worried me.

"Why didn't he ask you to arrange a meeting?"

"He wants her to see his house," she explained. "And your house is right next door."

"Oh!"

"I think he half-expected her to wander into one of his parties, some night," went on Jordan, "but she never did. Then he began asking people casually if they knew her, and I was the first one he found. It was that night he sent for me at his dance, and you should have heard the elaborate way he worked up to it. Of course, I immediately suggested a luncheon in New York—and I thought he'd go mad:

"'I don't want to do anything out of the way!' he kept saying. 'I want to see her right next door.'

"When I said you were a particular friend of Tom's, he started to abandon the whole idea. He doesn't know very much about Tom, though he says he's read a Chicago paper for years just on the chance of catching a glimpse of Daisy's name."

It was dark now, and as we dipped under a little bridge I put my arm around Jordan's golden shoulder and drew her toward me and asked her to dinner. Suddenly I wasn't thinking of Daisy and Gatsby any more, but of this clean, hard, limited[62] person, who dealt in universal skepticism, and who leaned back jauntily just within the circle of my arm. A phrase began to beat in my ears with a sort of heady[63] excitement: "There are only the pursued, the pursuing, the busy, and the tired."

"And Daisy ought to have something in her life," murmured Jordan to me.

[61] *tough*: Jordan means someone who is steadfast and firm, uncompromising. But Fitzgerald's word choice offers to the reader the more common implication "a person given to rough or violent behavior" (*OED*).

[62] *limited*: not necessarily in a deprecating sense; "having only modest accomplishments, ambitions, or potential" (*OED*).

[63] *heady*: exhilarating; intoxicating.

"Does she want to see Gatsby?"

"She's not to know about it. Gatsby doesn't want her to know. You're just supposed to invite her to tea."

We passed a barrier of dark trees, and then the façade of Fifty-ninth Street, a block of delicate pale light, beamed down into the Park. Unlike Gatsby and Tom Buchanan, I had no girl whose disembodied face floated along the dark cornices[64] and blinding signs, and so I drew up the girl beside me, tightening my arms. Her wan, scornful mouth smiled, and so I drew her up again closer, this time to my face.

[64] *cornices*: A cornice is "a horizontal molded projection which crowns or finishes a building" (*OED*).

CHAPTER V

WHEN I CAME HOME to West Egg that night I was afraid for a moment that my house was on fire. Two o'clock and the whole corner of the peninsula was blazing with light, which fell unreal on the shrubbery and made thin elongating glints upon the roadside wires. Turning a corner, I saw that it was Gatsby's house, lit from tower to cellar.

At first I thought it was another party, a wild rout[1] that had resolved itself into "hide-and-go-seek" or "sardines-in-the-box"[2] with all the house thrown open to the game. But there wasn't a sound. Only wind in the trees, which blew the wires and made the lights go off and on again as if the house had winked into the darkness. As my taxi groaned away I saw Gatsby walking toward me across his lawn.

"Your place looks like the World's Fair,"[3] I said.

"Does it?" He turned his eyes toward it absently. "I have been glancing into some of the rooms. Let's go to Coney Island,[4] old sport. In my car."

"It's too late."

"Well, suppose we take a plunge in the swimming-pool? I haven't made use of it all summer."

"I've got to go to bed."

"All right."

[1] *rout*: "fashionable gathering; a large evening party" (*OED*).

[2] *sardines … box*: opposite of hide-and-seek, where one person hides and each who finds the one hidden joins in the hiding until all are packed in one hiding spot.

[3] *World's Fair*: international exhibitions showcasing major accomplishments in industry, art, and the like. Several were mounted around the world while Fitzgerald worked on the novel.

[4] *Coney Island*: western end of the peninsula south of Brooklyn, famous for its beaches and amusement parks.

He waited, looking at me with suppressed eagerness.

"I talked with Miss Baker," I said after a moment. "I'm going to call up Daisy tomorrow and invite her over here to tea."

"Oh, that's all right," he said carelessly. "I don't want to put you to any trouble."

"What day would suit you?"

"What day would suit *you*?" he corrected me quickly. "I don't want to put you to any trouble, you see."

"How about the day after tomorrow?"

He considered for a moment. Then, with reluctance:

"I want to get the grass cut," he said.

We both looked at the grass—there was a sharp line where my ragged lawn ended and the darker, well-kept expanse of his began. I suspected that he meant my grass.

"There's another little thing," he said uncertainly, and hesitated.

"Would you rather put it off for a few days?" I asked.

"Oh, it isn't about that. At least—" He fumbled with a series of beginnings. "Why, I thought—why, look here, old sport, you don't make much money, do you?"

"Not very much."

This seemed to reassure him and he continued more confidently.

"I thought you didn't, if you'll pardon my—you see, I carry on a little business on the side, a sort of side line,[5] you understand. And I thought that if you don't make very much—You're selling bonds, aren't you, old sport?"

"Trying to."

"Well, this would interest you. It wouldn't take up much of your time and you might pick up a nice bit of money. It happens to be a rather confidential sort of thing."

I realize now that under different circumstances that conversation might have been one of the crises of my life. But, because the offer was obviously and tactlessly for a service to be rendered, I had no choice except to cut him off there.

[5] *side line*: extra job beyond one's main occupation to earn more money.

"I've got my hands full," I said. "I'm much obliged but I couldn't take on any more work."

"You wouldn't have to do any business with Wolfshiem." Evidently he thought that I was shying away from the "gonnegtion" mentioned at lunch, but I assured him he was wrong. He waited a moment longer, hoping I'd begin a conversation, but I was too absorbed[6] to be responsive, so he went unwillingly home.

The evening had made me light-headed and happy; I think I walked into a deep sleep as I entered my front door. So I don't know whether or not Gatsby went to Coney Island, or for how many hours he "glanced into rooms" while his house blazed gaudily on. I called up Daisy from the office next morning, and invited her to come to tea.

"Don't bring Tom," I warned her.

"What?"

"Don't bring Tom."

"Who is 'Tom'?" she asked innocently.

The day agreed upon was pouring rain. At eleven o'clock a man in a raincoat, dragging a lawn-mower, tapped at my front door and said that Mr. Gatsby had sent him over to cut my grass. This reminded me that I had forgotten to tell my Finn to come back, so I drove into West Egg Village to search for her among soggy whitewashed alleys and to buy some cups and lemons and flowers.

The flowers were unnecessary, for at two o'clock a greenhouse arrived from Gatsby's, with innumerable receptacles to contain it. An hour later the front door opened nervously, and Gatsby, in a white flannel suit, silver shirt, and gold-colored tie, hurried in. He was pale, and there were dark signs of sleeplessness beneath his eyes.

"Is everything all right?" he asked immediately.

"The grass looks fine, if that's what you mean."

"What grass?" he inquired blankly. "Oh, the grass in the yard." He looked out the window at it, but, judging from his expression, I don't believe he saw a thing.

[6] *absorbed*: i.e., preoccupied; having his full attention elsewhere.

"Looks very good," he remarked vaguely. "One of the papers said they thought the rain would stop about four. I think it was *The Journal*. Have you got everything you need in the shape of—of tea?"

I took him into the pantry, where he looked a little reproachfully at the Finn. Together we scrutinized the twelve lemon cakes from the delicatessen shop.

"Will they do?" I asked.

"Of course, of course! They're fine!" and he added hollowly, "... old sport."

The rain cooled about half-past three to a damp mist, through which occasional thin drops swam like dew. Gatsby looked with vacant eyes through a copy of Clay's *Economics*,[7] starting at the Finnish tread that shook the kitchen floor, and peering toward the bleared[8] windows from time to time as if a series of invisible but alarming happenings were taking place outside. Finally he got up and informed me, in an uncertain voice, that he was going home.

"Why's that?"

"Nobody's coming to tea. It's too late!" He looked at his watch as if there was some pressing demand on his time elsewhere. "I can't wait all day."

"Don't be silly; it's just two minutes to four."

He sat down miserably, as if I had pushed him, and simultaneously there was the sound of a motor turning into my lane. We both jumped up, and, a little harrowed[9] myself, I went out into the yard.

[7] *Clay's* Economics: Recognized even in its time for its erudition, Henry Clay's *Economics: An Introduction for the General Reader* first appeared in 1916 and is still in print today.

[8] *bleared*: usually blurred with tears, here figurative if the rain; but also, "said of the face or person: Blurred with running from the eyes" (*OED*), thus pointing to the famous cover of the book. Indeed, the cover was produced and seen by Fitzgerald, who before publication "maintained that he had 'written it into' his book" in *F. Scott Fitzgerald's* The Great Gatsby*: A Literary Reference*, ed. Matthew J. Bruccoli (New York: Carroll and Graf, 2000), pp. 160–68. See Charles Scribner III, "Celestial Eyes—from Metamorphosis to Masterpiece", in ibid.

[9] *harrowed*: distressed or disturbed. In Christianity, the Harrowing of Hell is Christ's descent into the underworld to free those faithfully waiting for him, all the way back to Adam and Eve.

Under the dripping bare lilac-trees a large open car was coming up the drive. It stopped. Daisy's face, tipped sideways beneath a three-cornered lavender hat, looked out at me with a bright ecstatic smile.

"Is this absolutely where you live, my dearest one?"

The exhilarating ripple of her voice was a wild tonic[10] in the rain. I had to follow the sound of it for a moment, up and down, with my ear alone, before any words came through. A damp streak of hair lay like a dash of blue paint across her cheek,[11] and her hand was wet with glistening drops as I took it to help her from the car.

"Are you in love with me," she said low in my ear, "or why did I have to come alone?"

"That's the secret of Castle Rackrent.[12] Tell your chauffeur to go far away and spend an hour."

"Come back in an hour, Ferdie." Then in a grave murmur: "His name is Ferdie."

"Does the gasoline affect his nose?"[13]

"I don't think so," she said innocently. "Why?"

We went in. To my overwhelming surprise the living-room was deserted.

"Well, that's funny!" I exclaimed.

"What's funny?"

She turned her head as there was a light dignified knocking at the front door. I went out and opened it. Gatsby, pale as death, with his hands plunged like weights in his coat pockets, was standing in a puddle of water glaring tragically into my eyes.

[10] *tonic*: both invigorating in itself (like a medicinal tonic) and acting as a musical anchor, i.e., the tonic note.

[11] *damp ... cheek*: almost a perfect description of the novel's cover, which Fitzgerald did see ahead of time (see note 8, "bleared").

[12] *Castle Rackrent*: novel by Maria Edgeworth first published in 1800 that chronicles multiple generations of the Rackrent family. The so-called secret that Nick alludes to may be that although Sir Condy Rackrent loses the castle by accruing too much debt, he had left his wife a substantial jointure or allowance, collectible upon his death.

[13] *gasoline ... nose*: part three of the running gag about butlers' overtaxed body parts.

With his hands still in his coat pockets he stalked by me into the hall, turned sharply as if he were on a wire, and disappeared into the living-room. It wasn't a bit funny. Aware of the loud beating of my own heart I pulled the door to against the increasing rain.

For half a minute there wasn't a sound. Then from the living-room I heard a sort of choking murmur and part of a laugh, followed by Daisy's voice on a clear artificial note:

"I certainly am awfully glad to see you again."

A pause; it endured horribly. I had nothing to do in the hall, so I went into the room.

Gatsby, his hands still in his pockets, was reclining against the mantelpiece in a strained counterfeit of perfect ease, even of boredom. His head leaned back so far that it rested against the face of a defunct[14] mantelpiece clock, and from this position his distraught[15] eyes stared down at Daisy, who was sitting, frightened but graceful, on the edge of a stiff chair.

"We've met before," muttered Gatsby. His eyes glanced momentarily at me, and his lips parted with an abortive attempt at a laugh. Luckily the clock took this moment to tilt dangerously at the pressure of his head, whereupon he turned and caught it with trembling fingers and set it back in place. Then he sat down, rigidly, his elbow on the arm of the sofa and his chin in his hand.

"I'm sorry about the clock," he said.

My own face had now assumed a deep tropical burn. I couldn't muster up a single commonplace out of the thousand in my head.

"It's an old clock," I told them idiotically.

I think we all believed for a moment that it had smashed in pieces on the floor.

"We haven't met for many years," said Daisy, her voice as matter-of-fact as it could ever be.

"Five years next November."

[14] *defunct*: forever out of working order; extinct.

[15] *distraught*: with conflicting or distracted emotions; deeply upset.

The automatic quality of Gatsby's answer set us all back at least another minute. I had them both on their feet with the desperate suggestion that they help me make tea in the kitchen when the demoniac[16] Finn brought it in on a tray.

Amid the welcome confusion of cups and cakes a certain physical decency established itself. Gatsby got himself into a shadow and, while Daisy and I talked, looked conscientiously from one to the other of us with tense, unhappy eyes. However, as calmness wasn't an end in itself, I made an excuse at the first possible moment, and got to my feet.

"Where are you going?" demanded Gatsby in immediate alarm.

"I'll be back."

"I've got to speak to you about something before you go."

He followed me wildly into the kitchen, closed the door, and whispered: "Oh, God!" in a miserable way.

"What's the matter?"

"This is a terrible mistake," he said, shaking his head from side to side, "a terrible, terrible mistake."

"You're just embarrassed, that's all," and luckily I added: "Daisy's embarrassed too."

"She's embarrassed?" he repeated incredulously.

"Just as much as you are."

"Don't talk so loud."

"You're acting like a little boy," I broke out impatiently. "Not only that, but you're rude. Daisy's sitting in there all alone."

He raised his hand to stop my words, looked at me with unforgettable reproach, and, opening the door cautiously, went back into the other room.

I walked out the back way—just as Gatsby had when he had made his nervous circuit of the house half an hour before—and ran for a huge black knotted tree, whose massed leaves made a fabric against the rain. Once more it was pouring, and my irregular lawn, well-shaved by Gatsby's gardener, abounded in small muddy swamps and prehistoric marshes. There was nothing to look at from under the tree except Gatsby's enormous

[16] *demoniac*: i.e., with farcically unsummoned entry.

house, so I stared at it, like Kant at his church steeple,[17] for half an hour. A brewer had built it early in the "period" craze,[18] a decade before, and there was a story that he'd agreed to pay five years' taxes on all the neighboring cottages if the owners would have their roofs thatched with straw. Perhaps their refusal took the heart out of his plan to Found a Family[19]—he went into an immediate decline. His children sold his house with the black wreath still on the door. Americans, while occasionally willing to be serfs, have always been obstinate[20] about being peasantry.

After half an hour, the sun shone again, and the grocer's automobile rounded Gatsby's drive with the raw material for his servants' dinner—I felt sure he wouldn't eat a spoonful. A maid began opening the upper windows of his house, appeared momentarily in each, and, leaning from a large central bay, spat meditatively into the garden. It was time I went back. While the rain continued it had seemed like the murmur of their voices, rising and swelling a little now and then with gusts of emotion. But in the new silence I felt that silence had fallen within the house too.

I went in—after making every possible noise in the kitchen, short of pushing over the stove—but I don't believe they heard a sound. They were sitting at either end of the couch, looking at each other as if some question had been asked, or was in the air, and every vestige[21] of embarrassment was gone. Daisy's face was smeared with tears, and when I came in she jumped up and began wiping at it with her handkerchief before a mirror. But there was a change in Gatsby that was simply confounding.[22]

[17] *Kant ... church steeple*: Immanuel Kant (1724–1804), philosopher of modern-day rationalism and human autonomy, would apparently engage in this practice. See Horst Kruse, "*The Great Gatsby*: A View from Kant's Window—Transatlantic Crosscurrents", *F. Scott Fitzgerald Review* 2 (2003): 72–84.

[18] *"period" craze*: "elaborate Châteauesque Style ... [for] enormously rich families". Curtis Dahl, "Fitzgerald's Use of American Architectural Styles in *The Great Gatsby*", *American Studies* 25, no. 1 (1984): 92.

[19] *Found a Family*: i.e., be the founder of a Family, or create a foundation of a family.

[20] *obstinate*: stubborn; inflexible; unwilling to change on a particular idea.

[21] *vestige*: trace; former indication.

[22] *confounding*: utterly surprising; dumbfounding.

He literally glowed; without a word or a gesture of exultation[23] a new well-being radiated from him and filled the little room.

"Oh, hello, old sport," he said, as if he hadn't seen me for years. I thought for a moment he was going to shake hands.

"It's stopped raining."

"Has it?" When he realized what I was talking about, that there were twinkle-bells of sunshine in the room, he smiled like a weather man, like an ecstatic patron of recurrent light, and repeated the news to Daisy. "What do you think of that? It's stopped raining."

"I'm glad, Jay." Her throat, full of aching, grieving[24] beauty, told only of her unexpected joy.

"I want you and Daisy to come over to my house," he said. "I'd like to show her around."

"You're sure you want me to come?"

"Absolutely, old sport."

Daisy went upstairs to wash her face—too late I thought with humiliation of my towels—while Gatsby and I waited on the lawn.

"My house looks well, doesn't it?" he demanded. "See how the whole front of it catches the light."

I agreed that it was splendid.

"Yes." His eyes went over it, every arched door and square tower. "It took me just three years to earn the money that bought it."

"I thought you inherited your money."

"I did, old sport," he said automatically, "but I lost most of it in the big panic—the panic of the war."

I think he hardly knew what he was saying, for when I asked him what business he was in he answered: "That's my affair," before he realized that it wasn't an appropriate reply.

"Oh, I've been in several things," he corrected himself. "I was in the drug business[25] and then I was in the oil business.

[23] *exultation*: joyful triumph.

[24] *grieving*: filled with deep sorrow, ordinarily out of loss, regret, or suffering.

[25] *drug business*: i.e., drugstores, retail medicines, or similar. However, drugstores at this time were often fronts for bootleggers and other organized crime setups.

But I'm not in either one now." He looked at me with more attention. "Do you mean you've been thinking over what I proposed the other night?"

Before I could answer, Daisy came out of the house and two rows of brass buttons on her dress gleamed in the sunlight.

"That huge place *there?*" she cried pointing.

"Do you like it?"

"I love it, but I don't see how you live there all alone."

"I keep it always full of interesting people, night and day. People who do interesting things. Celebrated people."

Instead of taking the short-cut along the Sound we went down to the road and entered by the big postern.[26] With enchanting murmurs Daisy admired this aspect or that of the feudal silhouette against the sky, admired the gardens, the sparkling odor of jonquils and the frothy odor of hawthorn and plum blossoms and the pale gold odor of kiss-me-at-the-gate.[27] It was strange to reach the marble steps and find no stir of bright dresses in and out the door, and hear no sound but bird voices in the trees.

And inside, as we wandered through Marie Antoinette music-rooms and Restoration salons,[28] I felt that there were guests concealed behind every couch and table, under orders to be breathlessly silent until we had passed through. As Gatsby closed the door of "the Merton College Library"[29] I could have sworn I heard the owl-eyed man break into ghostly laughter.

We went upstairs, through period bedrooms swathed in rose and lavender silk and vivid with new flowers, through

[26]*postern*: back door or gate.

[27]*jonquils … kiss-me-at-the-gate*: Jonquils are yellow or white highly aromatic flowers similar to daffodils. Hawthorns are shrubs or trees with strongly scented white and pink blossoms. Plum blossoms are trees that bear highly fragrant white, pink, and red flowers. Kiss-me-at-the-gate, called heartsease or London Pride (*OED*), is a small plant that produces dozens of small five-petaled, pink blossoms.

[28]*Marie … salons*: These very different architectural styles highlight the eclecticism of the aforementioned "period craze": Marie Antoinette, after the rich, luxurious eighteenth-century style of the Palace of Versailles; Restoration, seventeenth-century British style with elaborate and detailed ornamentation.

[29]*Merton College Library*: one of the oldest scholarly libraries in the world. Merton College is part of Oxford University.

dressing-rooms and poolrooms, and bathrooms with sunken baths—intruding into one chamber where a dishevelled[30] man in pajamas was doing liver exercises[31] on the floor. It was Mr. Klipspringer, the "boarder." I had seen him wandering hungrily about the beach that morning. Finally we came to Gatsby's own apartment, a bedroom and a bath, and an Adam study,[32] where we sat down and drank a glass of some Chartreuse[33] he took from a cupboard in the wall.

He hadn't once ceased looking at Daisy, and I think he revalued everything in his house according to the measure of response it drew from her well-loved eyes. Sometimes, too, he stared around at his possessions in a dazed way, as though in her actual and astounding presence none of it was any longer real. Once he nearly toppled down a flight of stairs.

His bedroom was the simplest room of all—except where the dresser was garnished with a toilet set[34] of pure dull gold. Daisy took the brush with delight, and smoothed her hair, whereupon Gatsby sat down and shaded his eyes and began to laugh.

"It's the funniest thing, old sport," he said hilariously. "I can't—When I try to——"

He had passed visibly through two states and was entering upon a third. After his embarrassment and his unreasoning joy he was consumed with wonder at her presence. He had been full of the idea so long, dreamed it right through to the end, waited with his teeth set, so to speak, at an inconceivable pitch of intensity. Now, in the reaction, he was running down like an overwound clock.[35]

[30] *dishevelled*: untidy; scruffy.

[31] *liver exercises*: body movements thought to cleanse the liver by indirectly massaging and gently squeezing it, forcing new blood to flow through it. See Adelle E. Burch, *Exercises for Health* (Kalamazoo, MI.: Silver Birch, 1916), p. 15.

[32] *Adam study*: i.e., in the Adam style of architecture, eighteenth-century neoclassical, far less busy than other styles already mentioned. See Dahl, "Fitzgerald's Use", pp. 92, 98.

[33] *Chartreuse*: exclusive liqueur made by Carthusian monks in France; only two monks at any given time know the secret recipe of more than 130 ingredients.

[34] *toilet set*: i.e., grooming basics, sold as a set.

[35] *overwound clock*: If a mechanical clock is wound too tightly, it will run fast for a while.

Recovering himself in a minute he opened for us two hulking[36] patent cabinets[37] which held his massed suits and dressing-gowns and ties, and his shirts, piled like bricks in stacks a dozen high.

"I've got a man in England who buys me clothes. He sends over a selection of things at the beginning of each season, spring and fall."

He took out a pile of shirts and began throwing them, one by one, before us, shirts of sheer linen and thick silk and fine flannel, which lost their folds as they fell and covered the table in many-colored disarray. While we admired he brought more and the soft rich heap mounted higher—shirts with stripes and scrolls and plaids in coral and apple-green and lavender and faint orange, with monograms of Indian blue. Suddenly, with a strained sound, Daisy bent her head into the shirts and began to cry stormily.

"They're such beautiful shirts," she sobbed, her voice muffled in the thick folds. "It makes me sad because I've never seen such—such beautiful shirts before."

* * * * *

After the house, we were to see the grounds and the swimming-pool, and the hydroplane and the mid-summer flowers—but outside Gatsby's window it began to rain again, so we stood in a row looking at the corrugated[38] surface of the Sound.

"If it wasn't for the mist we could see your home across the bay," said Gatsby. "You always have a green light that burns all night at the end of your dock."

Daisy put her arm through his abruptly, but he seemed absorbed in what he had just said. Possibly it had occurred to

[36] *hulking*: huge; overlarge. See chapter 1 for the only other use of this word in the novel, which Fitzgerald highlights for the reader by having Tom explicitly say, "I hate that word hulking."

[37] *patent cabinets*: late nineteenth- and early twentieth-century wooden furniture made for office desks, wardrobes, and the like.

[38] *corrugated*: with regular curves or grooves—here the soft waves.

him that the colossal[39] significance of that light had now vanished forever. Compared to the great distance that had separated him from Daisy it had seemed very near to her, almost touching her. It had seemed as close as a star to the moon. Now it was again a green light on a dock. His count of enchanted objects had diminished by one.

I began to walk about the room, examining various indefinite objects in the half-darkness. A large photograph of an elderly man in yachting costume attracted me, hung on the wall over his desk.

"Who's this?"

"That? That's Mr. Dan Cody, old sport."

The name sounded faintly familiar.

"He's dead now. He used to be my best friend years ago."

There was a small picture of Gatsby, also in yachting costume, on the bureau—Gatsby with his head thrown back defiantly—taken apparently when he was about eighteen.

"I adore it," exclaimed Daisy. "The pompadour![40] You never told me you had a pompadour—or a yacht."

"Look at this," said Gatsby quickly. "Here's a lot of clippings—about you."

They stood side by side examining it. I was going to ask to see the rubies[41] when the phone rang, and Gatsby took up the receiver.

"Yes.... Well, I can't talk now.... I can't talk now, old sport.... I said a *small* town.... He must know what a small town is.... Well, he's no use to us if Detroit is his idea of a small town...."

He rang off.

"Come here *quick!*" cried Daisy at the window.

The rain was still falling, but the darkness had parted in the west, and there was a pink and golden billow of foamy clouds above the sea.

[39] *colossal*: tremendous; extraordinary.

[40] *pompadour*: distinctive hairstyle in which all the hair is swept up and slightly back, with no part.

[41] *I ... rubies*: Nick's side joke to the reader plays off Gatsby's "rajah" speech in chapter 4.

"Look at that," she whispered, and then after a moment: "I'd like to just get one of those pink clouds and put you in it and push you around."

I tried to go then, but they wouldn't hear of it; perhaps my presence made them feel more satisfactorily alone.

"I know what we'll do," said Gatsby. "We'll have Klipspringer play the piano."

He went out of the room calling "Ewing!" and returned in a few minutes accompanied by an embarrassed, slightly worn young man, with shell-rimmed glasses and scanty blond hair. He was now decently clothed in a "sport-shirt,"[42] open at the neck, sneakers, and duck trousers[43] of a nebulous[44] hue.

"Did we interrupt your exercises?" inquired Daisy politely.

"I was asleep," cried Mr. Klipspringer, in a spasm of embarrassment. "That is, I'd *been* asleep. Then I got up.... "

"Klipspringer plays the piano," said Gatsby, cutting him off. "Don't you, Ewing, old sport?"

"I don't play well. I don't—I hardly play at all. I'm all out of prac——"

"We'll go downstairs," interrupted Gatsby. He flipped a switch. The gray windows disappeared as the house glowed full of light.

In the music-room Gatsby turned on a solitary lamp beside the piano. He lit Daisy's cigarette from a trembling match, and sat down with her on a couch far across the room, where there was no light save what the gleaming floor bounced in from the hall.

When Klipspringer had played "The Love Nest"[45] he turned around on the bench and searched unhappily for Gatsby in the gloom.

[42] *sport-shirt*: polo or casual shirt with two or three buttons, as opposed to a (more formal) button-down shirt.

[43] *duck trousers*: i.e., made of duck canvas, a heavy and durable cotton.

[44] *nebulous*: if descriptive, like a cloud or mist; if figurative, indistinct or hazy. Both senses work together here.

[45] "*The Love Nest*": hit song from the popular Broadway musical *Mary*, which originally ran from 1920 to 1921. The musical tells the story of Jack, who wants to build homes for poor families but loses almost everything, only to strike it rich with oil, whereupon he returns home triumphant to marry the titular Mary.

"I'm all out of practice, you see. I told you I couldn't play. I'm all out of prac——"

"Don't talk so much, old sport," commanded Gatsby. "Play!"

"In the morning,
In the evening,
  Ain't we got fun[46]——"

Outside the wind was loud and there was a faint flow of thunder along the Sound. All the lights were going on in West Egg now; the electric trains, men-carrying, were plunging home through the rain from New York. It was the hour of a profound human change, and excitement was generating on the air.

"One thing's sure and nothing's surer
The rich get richer and the poor get—children.
  In the meantime,
  In between time——"

As I went over to say good-bye I saw that the expression of bewilderment had come back into Gatsby's face, as though a faint doubt had occurred to him as to the quality of his present happiness. Almost five years! There must have been moments even that afternoon when Daisy tumbled short of his dreams—not through her own fault, but because of the colossal vitality of his illusion. It had gone beyond her, beyond everything. He had thrown himself into it with a creative passion, adding to it all the time, decking it out with every bright feather that drifted his way. No amount of fire or freshness can challenge what a man will store up in his ghostly heart.

As I watched him he adjusted himself a little, visibly. His hand took hold of hers, and as she said something low in his ear he turned toward her with a rush of emotion. I think that voice held him most, with its fluctuating, feverish[47] warmth, because it couldn't be overdreamed—that voice was a deathless song.

[46] *Ain't we got fun*: Billboard number-one song in 1921, in which a couple that cannot keep up with rent sing humorously of making the best of their circumstances.

[47] *feverish*: "excited, nervous, restless" (*OED*).

They had forgotten me, but Daisy glanced up and held out her hand; Gatsby didn't know me now at all. I looked once more at them and they looked back at me, remotely, possessed by intense life. Then I went out of the room and down the marble steps into the rain, leaving them there together.

CHAPTER VI

ABOUT THIS TIME an ambitious young reporter from New York arrived one morning at Gatsby's door and asked him if he had anything to say.

"Anything to say about what?" inquired Gatsby politely.

"Why—any statement to give out."

It transpired after a confused five minutes that the man had heard Gatsby's name around his office in a connection which he either wouldn't reveal or didn't fully understand. This was his day off and with laudable initiative he had hurried out "to see."

It was a random shot, and yet the reporter's instinct was right. Gatsby's notoriety,[1] spread about by the hundreds who had accepted his hospitality and so become authorities upon his past, had increased all summer until he fell just short of being news. Contemporary legends such as the "underground pipe-line to Canada"[2] attached themselves to him, and there was one persistent story that he didn't live in a house at all, but in a boat that looked like a house and was moved secretly up and down the Long Island shore. Just why these inventions were a source of satisfaction to James Gatz of North Dakota isn't easy to say.

James Gatz—that was really, or at least legally, his name. He had changed it at the age of seventeen and at the specific moment that witnessed the beginning of his career—when he saw Dan Cody's yacht drop anchor over the most insidious[3]

[1] *notoriety*: being well known or famous, usually for disreputable reasons.

[2] *"underground ... Canada"*: The front page of the *New York Times* on July 29, 1923, reported on the rum-running business in Detroit as a "storm center", with "liquor openly loaded on Canadian side in daylight". Readers will note that Detroit is mentioned twice in the novel (chaps. 5 and 8) in the context of Gatsby's shady business dealings.

[3] *insidious*: "lying in wait or seeking to entrap or ensnare" (*OED*).

flat on Lake Superior. It was James Gatz who had been loafing along the beach that afternoon in a torn green jersey and a pair of canvas pants, but it was already Jay Gatsby who borrowed a rowboat, pulled out to the *Tuolomee*,[4] and informed Cody that a wind might catch him and break him up[5] in half an hour.

I suppose he'd had the name ready for a long time, even then. His parents were shiftless and unsuccessful farm people—his imagination had never really accepted them as his parents at all. The truth was that Jay Gatsby of West Egg, Long Island, sprang from his Platonic[6] conception of himself. He was a son of God—a phrase which, if it means anything, means just that—and he must be about His Father's business, the service of a vast, vulgar,[7] and meretricious[8] beauty. So he invented just the sort of Jay Gatsby that a seventeen-year-old boy would be likely to invent, and to this conception[9] he was faithful to the end.

For over a year he had been beating his way along the south shore of Lake Superior as a clam-digger and a salmon-fisher or in any other capacity that brought him food and bed. His brown, hardening body lived naturally through the half-fierce, half-lazy work of the bracing[10] days. He knew[11] women early, and since they spoiled him he became contemptuous of

[4] Tuolomee: widely seen by scholars as an adaptation of the Tuolomne, the famous river that was one of the main sites of the California Gold Rush.

[5] *a wind ... break him up*: Cody's yacht has unknowingly dropped anchor in a shallow area (the "insidious flat"); on the Great Lakes, seiches or standing waves, especially with high winds, can unmoor vessels.

[6] *Platonic*: i.e., following Plato's philosophy of the "ideal forms". From Nick's perspective, Gatz has invented Gatsby as this ideal form, to which Gatz will conform himself obediently.

[7] *vulgar*: lacking good taste; unrefined.

[8] *meretricious*: Literally and etymologically, "related to befitting a prostitute". In this context, perhaps it is used euphemistically for something desirable but false, something "showily or superficially attractive but having in reality no value or integrity" (*OED*).

[9] *conception*: abstract idea or invention. In light of other words in this paragraph—"sprang from" and "son of"—conception also means to give birth to.

[10] *bracing*: invigorating (in reference to the weather).

[11] *knew*: shorthand for "had sexual intercourse with", but not excluding the sense of "got to know".

them, of young virgins because they were ignorant, of the others because they were hysterical about things which in his overwhelming self-absorption he took for granted.

But his heart was in a constant, turbulent riot. The most grotesque[12] and fantastic conceits[13] haunted him in his bed at night. A universe of ineffable[14] gaudiness[15] spun itself out in his brain while the clock ticked on the washstand and the moon soaked with wet light his tangled clothes upon the floor. Each night he added to the pattern of his fancies until drowsiness closed down upon some vivid scene with an oblivious embrace. For a while these reveries provided an outlet for his imagination; they were a satisfactory hint of the unreality of reality, a promise that the rock of the world was founded securely on a fairy's wing.

An instinct toward his future glory had led him, some months before, to the small Lutheran college of St. Olaf's in southern Minnesota. He stayed there two weeks, dismayed at its ferocious indifference to the drums of his destiny, to destiny itself, and despising the janitor's work with which he was to pay his way through. Then he drifted back to Lake Superior, and he was still searching for something to do on the day that Dan Cody's yacht dropped anchor in the shallows alongshore.

Cody was fifty years old then, a product of the Nevada silver fields, of the Yukon, of every rush for metal since seventy-five. The transactions in Montana copper that made him many times a millionaire found him physically robust but on the verge of soft-mindedness, and, suspecting this, an infinite number of women tried to separate him from his money. The none too savory ramifications by which Ella Kaye, the newspaper woman, played Madame de Maintenon[16] to his weakness

[12] *grotesque*: "characterized by distortion or unnatural combinations; fantastically extravagant; bizarre" (*OED*).

[13] *conceits*: A conceit is "a fanciful or ingenious action or practice; an affectation of behavior or manner" (*OED*).

[14] *ineffable*: beyond words; incapable of being expressed.

[15] *gaudiness*: extravagant showiness.

[16] *Madame de Maintenon*: Françoise d'Aubigné, second and secret wife of King Louis XIV, who had a very strong influence on her husband, though apparently for good (e.g., making him a more pious Catholic).

and sent him to sea in a yacht, were common property of the turgid[17] journalism of 1902. He had been coasting along all too hospitable shores for five years when he turned up as James Gatz's destiny in Little Girl Bay.[18]

To young Gatz, resting on his oars and looking up at the railed deck, that yacht represented all the beauty and glamour in the world. I suppose he smiled at Cody—he had probably discovered that people liked him when he smiled. At any rate Cody asked him a few questions (one of them elicited the brand new name) and found that he was quick and extravagantly ambitious. A few days later he took him to Duluth and bought him a blue coat, six pairs of white duck trousers, and a yachting cap. And when the *Tuolomee* left for the West Indies and the Barbary Coast, Gatsby left too.

He was employed in a vague personal capacity—while he remained with Cody he was in turn steward, mate, skipper, secretary, and even jailor, for Dan Cody sober knew what lavish[19] doings Dan Cody drunk might soon be about, and he provided for such contingencies by reposing[20] more and more trust in Gatsby. The arrangement lasted five years, during which the boat went three times around the Continent. It might have lasted indefinitely except for the fact that Ella Kaye came on board one night in Boston and a week later Dan Cody inhospitably[21] died.

I remember the portrait of him up in Gatsby's bedroom, a gray, florid man with a hard, empty face—the pioneer

[17] *turgid*: pompous; overinflated.

[18] *Little Girl Bay*: Fitzgerald's adaptation of Little Girl's Point on the southwest shore of Lake Superior, about six miles east of the Wisconsin border. See Julie Kenyon, "'Little Girl Bay,' Frontier, and Folklore: Fitzgerald's Use of Regional History in *The Great Gatsby*", *F. Scott Fitzgerald Review* 16, no. 1 (2018): 109–26.

[19] *lavish*: Given the "jailor" context, Nick's usage here is closest to the obsolete "unrestrained, impetuous; loose, wild, licentious" meaning used by Shakespeare and Milton (*OED*).

[20] *reposing*: "to entrust or confide (power, responsibility, etc.) to a person" (*OED*).

[21] *inhospitably*: Nick plays off three meanings at once: first, jokingly, as if Cody's death were rude and no longer afforded hospitality to Gatsby; second, in the transferred sense, as Cody died at sea, for no harbor would take him; third, in a dreadfully ironic pun, as Cody dies without the help of a hospital (implying that Kaye killed him).

debauchee,[22] who during one phase of American life brought back to the Eastern seaboard the savage violence of the frontier brothel and saloon. It was indirectly due to Cody that Gatsby drank so little. Sometimes in the course of gay parties women used to rub champagne into his hair; for himself he formed the habit of letting liquor alone.

And it was from Cody that he inherited money—a legacy of twenty-five thousand dollars. He didn't get it.[23] He never understood the legal device that was used against him, but what remained of the millions went intact to Ella Kaye. He was left with his singularly appropriate education; the vague contour of Jay Gatsby had filled out to the substantiality[24] of a man.

* * * * *

He told me all this very much later, but I've put it down here with the idea of exploding those first wild rumors about his antecedents, which weren't even faintly true. Moreover he told it to me at a time of confusion, when I had reached the point of believing everything and nothing about him. So I take advantage of this short halt, while Gatsby, so to speak, caught his breath, to clear this set of misconceptions away.

It was a halt, too, in my association with his affairs. For several weeks I didn't see him or hear his voice on the phone—mostly I was in New York, trotting around with Jordan and trying to ingratiate myself with her senile aunt—but finally I went over to his house one Sunday afternoon. I hadn't been there two minutes when somebody brought Tom Buchanan in for a drink. I was startled, naturally, but the really surprising thing was that it hadn't happened before.

[22] *debauchee*: someone debauched; one who overindulges in alcohol, drugs, or sexual intercourse.

[23] *get it*: I.e., he did not understand why he did not receive Cody's remaining millions.

[24] *substantiality*: Given the explicit reference to Plato earlier, Nick uses this word philosophically, i.e., "substance" from the Latin *substantia* or the Greek *ousia* (being). To put it another way, Gatz's ideal form of Gatsby has now become incarnate in him.

They were a party of three on horseback—Tom and a man named Sloane and a pretty woman in a brown riding-habit, who had been there previously.

"I'm delighted to see you," said Gatsby, standing on his porch. "I'm delighted that you dropped in."

As though they cared!

"Sit right down. Have a cigarette or a cigar." He walked around the room quickly, ringing bells. "I'll have something to drink for you in just a minute."

He was profoundly affected by the fact that Tom was there. But he would be uneasy anyhow until he had given them something, realizing in a vague way that that was all they came for. Mr. Sloane wanted nothing. A lemonade? No, thanks. A little champagne? Nothing at all, thanks.... I'm sorry——

"Did you have a nice ride?"

"Very good roads around here."

"I suppose the automobiles——"

"Yeah."

Moved by an irresistible impulse, Gatsby turned to Tom, who had accepted the introduction as a stranger.

"I believe we've met somewhere before, Mr. Buchanan."

"Oh, yes," said Tom, gruffly polite, but obviously not remembering. "So we did. I remember very well."

"About two weeks ago."

"That's right. You were with Nick here."

"I know[25] your wife," continued Gatsby, almost aggressively.

"That so?"

Tom turned to me.

"You live near here, Nick?"

"Next door."

"That so?"

Mr. Sloane didn't enter into the conversation, but lounged back haughtily in his chair; the woman said nothing either—until unexpectedly, after two highballs, she became cordial.

[25] *know*: See note 11 earlier in this chapter about "know" used to mean "to have sexual intercourse".

"We'll all come over to your next party, Mr. Gatsby," she suggested. "What do you say?"

"Certainly; I'd be delighted to have you."

"Be ver' nice," said Mr. Sloane, without gratitude. "Well—think ought to be starting home."

"Please don't hurry," Gatsby urged them. He had control of himself now, and he wanted to see more of Tom. "Why don't you—why don't you stay for supper? I wouldn't be surprised if some other people dropped in from New York."

"You come to supper with *me*," said the lady enthusiastically. "Both of you."

This included me. Mr. Sloane got to his feet.

"Come along," he said—but to her only.

"I mean it," she insisted. "I'd love to have you. Lots of room."

Gatsby looked at me questioningly. He wanted to go, and he didn't see that Mr. Sloane had determined he shouldn't.

"I'm afraid I won't be able to," I said.

"Well, you come," she urged, concentrating on Gatsby.

Mr. Sloane murmured something close to her ear.

"We won't be late if we start now," she insisted aloud.

"I haven't got a horse," said Gatsby. "I used to ride in the army, but I've never bought a horse. I'll have to follow you in my car. Excuse me for just a minute."

The rest of us walked out on the porch, where Sloane and the lady began an impassioned conversation aside.

"My God, I believe the man's coming," said Tom. "Doesn't he know she doesn't want him?"

"She says she does want him."

"She has a big dinner party and he won't know a soul there." He frowned. "I wonder where in the devil he met Daisy. By God, I may be old-fashioned in my ideas, but women run around too much these days to suit me. They meet all kinds of crazy fish."[26]

[26] *crazy fish*: "with prefixed adjective [...]: a person of a specified kind" (*OED*), i.e., crazy people.

Suddenly Mr. Sloane and the lady walked down the steps and mounted their horses.

"Come on," said Mr. Sloane to Tom, "we're late. We've got to go." And then to me: "Tell him we couldn't wait, will you?"

Tom and I shook hands, the rest of us exchanged a cool nod, and they trotted quickly down the drive, disappearing under the August foliage just as Gatsby, with hat and light overcoat in hand, came out the front door.

Tom was evidently perturbed at Daisy's running around alone, for on the following Saturday night he came with her to Gatsby's party. Perhaps his presence gave the evening its peculiar quality of oppressiveness—it stands out in my memory from Gatsby's other parties that summer. There were the same people, or at least the same sort of people, the same profusion of champagne, the same many-colored, many-keyed commotion, but I felt an unpleasantness in the air, a pervading harshness that hadn't been there before. Or perhaps I had merely grown used to it, grown to accept West Egg as a world complete in itself, with its own standards and its own great figures, second to nothing because it had no consciousness of being so, and now I was looking at it again, through Daisy's eyes. It is invariably saddening to look through new eyes at things upon which you have expended your own powers of adjustment.

They arrived at twilight, and, as we strolled out among the sparkling hundreds, Daisy's voice was playing murmurous tricks in her throat.

"These things excite me *so*," she whispered. "If you want to kiss me any time during the evening, Nick, just let me know and I'll be glad to arrange it for you. Just mention my name. Or present a green card.[27] I'm giving out green——"

"Look around," suggested Gatsby.

"I'm looking around. I'm having a marvellous——"

"You must see the faces of many people you've heard about."

Tom's arrogant eyes roamed the crowd.

[27] *green card*: joking reference to visitor cards used in Britain to request a meeting with an MP (member of Parliament).

"We don't go around very much," he said. "In fact, I was just thinking I don't know a soul here."

"Perhaps you know that lady." Gatsby indicated a gorgeous, scarcely human orchid of a woman who sat in state[28] under a white-plum tree. Tom and Daisy stared, with that peculiarly unreal feeling that accompanies the recognition of a hitherto ghostly celebrity of the movies.

"She's lovely," said Daisy.

"The man bending over her is her director."

He took them ceremoniously from group to group:

"Mrs. Buchanan ... and Mr. Buchanan—" After an instant's hesitation he added: "the polo player."

"Oh, no," objected Tom quickly, "not me."

But evidently the sound of it pleased Gatsby, for Tom remained "the polo player" for the rest of the evening.

"I've never met so many celebrities," Daisy exclaimed. "I liked that man—what was his name?—with the sort of blue nose."

Gatsby identified him, adding that he was a small producer.

"Well, I liked him anyhow."

"I'd a little rather not be the polo player," said Tom pleasantly. "I'd rather look at all these famous people in—in oblivion."

Daisy and Gatsby danced. I remember being surprised by his graceful, conservative fox-trot[29]—I had never seen him dance before. Then they sauntered over to my house and sat on the steps for half an hour, while at her request I remained watchfully in the garden. "In case there's a fire or a flood," she explained, "or any act of God."

Tom appeared from his oblivion as we were sitting down to supper together. "Do you mind if I eat with some people over here?" he said. "A fellow's getting off[30] some funny stuff."

[28] *in state*: "with ceremonial splendor, pomp, or magnificence ... with dignity, solemnity, or formality" (*OED*).

[29] *foxtrot*: ballroom dance first developed in 1914, usually danced to ragtime or jazz.

[30] *getting off*: "to succeed in uttering (something, esp. a joke)" (*OED*). Also, an unintentional pun, as Tom intends to "get off" (i.e., have sexual intercourse with) the girl Daisy points out to Nick.

"Go ahead," answered Daisy genially, "and if you want to take down any addresses here's my little gold pencil."... She looked around after a moment and told me the girl was "common but pretty," and I knew that except for the half-hour she'd been alone with Gatsby she wasn't having a good time.

We were at a particularly tipsy table. That was my fault—Gatsby had been called to the phone, and I'd enjoyed these same people only two weeks before. But what had amused me then turned septic[31] on the air now.

"How do you feel, Miss Baedeker?"

The girl addressed was trying, unsuccessfully, to slump against my shoulder. At this inquiry she sat up and opened her eyes.

"Wha'?"

A massive and lethargic[32] woman, who had been urging Daisy to play golf with her at the local club tomorrow, spoke in Miss Baedeker's defense:

"Oh, she's all right now. When she's had five or six cocktails she always starts screaming like that. I tell her she ought to leave it alone."

"I do leave it alone," affirmed the accused hollowly.

"We heard you yelling, so I said to Doc Civet here: 'There's somebody that needs your help, Doc.'"

"She's much obliged, I'm sure," said another friend, without gratitude, "but you got her dress all wet when you stuck her head in the pool."

"Anything I hate is to get my head stuck in a pool," mumbled Miss Baedeker. "They almost drowned me once over in New Jersey."

"Then you ought to leave it alone," countered Doctor Civet.

"Speak for yourself!" cried Miss Baedeker violently. "Your hand shakes. I wouldn't let you operate on me!"

It was like that. Almost the last thing I remember was standing with Daisy and watching the moving-picture director and his Star. They were still under the white-plum tree and their

[31] *septic*: "very bad or unpleasant, nasty, disagreeable" (*OED*).

[32] *lethargic*: sluggish; apathetic.

faces were touching except for a pale, thin ray of moonlight between. It occurred to me that he had been very slowly bending toward her all evening to attain this proximity, and even while I watched I saw him stoop one ultimate degree and kiss at her cheek.

"I like her," said Daisy. "I think she's lovely."

But the rest offended her—and inarguably, because it wasn't a gesture[33] but an emotion. She was appalled[34] by West Egg, this unprecedented "place" that Broadway had begotten[35] upon a Long Island fishing village—appalled by its raw vigor that chafed[36] under the old euphemisms and by the too obtrusive fate that herded its inhabitants along a short-cut from nothing to nothing. She saw something awful in the very simplicity she failed to understand.

I sat on the front steps with them while they waited for their car. It was dark here in front; only the bright door sent ten square feet of light volleying out into the soft black morning. Sometimes a shadow moved against a dressing-room blind above, gave way to another shadow, an indefinite procession of shadows that rouged and powdered in an invisible glass.[37]

"Who is this Gatsby anyhow?" demanded Tom suddenly. "Some big bootlegger?"

"Where'd you hear that?" I inquired.

"I didn't hear it. I imagined it. A lot of these newly rich people are just big bootleggers, you know."

"Not Gatsby," I said shortly.

He was silent for a moment. The pebbles of the drive crunched under his feet.

"Well, he certainly must have strained himself to get this menagerie[38] together."

[33] *gesture*: action or demonstration toward another, e.g., a gesture of sympathy.

[34] *appalled*: shocked, dismayed; to lose heart.

[35] *begotten*: brought into existence by another.

[36] *chafed*: "to display irritation of temper and impatience of restraint or obstacles" (*OED*).

[37] *glass*: i.e., a mirror (in this context, for applying or adjusting makeup).

[38] *menagerie*: neutral word meaning a collection of animals, usually for display. Tom adds his own derogatory slant.

A breeze stirred the gray haze of Daisy's fur collar.

"At least they are more interesting than the people we know," she said with an effort.

"You didn't look so interested."

"Well, I was."

Tom laughed and turned to me.

"Did you notice Daisy's face when that girl asked her to put her under a cold shower?"[39]

Daisy began to sing with the music in a husky, rhythmic whisper, bringing out a meaning in each word that it had never had before and would never have again. When the melody rose her voice broke up sweetly, following it, in a way contralto voices have, and each change tipped out a little of her warm human magic upon the air.

"Lots of people come who haven't been invited," she said suddenly. "That girl hadn't been invited. They simply force their way in and he's too polite to object."

"I'd like to know who he is and what he does," insisted Tom. "And I think I'll make a point of finding out."

"I can tell you right now," she answered. "He owned some drugstores, a lot of drugstores. He built them up himself."

The dilatory[40] limousine came rolling up the drive.

"Good night, Nick," said Daisy.

Her glance left me and sought the lighted top of the steps, where "Three O'Clock in the Morning," a neat, sad little waltz of that year,[41] was drifting out the open door. After all, in the very casualness of Gatsby's party there were romantic possibilities totally absent from her world. What was it up there in the song that seemed to be calling her back inside? What would happen now in the dim, incalculable hours? Perhaps some unbelievable guest would arrive, a person infinitely rare and to be marvelled at, some authentically radiant young girl

[39] *cold shower*: long-rumored cure for drunkenness.

[40] *dilatory*: delayed; late.

[41] *"Three O'Clock" ... that year*: The 1922 recording by Paul Whiteman sold over three million copies.

who with one fresh glance at Gatsby, one moment of magical encounter, would blot out those five years of unwavering devotion.

I stayed late that night, Gatsby asked me to wait until he was free, and I lingered in the garden until the inevitable swimming party had run up, chilled and exalted, from the black beach, until the lights were extinguished in the guest-rooms overhead. When he came down the steps at last the tanned skin was drawn unusually tight on his face, and his eyes were bright and tired.

"She didn't like it," he said immediately.

"Of course she did."

"She didn't like it," he insisted. "She didn't have a good time."

He was silent, and I guessed at his unutterable depression.

"I feel far away from her," he said. "It's hard to make her understand."

"You mean about the dance?"

"The dance?" He dismissed all the dances he had given with a snap of his fingers. "Old sport, the dance is unimportant."

He wanted nothing less of Daisy than that she should go to Tom and say: "I never loved you." After she had obliterated four years with that sentence they could decide upon the more practical measures to be taken. One of them was that, after she was free, they were to go back to Louisville and be married from her house—just as if it were five years ago.

"And she doesn't understand," he said. "She used to be able to understand. We'd sit for hours——"

He broke off and began to walk up and down a desolate path of fruit rinds and discarded favors[42] and crushed flowers.

"I wouldn't ask too much of her," I ventured. "You can't repeat the past."

"Can't repeat the past?" he cried incredulously.[43] "Why of course you can!"

[42] *favors*: i.e., party favors, small presents given to guests as mementos by the host.

[43] *incredulously*: with unbelief; unwilling to believe.

He looked around him wildly, as if the past were lurking here in the shadow of his house, just out of reach of his hand.

"I'm going to fix everything just the way it was before," he said, nodding determinedly. "She'll see."

He talked a lot about the past, and I gathered that he wanted to recover something, some idea of himself perhaps, that had gone into loving Daisy. His life had been confused and disordered since then, but if he could once return to a certain starting place and go over it all slowly, he could find out what that thing was....

... One autumn night, five years before, they had been walking down the street when the leaves were falling, and they came to a place where there were no trees and the sidewalk was white with moonlight. They stopped here and turned toward each other. Now it was a cool night with that mysterious excitement in it which comes at the two changes of the year. The quiet lights in the houses were humming out into the darkness and there was a stir and bustle among the stars. Out of the corner of his eye Gatsby saw that the blocks of the sidewalk really formed a ladder and mounted to a secret place above the trees—he could climb to it, if he climbed alone, and once there he could suck on the pap[44] of life, gulp down the incomparable milk of wonder.

His heart beat faster and faster as Daisy's white face came up to his own. He knew that when he kissed this girl, and forever wed his unutterable visions to her perishable breath, his mind would never romp again like the mind of God. So he waited, listening for a moment longer to the tuning-fork[45] that had been struck upon a star. Then he kissed her. At his lips' touch she blossomed for him like a flower and the incarnation[46] was complete.

[44] *pap*: mother's breast.

[45] *tuning-fork*: device that when struck emits a constant tone by which to tune an instrument.

[46] *incarnation*: to be made flesh. In Catholicism, God is made man in the miraculous birth of Jesus Christ, the Incarnation. Jesus is true God and true man, one Person in two natures.

Through all he said, even through his appalling sentimentality,[47] I was reminded of something—an elusive rhythm, a fragment of lost words, that I had heard somewhere a long time ago. For a moment a phrase tried to take shape in my mouth and my lips parted like a dumb man's, as though there was more struggling upon them than a wisp of startled air. But they made no sound, and what I had almost remembered was uncommunicable[48] forever.

[47] *sentimentality*: when emotion or feeling overcomes or overrides reason.

[48] *uncommunicable*: not able to be expressed. In the context of "incarnation" above, uncommunicable takes on a deeper meaning: not in communion; unable to be in communion.

CHAPTER VII

IT WAS WHEN CURIOSITY about Gatsby was at its highest that the lights in his house failed to go on one Saturday night—and, as obscurely as it had begun, his career as Trimalchio[1] was over. Only gradually did I become aware that the automobiles which turned expectantly into his drive stayed for just a minute and then drove sulkily[2] away. Wondering if he were sick I went over to find out—an unfamiliar butler with a villainous face squinted at me suspiciously from the door.

"Is Mr. Gatsby sick?"

"Nope." After a pause he added "sir" in a dilatory,[3] grudging way.

"I hadn't seen him around, and I was rather worried. Tell him Mr. Carraway came over."

"Who?" he demanded rudely.

"Carraway."

"Carraway. All right, I'll tell him."

Abruptly he slammed the door.

My Finn informed me that Gatsby had dismissed every servant in his house a week ago and replaced them with half a dozen others, who never went into West Egg Village to be bribed by the tradesmen, but ordered moderate supplies over the telephone. The grocery boy reported that the kitchen looked like a pigsty, and the general opinion in the village was that the new people weren't servants at all.

Next day Gatsby called me on the phone.

[1] *Trimalchio*: ostentatious host of Petronius' first-century work *The Satyricon*, who throws wild dinner parties and shows off his rather quickly obtained wealth. Fitzgerald considered for *Gatsby* the title *Trimalchio in West Egg* or just *Trimalchio*.

[2] *sulkily*: stubbornly silent, in a bad mood.

[3] *dilatory*: of a person's habits, i.e., with delay; slow.

"Going away?" I inquired.

"No, old sport."

"I hear you fired all your servants."

"I wanted somebody who wouldn't gossip. Daisy comes over quite often—in the afternoons."

So the whole caravansary[4] had fallen in like a card house[5] at the disapproval in her eyes.

"They're some people Wolfshiem wanted to do something for. They're all brothers and sisters. They used to run a small hotel."

"I see."

He was calling up at Daisy's request—would I come to lunch at her house tomorrow? Miss Baker would be there. Half an hour later Daisy herself telephoned and seemed relieved to find that I was coming. Something was up. And yet I couldn't believe that they would choose this occasion for a scene—especially for the rather harrowing[6] scene that Gatsby had outlined in the garden.

The next day was broiling, almost the last, certainly the warmest, of the summer. As my train emerged from the tunnel into sunlight, only the hot whistles of the National Biscuit Company[7] broke the simmering hush at noon. The straw seats of the car hovered on the edge of combustion; the woman next to me perspired delicately for a while into her white shirtwaist,[8] and then, as her newspaper dampened under her fingers, lapsed despairingly into deep heat with a desolate cry. Her pocketbook slapped to the floor.

"Oh, my!" she gasped.

[4] *caravansary*: hotel or inn for traveling merchants (caravans); in this way, a "hive of activity" (*OED*).

[5] *card house*: i.e., house of cards, a flimsy structure easily dismantled.

[6] *harrowing*: causing great distress or emotional pain. Rare as an adjective, it may be read as "scene in which harrowing is to be done", where Gatsby becomes the savior of Daisy, harrowing her out of Tom's hell.

[7] *National Biscuit Company*: Popularly known as Nabisco, the factory in the Meatpacking District was the largest bakery in the world when it opened in 1899. In 1912 it produced the first Oreo cookie.

[8] *shirtwaist*: "woman's bodice or blouse designed to resemble a shirt, buttoned down the front and usually somewhat loose-fitting" (*OED*).

I picked it up with a weary bend and handed it back to her, holding it at arm's length and by the extreme tip of the corners to indicate that I had no designs upon it—but everyone nearby, including the woman, suspected me just the same.

"Hot!" said the conductor to familiar faces. "Some weather! ... Hot! ... Hot! ... Hot! ... Is it hot enough for you? Is it hot? Is it ... ?"

My commutation ticket[9] came back to me with a dark stain from his hand. That anyone should care in this heat whose flushed lips he kissed, whose head made damp the pajama pocket over his heart!

... Through the hall of the Buchanans' house blew a faint wind, carrying the sound of the telephone bell out to Gatsby and me as we waited at the door.

"The master's body!" roared the butler[10] into the mouthpiece. "I'm sorry, madame, but we can't furnish it—it's far too hot to touch this noon!"

What he really said was: "Yes ... Yes ... I'll see."

He set down the receiver and came toward us, glistening slightly, to take our stiff straw hats.

"Madame expects you in the salon!" he cried, needlessly indicating the direction. In this heat every extra gesture was an affront[11] to the common store[12] of life.

The room, shadowed well with awnings, was dark and cool. Daisy and Jordan lay upon an enormous couch, like silver idols weighing down their own white dresses against the singing breeze of the fans.

"We can't move," they said together.

Jordan's fingers, powdered white over their tan, rested for a moment in mine.

"And Mr. Thomas Buchanan, the athlete?" I inquired.

Simultaneously I heard his voice, gruff, muffled, husky, at the hall telephone.

[9] *commutation ticket*: specifically one held by a regular traveler or commuter, with reduced fares.

[10] *butler*: another entry in the running gag of butlers and body parts.

[11] *affront*: offense, disrespect.

[12] *store*: reserve; to keep in reserve.

Gatsby stood in the center of the crimson carpet and gazed around with fascinated eyes. Daisy watched him and laughed, her sweet, exciting laugh; a tiny gust of powder rose from her bosom into the air.

"The rumor is," whispered Jordan, "that that's Tom's girl on the telephone."

We were silent. The voice in the hall rose high with annoyance: "Very well, then, I won't sell you the car at all ... I'm under no obligations to you at all ... and as for your bothering me about it at lunch time, I won't stand that at all!"

"Holding down the receiver,"[13] said Daisy cynically.

"No, he's not," I assured her. "It's a bona-fide deal. I happen to know about it."

Tom flung open the door, blocked out its space for a moment with his thick body, and hurried into the room.

"Mr. Gatsby!" He put out his broad, flat hand with well-concealed dislike. "I'm glad to see you, sir.... Nick...."

"Make us a cold drink," cried Daisy.

As he left the room again she got up and went over to Gatsby and pulled his face down, kissing him on the mouth.

"You know I love you," she murmured.

"You forget there's a lady present," said Jordan.

Daisy looked around doubtfully.

"You kiss Nick too."

"What a low, vulgar girl!"

"I don't care!" cried Daisy, and began to clog on the brick fireplace. Then she remembered the heat and sat down guiltily on the couch just as a freshly laundered nurse leading a little girl came into the room.

"Bles-sed pre-cious," she crooned, holding out her arms. "Come to your own mother that loves you."

The child, relinquished by the nurse, rushed across the room and rooted[14] shyly into her mother's dress.

[13] *Holding ... receiver*: I.e., he has disconnected the call and is now pretending to talk to someone else.

[14] *rooted*: "to pry or poke into something" (*OED*), as children might hide their faces nervously.

"The bles-sed pre-cious! Did mother get powder on your old yellowy hair? Stand up now, and say—How-de-do."

Gatsby and I in turn leaned down and took the small reluctant hand. Afterward he kept looking at the child with surprise. I don't think he had ever really believed in its existence before.

"I got dressed before luncheon," said the child, turning eagerly to Daisy.

"That's because your mother wanted to show you off." Her face bent into the single wrinkle of the small white neck. "You dream, you. You absolute little dream."

"Yes," admitted the child calmly. "Aunt Jordan's got on a white dress too."

"How do you like mother's friends?" Daisy turned her around so that she faced Gatsby. "Do you think they're pretty?"

"Where's Daddy?"

"She doesn't look like her father," explained Daisy. "She looks like me. She's got my hair and shape of the face."

Daisy sat back upon the couch. The nurse took a step forward and held out her hand.

"Come, Pammy."

"Good-bye, sweetheart!"

With a reluctant backward glance the well-disciplined child held to her nurse's hand and was pulled out the door, just as Tom came back, preceding[15] four gin rickeys[16] that clicked full of ice.

Gatsby took up his drink.

"They certainly look cool," he said, with visible tension.

We drank in long, greedy swallows.

"I read somewhere that the sun's getting hotter every year," said Tom genially. "It seems that pretty soon the earth's going

[15] *preceding*: going before or in front of, meaning that Tom is walking in backwards, presumably to open the door with his back while holding the drinks. James L.W. West in contrast believes that an unnamed butler is carrying them, who precedes Tom (James L. W. West III, ed., *The Great Gatsby: A Variorum Edition* [Cambridge: Cambridge University Press, 2019], p. 241).

[16] *gin rickeys*: highball with gin (40–45% alcohol), lime juice, and carbonated water, poured over ice.

to fall into the sun—or wait a minute—it's just the opposite—the sun's getting colder every year.

"Come outside," he suggested to Gatsby. "I'd like you to have a look at the place."

I went with them out to the veranda. On the green Sound, stagnant in the heat, one small sail crawled slowly toward the fresher sea. Gatsby's eyes followed it momentarily; he raised his hand and pointed across the bay.

"I'm right across from you."

"So you are."

Our eyes lifted over the rose-beds and the hot lawn and the weedy refuse of the dog-days[17] alongshore. Slowly the white wings of the boat moved against the blue cool limit of the sky. Ahead lay the scalloped ocean and the abounding blessed isles.[18]

"There's sport for you," said Tom, nodding. "I'd like to be out there with him for about an hour."

We had luncheon in the dining-room, darkened too against the heat, and drank down nervous gayety with the cold ale.

"What'll we do with ourselves this afternoon?" cried Daisy, "and the day after that, and the next thirty years?"

"Don't be morbid," Jordan said. "Life starts all over again when it gets crisp in the fall."

"But it's so hot," insisted Daisy, on the verge of tears, "and everything's so confused. Let's all go to town!"

Her voice struggled on through the heat, beating against it, molding its senselessness into forms.

"I've heard of making a garage out of a stable," Tom was saying to Gatsby, "but I'm the first man who ever made a stable out of a garage."

[17] *dog-days*: i.e., the dog days of summer, "the hottest part of the summer, associated in ancient times with the heliacal rising of the Dog Star in the Mediterranean area, and formerly considered to be the most unhealthy period of the year and a time of ill omen" (*OED*).

[18] *blessed isles*: in Greek mythology, a location at the farthest point west with a garden of golden fruit watched over by the Hesperides, the nymph-daughters of Hesperus.

"Who wants to go to town?" demanded Daisy insistently. Gatsby's eyes floated toward her. "Ah," she cried, "you look so cool."

Their eyes met, and they stared together at each other, alone in space. With an effort she glanced down at the table.

"You always look so cool," she repeated.

She had told him that she loved him, and Tom Buchanan saw. He was astounded. His mouth opened a little, and he looked at Gatsby, and then back at Daisy as if he had just recognized her as someone he knew a long time ago.

"You resemble the advertisement of the man," she went on innocently. "You know the advertisement of the man——"

"All right," broke in Tom quickly, "I'm perfectly willing to go to town. Come on—we're all going to town."

He got up, his eyes still flashing between Gatsby and his wife. No one moved.

"Come on!" His temper cracked a little. "What's the matter, anyhow? If we're going to town, let's start."

His hand, trembling with his effort at self-control, bore to his lips the last of his glass of ale. Daisy's voice got us to our feet and out on to the blazing gravel drive.

"Are we just going to go?" she objected. "Like this? Aren't we going to let anyone smoke a cigarette first?"

"Everybody smoked all through lunch."

"Oh, let's have fun," she begged him. "It's too hot to fuss."

He didn't answer.

"Have it your own way," she said. "Come on, Jordan."

They went upstairs to get ready while we three men stood there shuffling the hot pebbles with our feet. A silver curve of the moon hovered already in the western sky. Gatsby started to speak, changed his mind, but not before Tom wheeled and faced him expectantly.

"Have you got your stables here?" asked Gatsby with an effort.

"About a quarter of a mile down the road."

"Oh."

A pause.

"I don't see the idea of going to town," broke out Tom savagely. "Women get these notions in their heads——"

"Shall we take anything to drink?" called Daisy from an upper window.

"I'll get some whiskey," answered Tom. He went inside.

Gatsby turned to me rigidly:

"I can't say anything in his house, old sport."

"She's got an indiscreet[19] voice," I remarked. "It's full of—" I hesitated.

"Her voice is full of money," he said suddenly.

That was it. I'd never understood before. It was full of money—that was the inexhaustible charm that rose and fell in it, the jingle of it, the cymbals' song of it.... High in a white palace the king's daughter, the golden girl....

Tom came out of the house wrapping a quart bottle in a towel, followed by Daisy and Jordan wearing small tight hats of metallic cloth and carrying light capes over their arms.

"Shall we all go in my car?" suggested Gatsby. He felt the hot, green leather of the seat. "I ought to have left it in the shade."

"Is it standard shift?" demanded Tom.

"Yes."

"Well, you take my coupé and let me drive your car to town."

The suggestion was distasteful to Gatsby.

"I don't think there's much gas," he objected.

"Plenty of gas," said Tom boisterously. He looked at the gauge. "And if it runs out I can stop at a drugstore. You can buy anything at a drugstore nowadays."

A pause followed this apparently pointless remark. Daisy looked at Tom frowning, and an indefinable expression, at once definitely unfamiliar and vaguely recognizable, as if I had only heard it described in words, passed over Gatsby's face.

"Come on, Daisy," said Tom, pressing her with his hand toward Gatsby's car. "I'll take you in this circus wagon."[20]

[19] *indiscreet*: lacking good judgment; unwary.

[20] *circus wagon*: typically four-wheeled, gaudily colored and lavishly decorated traveling cage for animals. See the note for "menagerie" in chapter 6.

He opened the door, but she moved out from the circle of his arm.

"You take Nick and Jordan. We'll follow you in the coupé."

She walked close to Gatsby, touching his coat with her hand. Jordan and Tom and I got into the front seat of Gatsby's car, Tom pushed the unfamiliar gears tentatively, and we shot off into the oppressive heat, leaving them out of sight behind.

"Did you see that?" demanded Tom.

"See what?"

He looked at me keenly,[21] realizing that Jordan and I must have known all along.

"You think I'm pretty dumb, don't you?" he suggested. "Perhaps I am, but I have a—almost a second sight, sometimes, that tells me what to do. Maybe you don't believe that, but science——"

He paused. The immediate contingency[22] overtook him, pulled him back from the edge of the theoretical abyss.

"I've made a small investigation of this fellow," he continued. "I could have gone deeper if I'd known——"

"Do you mean you've been to a medium?"[23] inquired Jordan humorously.

"What?" Confused, he stared at us as we laughed. "A medium?"

"About Gatsby."

"About Gatsby! No, I haven't. I said I'd been making a small investigation of his past."

"And you found he was an Oxford man," said Jordan helpfully.

"An Oxford man!" He was incredulous. "Like hell he is! He wears a pink suit."

"Nevertheless he's an Oxford man."

[21] *keenly*: with sharp or piercing insight.

[22] *immediate contingency*: Nick plays off the commonplace "future contingency"—something that may happen or not in the future—by highlighting Tom's immediate sense that Gatsby may try to seduce Daisy.

[23] *medium*: someone who supposedly mediates between the spirit world and ours, providing access to occult knowledge, usually by so-called speaking with the dead.

"Oxford, New Mexico," snorted Tom contemptuously, "or something like that."

"Listen, Tom. If you're such a snob, why did you invite him to lunch?" demanded Jordan crossly.

"Daisy invited him; she knew him before we were married—God knows where!"

We were all irritable now with the fading ale, and aware of it we drove for a while in silence. Then as Doctor T. J. Eckleburg's faded eyes came into sight down the road, I remembered Gatsby's caution about gasoline.

"We've got enough to get us to town," said Tom.

"But there's a garage right here," objected Jordan. "I don't want to get stalled in this baking heat."

Tom threw on both brakes[24] impatiently, and we slid to an abrupt dusty stop under Wilson's sign. After a moment the proprietor emerged from the interior of his establishment and gazed hollow-eyed at the car.

"Let's have some gas!" cried Tom roughly. "What do you think we stopped for—to admire the view?"

"I'm sick," said Wilson without moving. "Been sick all day."

"What's the matter?"

"I'm all run down."

"Well, shall I help myself?" Tom demanded. "You sounded well enough on the phone."

With an effort Wilson left the shade and support of the doorway and, breathing hard, unscrewed the cap of the tank. In the sunlight his face was green.

"I didn't mean to interrupt your lunch," he said. "But I need money pretty bad, and I was wondering what you were going to do with your old car."

"How do you like this one?" inquired Tom. "I bought it last week."

"It's a nice yellow one," said Wilson, as he strained at the handle.

[24] *both brakes*: Assisted or power brakes did not emerge until the 1950s; until then, drivers had to apply all the braking power themselves, which ordinarily required both foot and hand brakes.

"Like to buy it?"

"Big chance," Wilson smiled faintly. "No, but I could make some money on the other."

"What do you want money for, all of a sudden?"

"I've been here too long. I want to get away. My wife and I want to go West."

"Your wife does," exclaimed Tom, startled.

"She's been talking about it for ten years." He rested for a moment against the pump, shading his eyes. "And now she's going whether she wants to or not. I'm going to get her away."

The coupé flashed by us with a flurry of dust and the flash of a waving hand.

"What do I owe you?" demanded Tom harshly.

"I just got wised up to something funny the last two days," remarked Wilson. "That's why I want to get away. That's why I been bothering you about the car."

"What do I owe you?"

"Dollar twenty."

The relentless beating heat was beginning to confuse me and I had a bad moment there before I realized that so far his suspicions hadn't alighted on Tom. He had discovered that Myrtle had some sort of life apart from him in another world, and the shock had made him physically sick. I stared at him and then at Tom, who had made a parallel discovery less than an hour before—and it occurred to me that there was no difference between men, in intelligence or race, so profound as the difference between the sick and the well. Wilson was so sick that he looked guilty, unforgivably guilty—as if he had just got some poor girl with child.

"I'll let you have that car," said Tom. "I'll send it over tomorrow afternoon."

That locality was always vaguely disquieting, even in the broad glare of afternoon, and now I turned my head as though I had been warned of something behind. Over the ashheaps the giant eyes of Doctor T. J. Eckleburg kept their vigil, but I perceived, after a moment, that other eyes were regarding us with peculiar intensity from less than twenty feet away.

In one of the windows over the garage the curtains had been moved aside a little, and Myrtle Wilson was peering down at the car. So engrossed was she that she had no consciousness of being observed, and one emotion after another crept into her face like objects into a slowly developing[25] picture. Her expression was curiously familiar—it was an expression I had often seen on women's faces, but on Myrtle Wilson's face it seemed purposeless and inexplicable until I realized that her eyes, wide with jealous terror, were fixed not on Tom, but on Jordan Baker, whom she took to be his wife.

* * * * *

There is no confusion like the confusion of a simple mind, and as we drove away Tom was feeling the hot whips of panic. His wife and his mistress, until an hour ago secure and inviolate, were slipping precipitately[26] from his control. Instinct made him step on the accelerator with the double purpose of overtaking Daisy and leaving Wilson behind, and we sped along toward Astoria at fifty miles an hour, until, among the spidery girders of the elevated, we came in sight of the easy-going blue coupé.

"Those big movies around Fiftieth Street are cool," suggested Jordan. "I love New York on summer afternoons when everyone's away. There's something very sensuous about it—overripe, as if all sorts of funny fruits were going to fall into your hands."

The word "sensuous" had the effect of further disquieting Tom, but before he could invent a protest the coupé came to a stop, and Daisy signalled us to draw up alongside.

"Where are we going?" she cried.

"How about the movies?"

"It's so hot," she complained. "You go. We'll ride around and meet you after." With an effort her wit rose faintly. "We'll meet you on some corner. I'll be the man smoking two cigarettes."

[25] *slowly developing*: Photographic prints were made by passing light through film negatives onto sensitive paper; the image on the paper would slowly develop as a result.

[26] *precipitately*: rapidly; suddenly.

"We can't argue about it here," Tom said impatiently, as a truck gave out a cursing whistle behind us. "You follow me to the south side of Central Park, in front of the Plaza."

Several times he turned his head and looked back for their car, and if the traffic delayed them he slowed up until they came into sight. I think he was afraid they would dart down a side street and out of his life forever.

But they didn't. And we all took the less explicable step of engaging[27] the parlor of a suite in the Plaza Hotel.

The prolonged and tumultuous argument that ended by herding us into that room eludes me, though I have a sharp physical memory that, in the course of it, my underwear kept climbing like a damp snake around my legs and intermittent beads of sweat raced cool across my back. The notion originated with Daisy's suggestion that we hire five bathrooms and take cold baths, and then assumed more tangible form as "a place to have a mint julep." Each of us said over and over that it was a "crazy idea"—we all talked at once to a baffled clerk and thought, or pretended to think, that we were being very funny....

The room was large and stifling, and, though it was already four o'clock, opening the windows admitted only a gust of hot shrubbery from the Park. Daisy went to the mirror and stood with her back to us, fixing her hair.

"It's a swell[28] suite," whispered Jordan respectfully, and everyone laughed.

"Open another window," commanded Daisy, without turning around.

"There aren't any more."

"Well, we'd better telephone for an axe——"

"The thing to do is to forget about the heat," said Tom impatiently. "You make it ten times worse by crabbing about it."

He unrolled the bottle of whiskey from the towel and put it on the table.

[27] *engaging*: i.e., rented it. Fitzgerald's hint at "engagement" plays off the wedding theme and the confrontation that will follow.

[28] *swell*: Jordan's joke plays off "swell" as handsome or splendid, against the "swell" or sweltering heat.

"Why not let her alone, old sport?" remarked Gatsby. "You're the one that wanted to come to town."

There was a moment of silence. The telephone book slipped from its nail and splashed to the floor, whereupon Jordan whispered, "Excuse me"—but this time no one laughed.

"I'll pick it up," I offered.

"I've got it." Gatsby examined the parted string, muttered "Hum!" in an interested way, and tossed the book on a chair.

"That's a great expression of yours, isn't it?" said Tom sharply.

"What is?"

"All this 'old sport' business. Where'd you pick that up?"

"Now see here, Tom," said Daisy, turning around from the mirror, "if you're going to make personal remarks I won't stay here a minute. Call up and order some ice for the mint julep."

As Tom took up the receiver the compressed heat exploded into sound and we were listening to the portentous[29] chords of Mendelssohn's Wedding March from the ballroom below.

"Imagine marrying anybody in this heat!" cried Jordan dismally.

"Still—I was married in the middle of June," Daisy remembered. "Louisville in June! Somebody fainted. Who was it fainted, Tom?"

"Biloxi," he answered shortly.

"A man named Biloxi. 'Blocks' Biloxi, and he made boxes—that's a fact—and he was from Biloxi, Mississippi."[30]

"They carried him into my house," appended Jordan, "because we lived just two doors from the church. And he stayed three weeks, until Daddy told him he had to get out. The day after he left Daddy died." After a moment she added, as if she might have sounded irreverent, "There wasn't any connection."

"I used to know a Bill Biloxi from Memphis," I remarked.

"That was his cousin. I knew his whole family history before he left. He gave me an aluminum putter that I use today."

[29] *portentous*: of music, very grand and with much pomp. Fitzgerald plays off the more common meaning: threatening, like a disastrous omen.

[30] *Mississippi*: The 1925 text has "Tennessee", which Fitzgerald corrected.

The music had died down as the ceremony began and now a long cheer floated in at the window, followed by intermittent cries of "Yea—ea—ea!" and finally by a burst of jazz as the dancing began.

"We're getting old," said Daisy. "If we were young we'd rise and dance."

"Remember Biloxi," Jordan warned her. "Where'd you know him, Tom?"

"Biloxi?" He concentrated with an effort. "I didn't know him. He was a friend of Daisy's."

"He was not," she denied. "I'd never seen him before. He came down in the private car."

"Well, he said he knew you. He said he was raised in Louisville. Asa Bird brought him around at the last minute and asked if we had room for him."

Jordan smiled.

"He was probably bumming his way home. He told me he was president of your class at Yale."

Tom and I looked at each other blankly.

"Biloxi?"

"First place, we didn't have any president——"

Gatsby's foot beat a short, restless tattoo[31] and Tom eyed him suddenly.

"By the way, Mr. Gatsby, I understand you're an Oxford man."

"Not exactly."

"Oh, yes, I understand you went to Oxford."

"Yes—I went there."

A pause. Then Tom's voice, incredulous and insulting:

"You must have gone there about the time Biloxi went to New Haven."

Another pause. A waiter knocked and came in with crushed mint and ice but the silence was unbroken by his "thank you"

[31] *tattoo*: "the action of beating, thumping, or rapping continuously upon something" (*OED*). Fitzgerald reminds the reader of Gatsby's military background, as the word derives from "tap-too", a military bugler playing "Taps" to signal soldiers to turn in for the night.

and the soft closing of the door. This tremendous detail was to be cleared up at last.

"I told you I went there," said Gatsby.

"I heard you, but I'd like to know when."

"It was in nineteen-nineteen. I only stayed five months. That's why I can't really call myself an Oxford man."

Tom glanced around to see if we mirrored his unbelief. But we were all looking at Gatsby.

"It was an opportunity they gave to some of the officers after the armistice," he continued. "We could go to any of the universities in England or France."

I wanted to get up and slap him on the back. I had one of those renewals of complete faith in him that I'd experienced before.

Daisy rose, smiling faintly, and went to the table.

"Open the whiskey, Tom," she ordered, "and I'll make you a mint julep. Then you won't seem so stupid to yourself.... Look at the mint!"

"Wait a minute," snapped Tom. "I want to ask Mr. Gatsby one more question."

"Go on," Gatsby said politely.

"What kind of a row[32] are you trying to cause in my house anyhow?"

They were out in the open at last and Gatsby was content.

"He isn't causing a row." Daisy looked desperately from one to the other. "You're causing a row. Please have a little self-control."

"Self-control!" repeated Tom incredulously. "I suppose the latest thing is to sit back and let Mr. Nobody from Nowhere make love[33] to your wife. Well, if that's the idea you can count

[32] *row*: "serious dispute [...] a fierce controversy about or over something" (*OED*). In this meaning, the word rhymes with "anyhow", which makes Tom's accusation sound ridiculous.

[33] *make love*: At this time, the normal meaning is to become romantic with, or to engage in courtship. Although "make love" as sexual intercourse would not become a published meaning until 1927 (*OED*), Fitzgerald allows the reader to engage in dramatic irony (i.e., the reader knows that Tom's phrase is more apt than Tom realizes).

me out.... Nowadays people begin by sneering at family life and family institutions, and next they'll throw everything overboard and have intermarriage between black and white."

Flushed with his impassioned gibberish, he saw himself standing alone on the last barrier of civilization.

"We're all white here," murmured Jordan.

"I know I'm not very popular. I don't give big parties. I suppose you've got to make your house into a pigsty in order to have any friends—in the modern world."

Angry as I was, as we all were, I was tempted to laugh whenever he opened his mouth. The transition from libertine[34] to prig[35] was so complete.

"I've got something to tell *you*, old sport—" began Gatsby. But Daisy guessed at his intention.

"Please don't!" she interrupted helplessly. "Please let's all go home. Why don't we all go home?"

"That's a good idea." I got up. "Come on, Tom. Nobody wants a drink."

"I want to know what Mr. Gatsby has to tell me."

"Your wife doesn't love you," said Gatsby. "She's never loved you. She loves me."

"You must be crazy!" exclaimed Tom automatically.

Gatsby sprang to his feet, vivid with excitement.

"She never loved you, do you hear?" he cried. "She only married you because I was poor and she was tired of waiting for me. It was a terrible mistake, but in her heart she never loved anyone except me!"

At this point Jordan and I tried to go, but Tom and Gatsby insisted with competitive firmness that we remain—as though neither of them had anything to conceal and it would be a privilege to partake vicariously of their emotions.

"Sit down, Daisy." Tom's voice groped unsuccessfully for the paternal note. "What's been going on? I want to hear all about it."

[34] *libertine*: morally loose, especially in sexual relations.

[35] *prig*: excessively precise or morally self-important person.

"I told you what's been going on," said Gatsby. "Going on for five years—and you didn't know."

Tom turned to Daisy sharply.

"You've been seeing this fellow for five years?"

"Not seeing," said Gatsby. "No, we couldn't meet. But both of us loved each other all that time, old sport, and you didn't know. I used to laugh sometimes"—but there was no laughter in his eyes—"to think that you didn't know."

"Oh—that's all." Tom tapped his thick fingers together like a clergyman and leaned back in his chair.

"You're crazy!" he exploded. "I can't speak about what happened five years ago because I didn't know Daisy then—and I'll be damned if I see how you got within a mile of her unless you brought the groceries to the back door. But all the rest of that's a God damned lie. Daisy loved me when she married me and she loves me now."

"No," said Gatsby, shaking his head.

"She does, though. The trouble is that sometimes she gets foolish ideas in her head and doesn't know what she's doing." He nodded sagely. "And what's more I love Daisy too. Once in a while I go off on a spree[36] and make a fool of myself, but I always come back, and in my heart I love her all the time."

"You're revolting," said Daisy. She turned to me, and her voice, dropping an octave lower, filled the room with thrilling scorn: "Do you know why we left Chicago? I'm surprised that they didn't treat you to the story of that little spree."

Gatsby walked over and stood beside her.

"Daisy, that's all over now," he said earnestly. "It doesn't matter any more. Just tell him the truth—that you never loved him—and it's all wiped out forever."

She looked at him blindly. "Why—how could I love him—possibly?"

"You never loved him."

[36] *spree*: any indulgence in wild or disorderly conduct; here, a sexual tryst or a fling.

She hesitated. Her eyes fell on Jordan and me with a sort of appeal, as though she realized at last what she was doing—and as though she had never, all along, intended doing anything at all. But it was done now. It was too late.

"I never loved him," she said, with perceptible reluctance.

"Not at Kapiolani?"[37] demanded Tom suddenly.

"No."

From the ballroom beneath, muffled and suffocating chords were drifting up on hot waves of air.

"Not that day I carried you down from the Punch Bowl[38] to keep your shoes dry?" There was a husky tenderness in his tone.... "Daisy?"

"Please don't." Her voice was cold, but the rancor[39] was gone from it. She looked at Gatsby. "There, Jay," she said—but her hand as she tried to light a cigarette was trembling. Suddenly she threw the cigarette and the burning match on the carpet.

"Oh, you want too much!" she cried to Gatsby. "I love you now—isn't that enough? I can't help what's past." She began to sob helplessly. "I did love him once—but I loved you too."

Gatsby's eyes opened[40] and closed.

"You loved me *too?*" he repeated.

"Even that's a lie," said Tom savagely. "She didn't know you were alive. Why—there're things between Daisy and me that you'll never know, things that neither of us can ever forget."

The words seemed to bite physically into Gatsby.

"I want to speak to Daisy alone," he insisted. "She's all excited now——"

[37] *Kapiolani*: large public park in Honolulu, Hawaii, after the queen of the same name.

[38] *Punch Bowl*: famous volcanic crater in Honolulu, at that time only a tourist attraction (but since 1949, the site of the National Memorial Cemetery of the Pacific).

[39] *rancor*: long-standing and bitter grudge or resentment.

[40] *opened*: a strange verb as presumably Gatsby's eyes were already open (and Nick has not indicated their being closed, which would be notable, nor has he specified a degree of more openness, as he does with Tom below).

"Even alone I can't say I never loved Tom," she admitted in a pitiful voice. "It wouldn't be true."

"Of course it wouldn't," agreed Tom.

She turned to her husband.

"As if it mattered to you," she said.

"Of course it matters. I'm going to take better care of you from now on."

"You don't understand," said Gatsby, with a touch of panic. "You're not going to take care of her any more."

"I'm not?" Tom opened his eyes wide and laughed. He could afford to control himself now. "Why's that?"

"Daisy's leaving you."

"Nonsense."

"I am, though," she said with a visible effort.

"She's not leaving me!" Tom's words suddenly leaned down over Gatsby. "Certainly not for a common swindler[41] who'd have to steal the ring he put on her finger."

"I won't stand this!" cried Daisy. "Oh, please let's get out."

"Who are you, anyhow?" broke out Tom. "You're one of that bunch that hangs around with Meyer Wolfshiem—that much I happen to know. I've made a little investigation into your affairs—and I'll carry it further tomorrow."

"You can suit yourself about that, old sport," said Gatsby steadily.

"I found out what your 'drugstores' were." He turned to us and spoke rapidly. "He and this Wolfshiem bought up a lot of side-street drugstores here and in Chicago and sold grain alcohol[42] over the counter. That's one of his little stunts.[43] I picked him for a bootlegger the first time I saw him, and I wasn't far wrong."

"What about it?" said Gatsby politely. "I guess your friend Walter Chase wasn't too proud to come in on it."

[41] *swindler*: con artist; someone who deceives others for material gain.

[42] *grain alcohol*: distilled spirit in its purest form, typically 190 proof or 95% alcohol.

[43] *stunts*: A stunt is "a piece of business, an act, enterprise, or exploit" (*OED*). Tom also plays off the meaning of stunt as a trick or feat to be pulled off.

"And you left him in the lurch,[44] didn't you? You let him go to jail for a month over in New Jersey. God! You ought to hear Walter on the subject of *you*."

"He came to us dead broke. He was very glad to pick up some money, old sport."

"Don't you call me 'old sport'!" cried Tom. Gatsby said nothing. "Walter could have you up on the betting laws too, but Wolfshiem scared him into shutting his mouth."

That unfamiliar yet recognizable look was back again in Gatsby's face.

"That drugstore business was just small change," continued Tom slowly, "but you've got something on now that Walter's afraid to tell me about."

I glanced at Daisy, who was staring terrified between Gatsby and her husband, and at Jordan, who had begun to balance an invisible but absorbing object on the tip of her chin. Then I turned back to Gatsby—and was startled at his expression. He looked—and this is said in all contempt for the babbled slander of his garden—as if he had "killed a man." For a moment the set of his face could be described in just that fantastic way.

It passed, and he began to talk excitedly to Daisy, denying everything, defending his name against accusations that had not been made. But with every word she was drawing further and further into herself, so he gave that up, and only the dead dream fought on as the afternoon slipped away, trying to touch what was no longer tangible, struggling unhappily, undespairingly, toward that lost voice across the room.

The voice begged again to go.

"*Please*, Tom! I can't stand this any more."

Her frightened eyes told that whatever intentions, whatever courage she had had, were definitely gone.

"You two start on home, Daisy," said Tom. "In Mr. Gatsby's car."

[44] *left ... lurch*: "to leave in adverse circumstances without assistance [or] in a position of unexpected difficulty" (*OED*).

She looked at Tom, alarmed now, but he insisted with magnanimous[45] scorn.

"Go on. He won't annoy you. I think he realizes that his presumptuous[46] little flirtation is over."

They were gone, without a word, snapped out, made accidental,[47] isolated, like ghosts, even from our pity.

After a moment Tom got up and began wrapping the unopened bottle of whiskey in the towel.

"Want any of this stuff? Jordan? ... Nick?"

I didn't answer.

"Nick?" He asked again.

"What?"

"Want any?"

"No ... I just remembered that today's my birthday."

I was thirty. Before me stretched the portentous, menacing road of a new decade.

It was seven o'clock when we got into the coupé with him and started for Long Island. Tom talked incessantly, exulting and laughing, but his voice was as remote from Jordan and me as the foreign clamor on the sidewalk or the tumult of the elevated overhead. Human sympathy has its limits, and we were content to let all their tragic arguments fade with the city lights behind. Thirty—the promise of a decade of loneliness, a thinning list of single men to know, a thinning brief-case of enthusiasm, thinning hair. But there was Jordan beside me, who, unlike Daisy, was too wise ever to carry well-forgotten dreams from age to age. As we passed over the dark bridge her

[45] *magnanimous*: Literally "great-souled", the virtue of magnanimity is treated by Saint Thomas Aquinas (*Summa* II-II, q. 129) and generally means generous and noble in spirit. Nick uses it sarcastically.

[46] *presumptuous*: like a usurper; arrogantly taking one's position for granted. In light of "magnanimous" above, "presumption" means one of the unforgivable sins (because its shuts one off from God's mercy).

[47] *accidental*: Fitzgerald plays off three meanings here: literally, by mistake or chance, unintentional; in light of magnanimous and presumptuous above, the philosophical meaning: insubstantial, nonessential; third, as foreshadowing: the unintended circumstance of the car accident at the climax of the novel.

wan face fell lazily against my coat's shoulder and the formidable stroke of thirty died away with the reassuring pressure of her hand.

So we drove on toward death through the cooling twilight.

The young Greek, Michaelis, who ran the coffee joint beside the ashheaps, was the principal witness at the inquest.[48] He had slept through the heat until after five, when he strolled over to the garage, and found George Wilson sick in his office—really sick, pale as his own pale hair and shaking all over. Michaelis advised him to go to bed, but Wilson refused, saying that he'd miss a lot of business if he did. While his neighbor was trying to persuade him a violent racket broke out overhead.

"I've got my wife locked in up there," explained Wilson calmly. "She's going to stay there till the day after tomorrow, and then we're going to move away."

Michaelis was astonished; they had been neighbors for four years, and Wilson had never seemed faintly capable of such a statement. Generally he was one of these worn-out men: when he wasn't working, he sat on a chair in the doorway and stared at the people and the cars that passed along the road. When anyone spoke to him he invariably laughed in an agreeable, colorless[49] way. He was his wife's man and not his own.

So naturally Michaelis tried to find out what had happened, but Wilson wouldn't say a word—instead he began to throw curious, suspicious glances at his visitor and ask him what he'd been doing at certain times on certain days. Just as the latter was getting uneasy, some workmen came past the door bound for his restaurant, and Michaelis took the opportunity to get away, intending to come back later. But he didn't. He supposed he forgot to, that's all. When he came outside again, a little after seven, he was reminded of the conversation because he

[48] *inquest*: "legal or judicial inquiry to ascertain or decide a matter of fact" (*OED*). Fitzgerald builds suspense as the modern usage is often a coroner's inquest.

[49] *colorless*: neutral, unbiased; undistinctive, bland.

heard Mrs. Wilson's voice, loud and scolding, downstairs in the garage.

"Beat me!" he heard her cry. "Throw me down and beat me, you dirty little coward!"

A moment later she rushed out into the dusk, waving her hands and shouting—before he could move from his door the business was over.

The "death car," as the newspapers called it, didn't stop; it came out of the gathering darkness, wavered[50] tragically for a moment, and then disappeared around the next bend. Michaelis wasn't even sure of its color—he told the first policeman that it was light green. The other car, the one going toward New York, came to rest a hundred yards beyond, and its driver hurried back to where Myrtle Wilson, her life violently extinguished, knelt in the road and mingled her thick dark blood with the dust.

Michaelis and this man reached her first, but when they had torn open her shirtwaist, still damp with perspiration, they saw that her left breast was swinging loose like a flap, and there was no need to listen for the heart beneath. The mouth was wide open and ripped at the corners, as though she had choked a little in giving up the tremendous vitality she had stored so long.

* * * * *

We saw the three or four automobiles and the crowd when we were still some distance away.

"Wreck!" said Tom. "That's good. Wilson'll have a little business at last."

He slowed down, but still without any intention of stopping, until, as we came nearer, the hushed, intent faces of the people at the garage door made him automatically put on the brakes.

"We'll take a look," he said doubtfully, "just a look."

[50] *wavered*: to "travel at random or without fixed destination" (*OED*). Fitzgerald adds suspense by playing off the meaning of "waver" as to have doubts or to lose one's courage.

I became aware now of a hollow, wailing sound which issued incessantly from the garage, a sound which as we got out of the coupé and walked toward the door resolved itself into the words "Oh, my God!" uttered over and over in a gasping moan.

"There's some bad trouble here," said Tom excitedly.

He reached up on tiptoes and peered over a circle of heads into the garage, which was lit only by a yellow light in a swinging wire basket overhead. Then he made a harsh sound in his throat, and with a violent thrusting movement of his powerful arms pushed his way through.

The circle closed up again with a running murmur of expostulation;[51] it was a minute before I could see anything at all. Then new arrivals disarranged the line, and Jordan and I were pushed suddenly inside.

Myrtle Wilson's body, wrapped in a blanket, and then in another blanket, as though she suffered from a chill in the hot night, lay on a work-table by the wall, and Tom, with his back to us, was bending over it, motionless. Next to him stood a motorcycle policeman taking down names with much sweat and correction in a little book. At first I couldn't find the source of the high, groaning words that echoed clamorously through the bare garage—then I saw Wilson standing on the raised threshold of his office, swaying back and forth and holding to the doorposts with both hands. Some man was talking to him in a low voice and attempting, from time to time, to lay a hand on his shoulder, but Wilson neither heard nor saw. His eyes would drop slowly from the swinging light to the laden table by the wall, and then jerk back to the light again, and he gave out incessantly his high, horrible call:

"Oh, my Ga-od! Oh, my Ga-od! Oh, Ga-od! Oh, my Ga-od!"

Presently Tom lifted his head with a jerk and, after staring around the garage with glazed eyes, addressed a mumbled incoherent remark to the policeman.

"M-a-v—" the policeman was saying, "—o——"

[51] *expostulation*: "remonstrating in a friendly manner; earnest and kindly protest" (*OED*).

"No, r—" corrected the man, "M-a-v-r-o——"

"Listen to me!" muttered Tom fiercely.

"r" said the policeman, "o——"

"g——"

"g—" He looked up as Tom's broad hand fell sharply on his shoulder. "What you want, fella?"

"What happened?—that's what I want to know."

"Auto hit her. Ins'antly killed."

"Instantly killed," repeated Tom, staring.

"She ran out ina road. Son-of-a-bitch didn't even stopus car."

"There was two cars," said Michaelis, "one comin', one goin', see?"

"Going where?" asked the policeman keenly.

"One goin' each way. Well, she"—his hand rose toward the blankets but stopped halfway and fell to his side—"she ran out there an' the one comin' from N'York knock right into her, goin' thirty or forty miles an hour."

"What's the name of this place here?" demanded the officer.

"Hasn't got any name."

A pale well-dressed negro stepped near.

"It was a yellow car," he said, "big yellow car. New."

"See the accident?" asked the policeman.

"No, but the car passed me down the road, going faster'n forty. Going fifty, sixty."

"Come here and let's have your name. Look out now. I want to get his name."

Some words of this conversation must have reached Wilson, swaying in the office door, for suddenly a new theme found voice among his gasping cries:

"You don't have to tell me what kind of car it was! I know what kind of car it was!"

Watching Tom, I saw the wad of muscle back of his shoulder tighten under his coat. He walked quickly over to Wilson and, standing in front of him, seized him firmly by the upper arms.

"You've got to pull yourself together," he said with soothing gruffness.

Wilson's eyes fell upon Tom; he started up on his tiptoes and then would have collapsed to his knees had not Tom held him upright.

"Listen," said Tom, shaking him a little. "I just got here a minute ago, from New York. I was bringing you that coupé we've been talking about. That yellow car I was driving this afternoon wasn't mine—do you hear? I haven't seen it all afternoon."

Only the negro and I were near enough to hear what he said, but the policeman caught something in the tone and looked over with truculent[52] eyes.

"What's all that?" he demanded.

"I'm a friend of his." Tom turned his head but kept his hands firm on Wilson's body. "He says he knows the car that did it.... It was a yellow car."

Some dim impulse moved the policeman to look suspiciously at Tom.

"And what color's your car?"

"It's a blue car, a coupé."

"We've come straight from New York," I said.

Someone who had been driving a little behind us confirmed this, and the policeman turned away.

"Now, if you'll let me have that name again correct——"

Picking up Wilson like a doll, Tom carried him into the office, set him down in a chair, and came back.

"If somebody'll come here and sit with him," he snapped authoritatively. He watched while the two men standing closest glanced at each other and went unwillingly into the room. Then Tom shut the door on them and came down the single step, his eyes avoiding the table. As he passed close to me he whispered: "Let's get out."

Self-consciously, with his authoritative arms breaking the way, we pushed through the still gathering crowd, passing a hurried doctor, case in hand, who had been sent for in wild hope half an hour ago.

[52] *truculent*: fierce; savage.

Tom drove slowly until we were beyond the bend—then his foot came down hard, and the coupé raced along through the night. In a little while I heard a low husky sob, and saw that the tears were overflowing down his face.

"The God damned coward!" he whimpered. "He didn't even stop his car."

* * * * *

The Buchanans' house floated suddenly toward us through the dark rustling trees. Tom stopped beside the porch and looked up at the second floor, where two windows bloomed with light among the vines.

"Daisy's home," he said. As we got out of the car he glanced at me and frowned slightly.

"I ought to have dropped you in West Egg, Nick. There's nothing we can do tonight."

A change had come over him, and he spoke gravely, and with decision. As we walked across the moonlight[53] gravel to the porch he disposed of the situation in a few brisk phrases.

"I'll telephone for a taxi to take you home, and while you're waiting you and Jordan better go in the kitchen and have them get you some supper—if you want any." He opened the door. "Come in."

"No, thanks. But I'd be glad if you'd order me the taxi. I'll wait outside."

Jordan put her hand on my arm.

"Won't you come in, Nick?"

"No, thanks."

I was feeling a little sick and I wanted to be alone. But Jordan lingered for a moment more.

"It's only half-past nine," she said.

I'd be damned if I'd go in; I'd had enough of all of them for one day, and suddenly that included Jordan too. She must have seen something of this in my expression, for she turned

[53] *moonlight*: i.e., moonlit; e.g., "a moonlight getaway" (*OED*).

abruptly away and ran up the porch steps into the house. I sat down for a few minutes with my head in my hands, until I heard the phone taken up inside and the butler's voice[54] calling a taxi. Then I walked slowly down the drive away from the house, intending to wait by the gate.

I hadn't gone twenty yards when I heard my name and Gatsby stepped from between two bushes into the path. I must have felt pretty weird[55] by that time, because I could think of nothing except the luminosity of his pink suit under the moon.

"What are you doing?" I inquired.

"Just standing here, old sport."

Somehow, that seemed a despicable occupation. For all I knew he was going to rob the house in a moment; I wouldn't have been surprised to see sinister faces, the faces of "Wolfshiem's people," behind him in the dark shrubbery.

"Did you see any trouble on the road?" he asked after a minute.

"Yes."

He hesitated.

"Was she killed?"

"Yes."

"I thought so; I told Daisy I thought so. It's better that the shock should all come at once. She stood it pretty well."

He spoke as if Daisy's reaction was the only thing that mattered.

"I got to West Egg by a side road," he went on, "and left the car in my garage. I don't think anybody saw us, but of course I can't be sure."

I disliked him so much by this time that I didn't find it necessary to tell him he was wrong.

"Who was the woman?" he inquired.

"Her name was Wilson. Her husband owns the garage. How the devil did it happen?"

[54] *butler's voice*: another entry in the running gag of butlers' body parts; Nick's synecdochic phrasing adds to the haunting tone of the scene.

[55] *weird*: strange and unusual. Fitzgerald plays off the mythological meaning: having to do with one's destiny or ultimate fate, e.g., the Weird Sisters (*OED*).

"Well, I tried to swing the wheel—" He broke off, and suddenly I guessed at the truth.

"Was Daisy driving?"

"Yes," he said after a moment, "but of course I'll say I was. You see, when we left New York she was very nervous and she thought it would steady her to drive—and this woman rushed out at us just as we were passing a car coming the other way. It all happened in a minute, but it seemed to me that she wanted to speak to us, thought we were somebody she knew. Well, first Daisy turned away from the woman toward the other car, and then she lost her nerve and turned back. The second my hand reached the wheel I felt the shock—it must have killed her instantly."

"It ripped her open——"

"Don't tell me, old sport." He winced. "Anyhow—Daisy stepped on it. I tried to make her stop, but she couldn't, so I pulled on the emergency brake. Then she fell over into my lap and I drove on.

"She'll be all right tomorrow," he said presently. "I'm just going to wait here and see if he tries to bother her about that unpleasantness this afternoon. She's locked herself into her room, and if he tries any brutality she's going to turn the light out and on again."

"He won't touch her," I said. "He's not thinking about her."

"I don't trust him, old sport."

"How long are you going to wait?"

"All night, if necessary. Anyhow, till they all go to bed."

A new point of view occurred to me. Suppose Tom found out that Daisy had been driving. He might think he saw a connection in it—he might think anything. I looked at the house; there were two or three bright windows downstairs and the pink glow from Daisy's room on the second floor.

"You wait here," I said. "I'll see if there's any sign of a commotion."

I walked back along the border of the lawn, traversed the gravel softly, and tiptoed up the veranda steps. The drawing-room curtains were open, and I saw that the room was empty.

Crossing the porch where we had dined that June night three months before, I came to a small rectangle of light which I guessed was the pantry window. The blind was drawn, but I found a rift[56] at the sill.

Daisy and Tom were sitting opposite each other at the kitchen table, with a plate of cold fried chicken between them, and two bottles of ale. He was talking intently across the table at her, and in his earnestness his hand had fallen upon and covered her own. Once in a while she looked up at him and nodded in agreement.

They weren't happy, and neither of them had touched the chicken or the ale—and yet they weren't unhappy either. There was an unmistakable air of natural intimacy about the picture, and anybody would have said that they were conspiring[57] together.

As I tiptoed from the porch I heard my taxi feeling its way along the dark road toward the house. Gatsby was waiting where I had left him in the drive.

"Is it all quiet up there?" he asked anxiously.

"Yes, it's all quiet." I hesitated. "You'd better come home and get some sleep."

He shook his head.

"I want to wait here till Daisy goes to bed. Good night, old sport."

He put his hands in his coat pockets and turned back eagerly to his scrutiny[58] of the house, as though my presence marred the sacredness of the vigil. So I walked away and left him standing there in the moonlight—watching over nothing.

[56] *rift*: literally, a crack or break; figuratively, a serious division between people that breaks friendship.

[57] *conspiring*: agreeing secretly to a criminal activity, e.g., co-conspirators.

[58] *scrutiny*: literally, a watchful searching. In light of "sacredness" and "vigil" below, "scrutiny" means the ancient Christian practice of examining candidates for holy orders and later for baptism.

CHAPTER VIII

I COULDN'T SLEEP all night; a fog-horn was groaning incessantly on the Sound, and I tossed half-sick between grotesque reality and savage, frightening dreams. Toward dawn I heard a taxi go up Gatsby's drive, and immediately I jumped out of bed and began to dress—I felt that I had something to tell him, something to warn him about, and morning would be too late.

Crossing his lawn, I saw that his front door was still open and he was leaning against a table in the hall, heavy with dejection or sleep.

"Nothing happened," he said wanly. "I waited, and about four o'clock she came to the window and stood there for a minute and then turned out the light."

His house had never seemed so enormous to me as it did that night when we hunted through the great rooms for cigarettes. We pushed aside curtains that were like pavilions,[1] and felt over innumerable feet of dark wall for electric light switches—once I tumbled with a sort of splash upon the keys of a ghostly piano. There was an inexplicable amount of dust everywhere, and the rooms were musty, as though they hadn't been aired for many days. I found the humidor[2] on an unfamiliar table, with two stale, dry cigarettes inside. Throwing open the French windows of the drawing-room, we sat smoking out into the darkness.

"You ought to go away," I said. "It's pretty certain they'll trace your car."

"Go away *now*, old sport?"

"Go to Atlantic City for a week, or up to Montreal."

[1] *pavilions*: i.e., like a large, stately tent.

[2] *humidor*: airtight box with a humidifying element for keeping tobacco products fresh.

He wouldn't consider it. He couldn't possibly leave Daisy until he knew what she was going to do. He was clutching at some last hope and I couldn't bear to shake him free.

It was this night that he told me the strange story of his youth with Dan Cody—told it to me because "Jay Gatsby" had broken up like glass against Tom's hard malice, and the long secret extravaganza[3] was played out. I think that he would have acknowledged anything now, without reserve, but he wanted to talk about Daisy.

She was the first "nice" girl he had ever known. In various unrevealed capacities he had come in contact with such people, but always with indiscernible barbed wire between. He found her excitingly desirable. He went to her house, at first with other officers from Camp Taylor,[4] then alone. It amazed him—he had never been in such a beautiful house before. But what gave it an air of breathless intensity was that Daisy lived there—it was as casual a thing to her as his tent out at camp was to him. There was a ripe mystery about it, a hint of bedrooms upstairs more beautiful and cool than other bedrooms, of gay and radiant activities taking place through its corridors, and of romances that were not musty and laid away already in lavender but fresh and breathing and redolent[5] of this year's shining motor-cars and of dances whose flowers were scarcely withered. It excited him, too, that many men had already loved Daisy—it increased her value in his eyes. He felt their presence all about the house, pervading the air with the shades and echoes of still vibrant emotions.

But he knew that he was in Daisy's house by a colossal[6] accident. However glorious might be his future as Jay Gatsby, he was at present a penniless young man without a past, and at any moment the invisible cloak of his uniform might slip from

[3] *extravaganza*: aesthetic creation at once fantastical, unrestrained, and inflated.

[4] *Camp Taylor*: one-time military base near Louisville.

[5] *redolent*: literally, with a pleasing aroma, and evocative of such; figuratively, "imbued with or rich in a quality, a feeling" (*OED*).

[6] *colossal*: Here, Fitzgerald uses the less common meaning: "as a depreciative intensifier: complete, utter" (*OED*), e.g., "colossal nonsense".

his shoulders. So he made the most of his time. He took what he could get, ravenously and unscrupulously[7]—eventually he took Daisy one still October night, took her because he had no real right to touch her hand.

He might have despised himself, for he had certainly taken her under false pretenses. I don't mean that he had traded on his phantom millions, but he had deliberately given Daisy a sense of security; he let her believe that he was a person from much the same strata as herself—that he was fully able to take care of her. As a matter of fact, he had no such facilities—he had no comfortable family standing behind him, and he was liable at the whim of an impersonal government to be blown anywhere about the world.

But he didn't despise himself and it didn't turn out as he had imagined. He had intended, probably, to take what he could and go—but now he found that he had committed himself to the following of a grail.[8] He knew that Daisy was extraordinary, but he didn't realize just how extraordinary a "nice" girl could be. She vanished into her rich house, into her rich, full life, leaving Gatsby—nothing. He felt married to her, that was all.

When they met again, two days later, it was Gatsby who was breathless, who was, somehow, betrayed. Her porch was bright with the bought luxury of star-shine; the wicker of the settee squeaked fashionably as she turned toward him and he kissed her curious and lovely mouth. She had caught a cold, and it made her voice huskier and more charming than ever, and Gatsby was overwhelmingly aware of the youth and mystery that wealth imprisons and preserves, of the freshness of many clothes, and of Daisy, gleaming like silver, safe and proud above the hot struggles of the poor.

* * * * *

[7] *unscrupulously*: with no regard to morals, ethics, or one's conscience. In Catholicism, scrupulosity is the opposite: treating mistakes, accidents, or common faults as grave sins.

[8] *following … grail*: i.e., on an impossible quest for the most valuable treasure, such as that for the Holy Grail.

"I can't describe to you how surprised I was to find out I loved her, old sport. I even hoped for a while that she'd throw me over,[9] but she didn't, because she was in love with me too. She thought I knew a lot because I knew different things from her.... Well, there I was, way off my ambitions, getting deeper in love every minute, and all of a sudden I didn't care. What was the use of doing great things if I could have a better time telling her what I was going to do?"

On the last afternoon before he went abroad, he sat with Daisy in his arms for a long, silent time. It was a cold fall day, with fire in the room and her cheeks flushed. Now and then she moved and he changed his arm a little, and once he kissed her dark shining hair. The afternoon had made them tranquil for a while, as if to give them a deep memory for the long parting the next day promised. They had never been closer in their month of love, nor communicated more profoundly one with another, than when she brushed silent lips against his coat's shoulder or when he touched the end of her finger, gently, as though she were asleep.

* * * * *

He did extraordinarily well in the war. He was a captain before he went to the front, and following the Argonne battles he got his majority and the command of the divisional machine-guns. After the armistice he tried frantically to get home, but some complication or misunderstanding sent him to Oxford instead. He was worried now—there was a quality of nervous despair in Daisy's letters. She didn't see why he couldn't come. She was feeling the pressure of the world outside, and she wanted to see him and feel his presence beside her and be reassured that she was doing the right thing after all.

For Daisy was young and her artificial world was redolent of orchids and pleasant, cheerful snobbery and orchestras which set the rhythm of the year, summing up the sadness and

[9] *throw me over*: i.e., break up with him.

suggestiveness of life in new tunes. All night the saxophones wailed the hopeless comment of the "Beale Street Blues"[10] while a hundred pairs of golden and silver slippers shuffled the shining dust. At the gray tea hour there were always rooms that throbbed incessantly with this low, sweet fever, while fresh faces drifted here and there like rose petals blown by the sad horns around the floor.

Through this twilight universe Daisy began to move again with the season; suddenly she was again keeping half a dozen dates a day with half a dozen men, and drowsing asleep at dawn with the beads and chiffon of an evening dress tangled among dying orchids on the floor beside her bed. And all the time something within her was crying for a decision. She wanted her life shaped now, immediately—and the decision must be made by some force—of love, of money, of unquestionable practicality—that was close at hand.

That force took shape in the middle of spring with the arrival of Tom Buchanan. There was a wholesome bulkiness about his person and his position, and Daisy was flattered. Doubtless there was a certain struggle and a certain relief. The letter reached Gatsby while he was still at Oxford.

* * * * *

It was dawn now on Long Island and we went about opening the rest of the windows downstairs, filling the house with gray-turning, gold-turning light. The shadow of a tree fell abruptly across the dew and ghostly birds began to sing among the blue leaves. There was a slow, pleasant movement in the air, scarcely a wind, promising a cool, lovely day.

"I don't think she ever loved him." Gatsby turned around from a window and looked at me challengingly. "You must remember, old sport, she was very excited this afternoon. He told her those things in a way that frightened her—that made

[10] "*Beale Street Blues*": jazz standard written by W.C. Handy in 1917; Marion Harris' best-selling rendition dates to December 1921.

it look as if I was some kind of cheap sharper.[11] And the result was she hardly knew what she was saying."

He sat down gloomily.

"Of course she might have loved him just for a minute, when they were first married—and loved me more even then, do you see?"

Suddenly he came out with a curious remark.

"In any case," he said, "it was just personal."

What could you make of that, except to suspect some intensity in his conception of the affair that couldn't be measured?

He came back from France when Tom and Daisy were still on their wedding trip, and made a miserable but irresistible journey to Louisville on the last of his army pay. He stayed there a week, walking the streets where their footsteps had clicked together through the November night and revisiting the out-of-the-way places to which they had driven in her white car. Just as Daisy's house had always seemed to him more mysterious and gay than other houses, so his idea of the city itself, even though she was gone from it, was pervaded with a melancholy beauty.

He left feeling that if he had searched harder, he might have found her—that he was leaving her behind. The day-coach[12]—he was penniless now—was hot. He went out to the open vestibule[13] and sat down on a folding-chair, and the station slid away and the backs of unfamiliar buildings moved by. Then out into the spring fields, where a yellow trolley raced them for a minute with people in it who might once have seen the pale magic of her face along the casual street.

The track curved and now it was going away from the sun, which, as it sank lower, seemed to spread itself in benediction over the vanishing city where she had drawn her breath. He stretched out his hand desperately as if to snatch only a wisp of air, to save a fragment of the spot that she had made lovely

[11] *sharper*: swindler; conman.

[12] *day-coach*: i.e., not a sleeper car; a standard (and cheaper) railroad car.

[13] *vestibule*: "enclosed and covered-in portion at either end of a railway carriage, serving as a means of passage from one carriage to another" (*OED*).

for him. But it was all going by too fast now for his blurred eyes and he knew that he had lost that part of it, the freshest and the best, forever.

It was nine o'clock when we finished breakfast and went out on the porch. The night had made a sharp difference in the weather and there was an autumn flavor in the air. The gardener, the last one of Gatsby's former servants, came to the foot of the steps.

"I'm going to drain the pool today, Mr. Gatsby. Leaves'll start falling pretty soon, and then there's always trouble with the pipes."

"Don't do it today," Gatsby answered. He turned to me apologetically. "You know, old sport, I've never used that pool all summer?"

I looked at my watch and stood up.

"Twelve minutes to my train."

I didn't want to go to the city. I wasn't worth a decent stroke of work, but it was more than that—I didn't want to leave Gatsby. I missed that train, and then another, before I could get myself away.

"I'll call you up," I said finally.

"Do, old sport."

"I'll call you about noon."

We walked slowly down the steps.

"I suppose Daisy'll call too." He looked at me anxiously, as if he hoped I'd corroborate this.

"I suppose so."

"Well, good-bye."

We shook hands and I started away. Just before I reached the hedge I remembered something and turned around.

"They're a rotten crowd," I shouted across the lawn. "You're worth the whole damn bunch put together."

I've always been glad I said that. It was the only compliment I ever gave him, because I disapproved of him from beginning to end. First he nodded politely, and then his face broke into that radiant and understanding smile, as if we'd been in ecstatic cahoots[14] on that fact all the time. His gorgeous pink rag of a suit made a bright spot of color against the white steps, and I thought of the night when I first came to his ancestral[15] home, three months before. The lawn and drive had been crowded with the faces of those who guessed at his corruption—and he had stood on those steps, concealing his incorruptible dream, as he waved them good-bye.

I thanked him for his hospitality. We were always thanking him for that—I and the others.

"Good-bye," I called. "I enjoyed breakfast, Gatsby."

* * * * *

Up in the city, I tried for a while to list the quotations on an interminable amount of stock, then I fell asleep in my swivel-chair. Just before noon the phone woke me, and I started up with sweat breaking out on my forehead. It was Jordan Baker; she often called me up at this hour because the uncertainty of her own movements between hotels and clubs and private houses made her hard to find in any other way. Usually her voice came over the wire as something fresh and cool, as if a divot from a green golf-links had come sailing in at the office window, but this morning it seemed harsh and dry.

"I've left Daisy's house," she said. "I'm at Hempstead, and I'm going down to Southampton this afternoon."

Probably it had been tactful to leave Daisy's house, but the act annoyed me, and her next remark made me rigid.

"You weren't so nice to me last night."

"How could it have mattered then?"

Silence for a moment. Then:

"However—I want to see you."

[14] *in ... cahoots*: regional expression meaning to be in comical or unexpected partnership with someone.

[15] *ancestral*: As Gatsby has no ancestors (Gatz does, but Gatsby does not), Nick means "ancestral" here as a thing that "precedes or gives rise to the invention or development of something" (*OED*), namely, Gatsby himself.

"I want to see you, too."

"Suppose I don't go to Southampton, and come into town this afternoon?"

"No—I don't think this afternoon."

"Very well."

"It's impossible this afternoon. Various——"

We talked like that for a while, and then abruptly we weren't talking any longer. I don't know which of us hung up with a sharp click, but I know I didn't care. I couldn't have talked to her across a tea-table that day if I never talked to her again in this world.

I called Gatsby's house a few minutes later, but the line was busy. I tried four times; finally an exasperated central told me the wire was being kept open for long distance from Detroit. Taking out my time-table, I drew a small circle around the three-fifty train. Then I leaned back in my chair and tried to think. It was just noon.

* * * * *

When I passed the ash-heaps on the train that morning I had crossed deliberately to the other side of the car. I supposed there'd be a curious crowd around there all day with little boys searching for dark spots in the dust, and some garrulous[16] man telling over and over what had happened, until it became less and less real even to him and he could tell it no longer, and Myrtle Wilson's tragic achievement was forgotten. Now I want to go back a little and tell what happened at the garage after we left there the night before.

They had difficulty in locating the sister, Catherine. She must have broken her rule against drinking that night, for when she arrived she was stupid with liquor and unable to understand that the ambulance had already gone to Flushing. When they convinced her of this, she immediately fainted, as if that was the intolerable part of the affair. Someone, kind or

[16] *garrulous*: talkative, and enjoyably so.

curious, took her in his car and drove her in the wake[17] of her sister's body.

Until long after midnight a changing crowd lapped up[18] against the front of the garage, while George Wilson rocked himself back and forth on the couch inside. For a while the door of the office was open, and everyone who came into the garage glanced irresistibly through it. Finally someone said it was a shame, and closed the door. Michaelis and several other men were with him; first, four or five men, later two or three men. Still later Michaelis had to ask the last stranger to wait there fifteen minutes longer, while he went back to his own place and made a pot of coffee. After that, he stayed there alone with Wilson until dawn.

About three o'clock the quality of Wilson's incoherent muttering changed—he grew quieter and began to talk about the yellow car. He announced that he had a way of finding out whom the yellow car belonged to, and then he blurted out that a couple of months ago his wife had come from the city with her face bruised and her nose swollen.

But when he heard himself say this, he flinched and began to cry "Oh, my God!" again in his groaning voice. Michaelis made a clumsy attempt to distract him.

"How long have you been married, George? Come on there, try and sit still a minute and answer my question. How long have you been married?"

"Twelve years."

"Ever had any children? Come on, George, sit still—I asked you a question. Did you ever have any children?"

The hard brown beetles kept thudding against the dull light, and whenever Michaelis heard a car go tearing along the road outside it sounded to him like the car that hadn't stopped a

[17] *wake*: morbid pun, as the car follows in the "wake" or turbulent waves and motion created by the vehicle in front, and she will soon be visiting her sister's "wake" or formal funeral visitation. It also functions as a callback to Nick's opening statement about Gatsby in chapter 1: "What foul dust floated in the wake of his dreams."

[18] *lapped up*: i.e., like waves lapping against a shore.

few hours before. He didn't like to go into the garage, because the work bench was stained where the body had been lying, so he moved uncomfortably around the office—he knew every object in it before morning—and from time to time sat down beside Wilson trying to keep him more quiet.

"Have you got a church you go to sometimes, George? Maybe even if you haven't been there for a long time? Maybe I could call up the church and get a priest to come over and he could talk to you, see?"

"Don't belong to any."

"You ought to have a church, George, for times like this. You must have gone to church once. Didn't you get married in a church? Listen, George, listen to me. Didn't you get married in a church?"

"That was a long time ago."

The effort of answering broke the rhythm of his rocking—for a moment he was silent. Then the same half-knowing, half-bewildered look came back into his faded eyes.

"Look in the drawer there," he said, pointing at the desk.

"Which drawer?"

"That drawer—that one."

Michaelis opened the drawer nearest his hand. There was nothing in it but a small, expensive dog-leash, made of leather and braided silver. It was apparently new.

"This?" he inquired, holding it up.

Wilson stared and nodded.

"I found it yesterday afternoon. She tried to tell me about it, but I knew it was something funny."

"You mean your wife bought it?"

"She had it wrapped in tissue paper on her bureau."

Michaelis didn't see anything odd in that, and he gave Wilson a dozen reasons why his wife might have bought the dog-leash. But conceivably Wilson had heard some of these same explanations before, from Myrtle, because he began saying "Oh, my God!" again in a whisper—his comforter left several explanations in the air.

"Then he killed her," said Wilson. His mouth dropped open suddenly.

"Who did?"

"I have a way of finding out."

"You're morbid, George," said his friend. "This has been a strain to you and you don't know what you're saying. You'd better try and sit quiet till morning."

"He murdered her."

"It was an accident, George."

Wilson shook his head. His eyes narrowed and his mouth widened slightly with the ghost of a superior "Hm!"

"I know," he said definitely. "I'm one of these trusting fellas and I don't think any harm to *no*body, but when I get to know a thing I know it. It was the man in that car. She ran out to speak to him and he wouldn't stop."

Michaelis had seen this too, but it hadn't occurred to him that there was any special significance in it. He believed that Mrs. Wilson had been running away from her husband, rather than trying to stop any particular car.

"How could she of been like that?"

"She's a deep one," said Wilson, as if that answered the question. "Ah-h-h——"

He began to rock again, and Michaelis stood twisting the leash in his hand.

"Maybe you got some friend that I could telephone for, George?"

This was a forlorn[19] hope—he was almost sure that Wilson had no friend: there was not enough of him for his wife. He was glad a little later when he noticed a change in the room, a blue quickening by the window, and realized that dawn wasn't far off. About five o'clock it was blue enough outside to snap off the light.

Wilson's glazed eyes turned out to the ashheaps, where small gray clouds took on fantastic shapes and scurried here and there in the faint dawn wind.

"I spoke to her," he muttered, after a long silence. "I told her she might fool me but she couldn't fool God. I took her to the window"—with an effort he got up and walked to the rear

[19] *forlorn*: "desperate; hopeless" (*OED*).

window and leaned with his face pressed against it—"and I said 'God knows what you've been doing, everything you've been doing. You may fool me, but you can't fool God!'"

Standing behind him, Michaelis saw with a shock that he was looking at the eyes of Doctor T. J. Eckleburg, which had just emerged, pale and enormous, from the dissolving[20] night.

"God sees everything," repeated Wilson.

"That's an advertisement," Michaelis assured him. Something made him turn away from the window and look back into the room. But Wilson stood there a long time, his face close to the window pane, nodding into the twilight.

By six o'clock Michaelis was worn out, and grateful for the sound of a car stopping outside. It was one of the watchers of the night before who had promised to come back, so he cooked breakfast for three, which he and the other man ate together. Wilson was quieter now, and Michaelis went home to sleep; when he awoke four hours later and hurried back to the garage, Wilson was gone.

His movements—he was on foot all the time—were afterward traced to Port Roosevelt and then to Gad's Hill,[21] where he bought a sandwich that he didn't eat, and a cup of coffee. He must have been tired and walking slowly, for he didn't reach Gad's Hill until noon. Thus far there was no difficulty in accounting for his time—there were boys who had seen a man "acting sort of crazy," and motorists at whom he stared oddly from the side of the road. Then for three hours he disappeared from view. The police, on the strength of what he said to Michaelis, that he "had a way of finding out," supposed that he spent that time going from garage to garage thereabout, inquiring for a yellow car. On the other hand, no garage man who had seen him ever came forward, and perhaps he had an easier, surer way of finding out what he

[20] *dissolving*: gradually disappearing.

[21] *Gad's Hill*: Gads Hill Place was the rural home of Charles Dickens, just outside of London, but Fitzgerald likely had the American reference in mind: Gad's Hill, Missouri, was the site of that state's first train robbery, perpetrated by the Jesse James gang.

wanted to know. By half-past two he was in West Egg, where he asked someone the way to Gatsby's house. So by that time he knew Gatsby's name.

* * * * *

At two o'clock Gatsby put on his bathing-suit and left word with the butler that if anyone phoned word was to be brought to him at the pool. He stopped at the garage for a pneumatic[22] mattress that had amused his guests during the summer, and the chauffeur helped him pump it up. Then he gave instructions that the open car wasn't to be taken out under any circumstances—and this was strange, because the front right fender needed repair.

Gatsby shouldered the mattress and started for the pool. Once he stopped and shifted it a little, and the chauffeur asked him if he needed help, but he shook his head and in a moment disappeared among the yellowing trees.

No telephone message arrived, but the butler went without his sleep and waited for it until four o'clock—until long after there was anyone to give it to if it came. I have an idea that Gatsby himself didn't believe it would come, and perhaps he no longer cared. If that was true he must have felt that he had lost the old warm world, paid a high price for living too long with a single dream. He must have looked up at an unfamiliar sky through frightening leaves and shivered as he found what a grotesque thing a rose is and how raw the sunlight was upon the scarcely created grass. A new world, material without being real, where poor ghosts, breathing dreams like air, drifted fortuitously[23] about ... like that ashen, fantastic figure gliding toward him through the amorphous trees.

The chauffeur—he was one of Wolfshiem's protégés—heard the shots—afterward he could only say that he hadn't thought

[22] *pneumatic*: inflatable. Fitzgerald's use of this synonym brings to mind "pneuma", or spirit, and in Catholic context especially the Holy Spirit's workings, as in "pneumatology".

[23] *fortuitously*: by chance or accident.

anything much about them. I drove from the station directly to Gatsby's house and my rushing anxiously up the front steps was the first thing that alarmed anyone. But they knew then, I firmly believe. With scarcely a word said, four of us, the chauffeur, butler, gardener, and I, hurried down to the pool.

There was a faint, barely perceptible movement of the water as the fresh flow from one end urged its way toward the drain at the other. With little ripples that were hardly the shadows of waves, the laden mattress moved irregularly down the pool. A small gust of wind that scarcely corrugated the surface was enough to disturb its accidental course with its accidental burden. The touch of a cluster of leaves revolved[24] it slowly, tracing, like the leg of transit, a thin red circle in the water.

It was after we started with Gatsby toward the house that the gardener saw Wilson's body a little way off in the grass, and the holocaust[25] was complete.

[24] *revolved*: morbid pun, as the cluster of leaves revolves or turns, with Gatsby's body literally revolved, i.e., shot by a revolver; e.g., "to go revolvering" (*OED*).

[25] *holocaust*: religious, destructive sacrifice; Nick's word choice highlights his ironic disapproval of Wilson's disordered religious fanaticism. Note: the word does not come to be used of the Jewish extermination by the Nazis until 1942 (*OED*).

CHAPTER IX

After two years I remember the rest of that day, and that night and the next day, only as an endless drill of police and photographers and newspaper men in and out of Gatsby's front door. A rope stretched across the main gate and a policeman by it kept out the curious, but little boys soon discovered that they could enter through my yard, and there were always a few of them clustered open-mouthed about the pool. Someone with a positive manner, perhaps a detective, used the expression "madman" as he bent over Wilson's body that afternoon, and the adventitious[1] authority of his voice set the key for the newspaper reports next morning.

Most of those reports were a nightmare—grotesque, circumstantial,[2] eager, and untrue. When Michaelis's testimony at the inquest brought to light Wilson's suspicions of his wife I thought the whole tale would shortly be served up in racy pasquinade[3]—but Catherine, who might have said anything, didn't say a word. She showed a surprising amount of character about it too—looked at the coroner with determined eyes under that corrected brow of hers, and swore that her sister had never seen Gatsby, that her sister was completely happy with her husband, that her sister had been into no mischief whatever. She convinced herself of it, and cried into her handkerchief, as if the very suggestion was more than she could endure. So Wilson was reduced to a man "deranged by grief" in order that the case might remain in its simplest form. And it rested there.

[1] *adventitious*: external; from the outside. Especially in light of "ancestral" in the previous chapter, Fitzgerald is also playing off the legal meaning as applied to Gatsby: money or wealth acquired some other way than inheritance.

[2] *circumstantial*: in law, "indirect evidence inferred from circumstances which afford a certain presumption" (*OED*).

[3] *pasquinade*: wild satire or lampoon made public.

But all this part of it seemed remote and unessential. I found myself on Gatsby's side, and alone. From the moment I telephoned news of the catastrophe to West Egg Village, every surmise about him, and every practical question, was referred to me. At first I was surprised and confused; then, as he lay in his house and didn't move or breathe or speak, hour upon hour, it grew upon me that I was responsible, because no one else was interested—interested, I mean, with that intense personal interest to which everyone has some vague right at the end.

I called up Daisy half an hour after we found him, called her instinctively and without hesitation. But she and Tom had gone away early that afternoon, and taken baggage with them.

"Left no address?"

"No."

"Say when they'd be back?"

"No."

"Any idea where they are? How I could reach them?"

"I don't know. Can't say."

I wanted to get somebody for him. I wanted to go into the room where he lay and reassure him: "I'll get somebody for you, Gatsby. Don't worry. Just trust me and I'll get somebody for you——"

Meyer Wolfshiem's name wasn't in the phone book. The butler gave me his office address on Broadway, and I called Information, but by the time I had the number it was long after five, and no one answered the phone.

"Will you ring again?"

"I've rung them three times."

"It's very important."

"Sorry. I'm afraid no one's there."

I went back to the drawing-room[4] and thought for an instant that they were chance visitors, all these official people who suddenly filled it. But, as they drew back the sheet and looked at Gatsby with unmoved eyes, his protest continued in my brain:

[4] *drawing-room*: separate room for receiving guests (who would ordinarily not proceed to other rooms unless specially invited, e.g., for a dinner).

"Look here, old sport, you've got to get somebody for me. You've got to try hard. I can't go through this alone."

Someone started to ask me questions, but I broke away and going upstairs looked hastily through the unlocked parts of his desk—he'd never told me definitely that his parents were dead. But there was nothing—only the picture of Dan Cody, a token of forgotten violence, staring down from the wall.

Next morning I sent the butler to New York with a letter to Wolfshiem, which asked for information and urged him to come out on the next train. That request seemed superfluous when I wrote it. I was sure he'd start when he saw the newspapers, just as I was sure there'd be a wire from Daisy before noon—but neither a wire nor Mr. Wolfshiem arrived; no one arrived except more police and photographers and newspaper men. When the butler brought back Wolfshiem's answer I began to have a feeling of defiance, of scornful solidarity between Gatsby and me against them all.

> Dear Mr. Carraway. This has been one of the most terrible shocks of my life to me I hardly can believe it that it is true at all. Such a mad act as that man did should make us all think. I cannot come down now as I am tied up in some very important business and cannot get mixed up in this thing now. If there is anything I can do a little later let me know in a letter by Edgar. I hardly know where I am when I hear about a thing like this and am completely knocked down and out.[5]
>
> Yours truly
> MEYER WOLFSHIEM

and then hasty addenda beneath:

> Let me know about the funeral etc do not know his family at all.

When the phone rang that afternoon and Long Distance said Chicago was calling I thought this would be Daisy at last.

[5] *knocked ... out*: boxing metaphor, as if the news has hit Wolfshiem like a knock-out punch.

But the connection came through as a man's voice, very thin and far away.

"This is Slagle speaking ... "

"Yes?" The name was unfamiliar.

"Hell of a note, isn't it? Get my wire?"

"There haven't been any wires."

"Young Parke's in trouble," he said rapidly. "They picked him up when he handed the bonds over the counter.[6] They got a circular from New York giving 'em the numbers just five minutes before. What d'you know about that, hey? You never can tell in these hick[7] towns——"

"Hello!" I interrupted breathlessly. "Look here—this isn't Mr. Gatsby. Mr. Gatsby's dead."

There was a long silence on the other end of the wire, followed by an exclamation ... then a quick squawk as the connection was broken.

I think it was on the third day that a telegram signed Henry C. Gatz arrived from a town in Minnesota. It said only that the sender was leaving immediately and to postpone the funeral until he came.

It was Gatsby's father, a solemn old man, very helpless and dismayed, bundled up in a long cheap ulster[8] against the warm September day. His eyes leaked continuously with excitement, and when I took the bag and umbrella from his hands he began to pull so incessantly at his sparse gray beard that I had difficulty in getting off his coat. He was on the point of collapse, so I took him into the music-room and made him sit down while I sent for something to eat. But he wouldn't eat, and the glass of milk spilled from his trembling hand.

[6] *bonds ... counter*: Parke was handling either stolen or counterfeit bonds; as the next sentence shows, he was caught and detained by police ("picked him up") because "the numbers", i.e., the unique identifiers on the bonds, matched the information the clerk received.

[7] *hick*: derogatory term meaning unsophisticated, ignorant, and foolish. Wolfshiem's crime ring has been targeting small towns for their stolen or counterfeit bond scheme, assuming they would be less informed, more easily overlooked, and more susceptible.

[8] *ulster*: ankle-length or otherwise long overcoat.

"I saw it in the Chicago newspaper," he said. "It was all in the Chicago newspaper. I started right away."

"I didn't know how to reach you."

His eyes, seeing nothing, moved ceaselessly about the room.

"It was a madman," he said. "He must have been mad."

"Wouldn't you like some coffee?" I urged him.

"I don't want anything. I'm all right now, Mr.——"

"Carraway."

"Well, I'm all right now. Where have they got Jimmy?"

I took him into the drawing-room, where his son lay, and left him there. Some little boys had come up on the steps and were looking into the hall; when I told them who had arrived, they went reluctantly away.

After a little while Mr. Gatz opened the door and came out, his mouth ajar, his face flushed slightly, his eyes leaking isolated and unpunctual[9] tears. He had reached an age where death no longer has the quality of ghastly[10] surprise, and when he looked around him now for the first time and saw the height and splendor of the hall and the great rooms opening out from it into other rooms, his grief began to be mixed with an awed pride. I helped him to a bedroom upstairs; while he took off his coat and vest I told him that all arrangements had been deferred until he came.

"I didn't know what you'd want, Mr. Gatsby——"

"Gatz is my name."

"—Mr. Gatz. I thought you might want to take the body West."

He shook his head.

"Jimmy always liked it better down East. He rose up to his position in the East. Were you a friend of my boy's, Mr.——?"

"We were close friends."

"He had a big future before him, you know. He was only a young man, but he had a lot of brain power here."

He touched his head impressively, and I nodded.

[9] *unpunctual*: not on time; late.

[10] *ghastly*: "suggestive of the kind of horror evoked by the sight of death" (*OED*).

"If he'd of lived, he'd of been a great man. A man like James J. Hill.[11] He'd of helped build up the country."

"That's true," I said, uncomfortably.

He fumbled at the embroidered coverlet, trying to take it from the bed, and lay down stiffly—was instantly asleep.

That night an obviously frightened person called up, and demanded to know who I was before he would give his name.

"This is Mr. Carraway," I said.

"Oh!" He sounded relieved. "This is Klipspringer."

I was relieved too, for that seemed to promise another friend at Gatsby's grave. I didn't want it to be in the papers and draw a sightseeing crowd, so I'd been calling up a few people myself. They were hard to find.

"The funeral's tomorrow," I said. "Three o'clock, here at the house. I wish you'd tell anybody who'd be interested."

"Oh, I will," he broke out hastily. "Of course I'm not likely to see anybody, but if I do."

His tone made me suspicious.

"Of course you'll be there yourself."

"Well, I'll certainly try. What I called up about is——"

"Wait a minute," I interrupted. "How about saying you'll come?"

"Well, the fact is—the truth of the matter is that I'm staying with some people up here in Greenwich,[12] and they rather expect me to be with them tomorrow. In fact, there's a sort of picnic or something. Of course I'll do my very best to get away."

I ejaculated[13] an unrestrained "Huh!" and he must have heard me, for he went on nervously:

"What I called up about was a pair of shoes I left there. I wonder if it'd be too much trouble to have the butler send

[11] *James J. Hill*: railroad tycoon who embodied the "rags to riches" American dream; Canadian-born but made Minnesota home for his wife and ten children. He died in 1916 with an estate worth at least $250 million at that time.

[12] *Greenwich*: town in Connecticut about thirty miles by road from Great Neck, New York.

[13] *ejaculated*: made a quick or sudden expression, often emotional. Until recently, "ejaculations" was the commonly used word in Catholicism for short, immediate prayers.

them on. You see, they're tennis shoes, and I'm sort of helpless without them. My address is care of B. F.——"

I didn't hear the rest of the name, because I hung up the receiver.

After that I felt a certain shame for Gatsby—one gentleman to whom I telephoned implied that he had got what he deserved. However, that was my fault, for he was one of those who used to sneer most bitterly at Gatsby on the courage of Gatsby's liquor, and I should have known better than to call him.

The morning of the funeral I went up to New York to see Meyer Wolfshiem; I couldn't seem to reach him any other way. The door that I pushed open, on the advice of an elevator boy, was marked "The Swastika[14] Holding Company," and at first there didn't seem to be anyone inside. But when I'd shouted "hello" several times in vain, an argument broke out behind a partition, and presently a lovely Jewess appeared at an interior door and scrutinized me with black hostile eyes.

"Nobody's in," she said. "Mr. Wolfshiem's gone to Chicago."

The first part of this was obviously untrue, for someone had begun to whistle "The Rosary,"[15] tunelessly, inside.

"Please say that Mr. Carraway wants to see him."

"I can't get him back from Chicago, can I?"

At this moment a voice, unmistakably Wolfshiem's, called "Stella!" from the other side of the door.

"Leave your name on the desk," she said quickly. "I'll give it to him when he gets back."

"But I know he's there."

She took a step toward me and began to slide her hands indignantly up and down her hips.

[14] *Swastika*: ancient and widely popular symbol for goodness and well-being in the form of a cross with all arms bent at ninety degrees the same way. The Nazi flag—a black swastika twisted forty-five degrees in a white circle on a red background—would be described by Hitler in 1925's *Mein Kampf* and would see widespread use when nationally adopted by Germany in 1933.

[15] "*The Rosary*": popular song written in 1898 by Ethelbert Nevin, with lyrics by Robert Cameron Rogers. The speaker, praying the Rosary, laments "a heart in absence wrung" and hopes "to learn / To kiss the cross".

"You young men think you can force your way in here any time," she scolded. "We're getting sickantired of it. When I say he's in Chicago, he's in Chic*ago*."

I mentioned Gatsby.

"Oh-h!" She looked me over again. "Will you just—What was your name?"

She vanished. In a moment Meyer Wolfshiem stood solemnly in the doorway, holding out both hands. He drew me into his office, remarking in a reverent voice that it was a sad time for all of us, and offered me a cigar.

"My memory goes back to when first I met him," he said. "A young major just out of the army and covered over with medals he got in the war. He was so hard up he had to keep on wearing his uniform because he couldn't buy some regular clothes. First time I saw him was when he come into Winebrenner's poolroom[16] at Forty-third Street and asked for a job. He hadn't eat anything for a couple of days. 'Come on have some lunch with me,' I sid. He ate more than four dollars' worth of food in half an hour."

"Did you start him in business?" I inquired.

"Start him! I made him."

"Oh."

"I raised him up out of nothing, right out of the gutter. I saw right away he was a fine-appearing, gentlemanly young man, and when he told me he was an Oggsford I knew I could use him good. I got him to join up in the American Legion[17] and he used to stand high there. Right off he did some work for a client of mine up to Albany. We were so thick like that in everything"—he held up two bulbous fingers—"always together."

I wondered if this partnership had included the World's Series transaction in 1919.

"Now he's dead," I said after a moment. "You were his closest friend, so I know you'll want to come to his funeral this afternoon."

[16] *poolroom*: i.e., a pool parlor or billiards hall. Winebrenner's is fictional.

[17] *American Legion*: founded in 1919, a national organization of ex-military and ex-servicemen. Fitzgerald may be playing off the Legion's strong presence in baseball.

"I'd like to come."

"Well, come then."

The hair in his nostrils quivered slightly, and as he shook his head his eyes filled with tears.

"I can't do it—I can't get mixed up in it," he said.

"There's nothing to get mixed up in. It's all over now."

"When a man gets killed I never like to get mixed up in it in any way. I keep out. When I was a young man it was different—if a friend of mine died, no matter how, I stuck with them to the end. You may think that's sentimental, but I mean it—to the bitter end."

I saw that for some reason of his own he was determined not to come, so I stood up.

"Are you a college man?" he inquired suddenly.

For a moment I thought he was going to suggest a "gonnegtion," but he only nodded and shook my hand.

"Let us learn to show our friendship for a man when he is alive and not after he is dead," he suggested. "After that my own rule is to let everything alone."

When I left his office the sky had turned dark and I got back to West Egg in a drizzle. After changing my clothes I went next door and found Mr. Gatz walking up and down excitedly in the hall. His pride in his son and in his son's possessions was continually increasing and now he had something to show me.

"Jimmy sent me this picture." He took out his wallet with trembling fingers. "Look there."

It was a photograph of the house, cracked in the corners and dirty with many hands. He pointed out every detail to me eagerly. "Look there!" and then sought admiration from my eyes. He had shown it so often that I think it was more real to him now than the house itself.

"Jimmy sent it to me. I think it's a very pretty picture. It shows up well."

"Very well. Had you seen him lately?"

"He come out to see me two years ago and bought me the house I live in now. Of course we was broke up when he run off from home, but I see now there was a reason for it. He knew he had a big future in front of him. And ever since he made a success he was very generous with me."

He seemed reluctant to put away the picture, held it for another minute, lingeringly, before my eyes. Then he returned the wallet and pulled from his pocket a ragged old copy of a book called *Hopalong Cassidy*.[18]

"Look here, this is a book he had when he was a boy. It just shows you."

He opened it at the back cover and turned it around for me to see. On the last fly-leaf was printed the word SCHEDULE[19] and the date September 12, 1906.[20] And underneath:

Rise from bed	6.00	A.M.
Dumbbell exercise and wall-scaling.........	6.15–6.30	"
Study electricity, etc	7.15–8.15	"
Work	8.30–4.30	P.M.
Baseball and sports	4.30–5.00	"
Practice elocution, poise and how to attain it..	5.00–6.00	"
Study needed inventions	7.00–9.00	"

GENERAL RESOLVES

No wasting time at Shafters or [a name, indecipherable]
No more smokeing or chewing.
Bath every other day
Read one improving book or magazine per week
Save $5.00 [crossed out] $3.00 per week
Be better to parents

[18] Hopalong Cassidy: popular fictional, rough-and-tough cowboy hero; author Clarence E. Mulford published nearly thirty novels about the character and his world from 1906 to 1941.

[19] *SCHEDULE*: This entire section obviously alludes to Benjamin Franklin's *Autobiography*, down to the formatting of the tables and the advice itself, such as the mentions of electricity and inventions, and the virtue of cleanliness. Franklin, of course, was widely seen as the very model of the "rags to riches" American dream.

[20] *1906*: The eponymous *Hopalong Cassidy* was published in 1910. Perhaps Fitzgerald had in mind the 1906 title *Hopalong Cassidy's Rustler Round-Up*.

"I come across this book by accident," said the old man. "It just shows you, don't it?"

"It just shows you."

"Jimmy was bound to get ahead. He always had some resolves like this or something. Do you notice what he's got about improving his mind? He was always great for that. He told me I et like a hog once, and I beat him for it."

He was reluctant to close the book, reading each item aloud and then looking eagerly at me. I think he rather expected me to copy down the list for my own use.

A little before three the Lutheran minister arrived from Flushing, and I began to look involuntarily out the windows for other cars. So did Gatsby's father. And as the time passed and the servants came in and stood waiting in the hall, his eyes began to blink anxiously, and he spoke of the rain in a worried, uncertain way. The minister glanced several times at his watch, so I took him aside and asked him to wait for half an hour. But it wasn't any use. Nobody came.

* * * * *

About five o'clock our procession of three cars reached the cemetery and stopped in a thick drizzle beside the gate—first a motor hearse, horribly black and wet, then Mr. Gatz and the minister and I in the limousine, and a little later four or five servants and the postman from West Egg, in Gatsby's station wagon,[21] all wet to the skin. As we started through the gate into the cemetery I heard a car stop and then the sound of someone splashing after us over the soggy ground. I looked around. It was the man with owl-eyed glasses whom I had found marvelling over Gatsby's books in the library one night three months before.

I'd never seen him since then. I don't know how he knew about the funeral, or even his name. The rain poured down his thick glasses, and he took them off and wiped them to see the protecting canvas unrolled from Gatsby's grave.

[21] *station wagon*: car outfitted to transport passengers and their luggage to or from a railway station, typically without glass or curtains in the window holes.

I tried to think about Gatsby then for a moment, but he was already too far away, and I could only remember, without resentment, that Daisy hadn't sent a message or a flower. Dimly I heard someone murmur "Blessed are the dead that the rain falls on,"[22] and then the owl-eyed man said "Amen to that," in a brave voice.

We straggled[23] down quickly through the rain to the cars. Owl-eyes spoke to me by the gate.

"I couldn't get to the house," he remarked.

"Neither could anybody else."

"Go on!" He started. "Why, my God! they used to go there by the hundreds."

He took off his glasses and wiped them again, outside and in.

"The poor son-of-a-bitch,"[24] he said.

* * * * *

One of my most vivid memories is of coming back West from prep school and later from college at Christmas time. Those who went farther than Chicago would gather in the old dim Union Station at six o'clock of a December evening, with a few Chicago friends, already caught up into their own holiday gayeties, to bid them a hasty good-bye. I remember the fur coats of the girls returning from Miss This-or-That's and the chatter of frozen breath and the hands waving overhead as we caught sight of old acquaintances, and the matchings of invitations: "Are you going to the Ordways'? the Herseys'? the Schultzes'?" and the long green tickets clasped tight in our gloved hands. And last the murky yellow cars of the Chicago, Milwaukee & St. Paul railroad looking cheerful as Christmas itself on the tracks beside the gate.

22 "*Blessed … on*": familiar proverb, with the earliest source typically cited as 1607's *The Puritan*. See Jennifer Speake, ed., *The Oxford Dictionary of Proverbs*, 6th ed. (Oxford: Oxford University Press, 2015), p. 69.

23 *straggled*: wandered or dispersed, especially without one's proper group; like a straggler.

24 *son-of-a-bitch*: "in neutral or approving contexts: a man, a fellow" (*OED*).

When we pulled out into the winter night and the real snow, our snow, began to stretch out beside us and twinkle against the windows, and the dim lights of small Wisconsin stations moved by, a sharp wild brace came suddenly into the air. We drew in deep breaths of it as we walked back from dinner through the cold vestibules, unutterably aware of our identity with this country for one strange hour, before we melted indistinguishably into it again.

That's my Middle West—not the wheat or the prairies or the lost Swede towns, but the thrilling returning trains of my youth, and the street lamps and sleigh bells in the frosty dark and the shadows of holly wreaths thrown by lighted windows on the snow. I am part of that, a little solemn with the feel of those long winters, a little complacent from growing up in the Carraway house in a city where dwellings are still called through decades by a family's name. I see now that this has been a story of the West, after all—Tom and Gatsby, Daisy and Jordan and I, were all Westerners, and perhaps we possessed some deficiency in common which made us subtly unadaptable to Eastern life.

Even when the East excited me most, even when I was most keenly aware of its superiority to the bored, sprawling, swollen towns beyond the Ohio, with their interminable inquisitions[25] which spared only the children and the very old—even then it had always for me a quality of distortion. West Egg, especially, still figures in my more fantastic dreams. I see it as a night scene by El Greco:[26] a hundred houses, at once conventional and grotesque, crouching under a sullen, overhanging sky and a lustreless moon. In the foreground four solemn men in dress suits are walking along the sidewalk with a stretcher on which lies a drunken woman in a white evening dress. Her hand, which dangles over the side, sparkles cold with jewels.

[25] *inquisitions*: "any intensive, sustained, or unwelcome questioning; a 'grilling'" (*OED*).

[26] *El Greco*: Greek painter famous for his mystical yet humanizing portrayal of Catholic subjects, his highly elongated style of drawing bodies, and his use of stark contrasts.

Gravely the men turn in at a house—the wrong house. But no one knows the woman's name, and no one cares.

After Gatsby's death the East was haunted for me like that, distorted beyond my eyes' power of correction. So when the blue smoke of brittle leaves was in the air and the wind blew the wet laundry stiff on the line I decided to come back home.

There was one thing to be done before I left, an awkward, unpleasant thing that perhaps had better have been let alone. But I wanted to leave things in order and not just trust that obliging and indifferent sea to sweep my refuse away. I saw Jordan Baker and talked over and around what had happened to us together, and what had happened afterward to me, and she lay perfectly still, listening, in a big chair.

She was dressed to play golf, and I remember thinking she looked like a good illustration, her chin raised a little jauntily, her hair the color of an autumn leaf, her face the same brown tint as the fingerless glove on her knee. When I had finished she told me without comment that she was engaged to another man. I doubted that, though there were several she could have married at a nod of her head, but I pretended to be surprised. For just a minute I wondered if I wasn't making a mistake, then I thought it all over again quickly and got up to say good-bye.

"Nevertheless you did throw me over," said Jordan suddenly. "You threw me over on the telephone. I don't give a damn about you now, but it was a new experience for me, and I felt a little dizzy for a while."

We shook hands.

"Oh, and do you remember"—she added—"a conversation we had once about driving a car?"

"Why—not exactly."

"You said a bad driver was only safe until she met another bad driver? Well, I met another bad driver, didn't I? I mean it was careless of me to make such a wrong guess. I thought you were rather an honest, straightforward person. I thought it was your secret pride."

"I'm thirty," I said. "I'm five years too old to lie to myself and call it honor."

She didn't answer. Angry, and half in love with her, and tremendously sorry, I turned away.

* * * * *

One afternoon late in October I saw Tom Buchanan. He was walking ahead of me along Fifth Avenue in his alert, aggressive way, his hands out a little from his body as if to fight off interference, his head moving sharply here and there, adapting itself to his restless eyes. Just as I slowed up to avoid overtaking him he stopped and began frowning into the windows of a jewelry store. Suddenly he saw me and walked back, holding out his hand.

"What's the matter, Nick? Do you object to shaking hands with me?"

"Yes. You know what I think of you."

"You're crazy, Nick," he said quickly. "Crazy as hell. I don't know what's the matter with you."

"Tom," I inquired, "what did you say to Wilson that afternoon?"

He stared at me without a word, and I knew I had guessed right about those missing hours. I started to turn away, but he took a step after me and grabbed my arm.

"I told him the truth," he said. "He came to the door while we were getting ready to leave, and when I sent down word that we weren't in he tried to force his way upstairs. He was crazy enough to kill me if I hadn't told him who owned the car. His hand was on a revolver[27] in his pocket every minute he was in the house—" He broke off defiantly. "What if I did tell him? That fellow had it coming to him. He threw dust into your eyes[28] just like he did in Daisy's, but he was a tough one. He ran over Myrtle like you'd run over a dog and never even stopped his car."

[27] *revolver*: handgun with a chamber that rotates (revolves) the next cartridge into place for firing. See note 24 in chapter 8 on "revolved".

[28] *threw dust ... eyes*: "to confuse, mislead, or dupe by making 'blind' to the actual facts of the case" (*OED*).

There was nothing I could say, except the one unutterable fact that it wasn't true.

"And if you think I didn't have my share of suffering—look here, when I went to give up that flat and saw that damn box of dog biscuits sitting there on the sideboard, I sat down and cried like a baby. By God it was awful——"

I couldn't forgive him or like him, but I saw that what he had done was, to him, entirely justified. It was all very careless and confused. They were careless people, Tom and Daisy—they smashed up things and creatures and then retreated back into their money or their vast carelessness, or whatever it was that kept them together, and let other people clean up the mess they had made....

I shook hands with him; it seemed silly not to, for I felt suddenly as though I were talking to a child. Then he went into the jewelry store to buy a pearl necklace—or perhaps only a pair of cuff buttons[29]—rid of my provincial squeamishness[30] forever.

Gatsby's house was still empty when I left—the grass on his lawn had grown as long as mine. One of the taxi drivers in the village never took a fare past the entrance gate without stopping for a minute and pointing inside; perhaps it was he who drove Daisy and Gatsby over to East Egg the night of the accident, and perhaps he had made a story about it all his own. I didn't want to hear it and I avoided him when I got off the train.

I spent my Saturday nights in New York because those gleaming, dazzling parties of his were with me so vividly that I could still hear the music and the laughter, faint and incessant, from his garden, and the cars going up and down his drive. One night I did hear a material car there, and saw its lights stop at his front steps. But I didn't investigate. Probably it was some final guest who had been away at the ends of the earth and didn't know that the party was over.

[29] *cuff buttons*: i.e., cuff links. See note 45 in chapter 4 on "human molars".

[30] *provincial squeamishness*: provincial: narrow-minded or unsophisticated; squeamishness: being excessively scrupulous or easily offended.

On the last night, with my trunk packed and my car sold to the grocer, I went over and looked at that huge incoherent failure of a house once more. On the white steps an obscene word, scrawled by some boy with a piece of brick, stood out clearly in the moonlight, and I erased it, drawing my shoe raspingly along the stone. Then I wandered down to the beach and sprawled out on the sand.

Most of the big shore places were closed now and there were hardly any lights except the shadowy, moving glow of a ferryboat across the Sound. And as the moon rose higher the inessential[31] houses began to melt away until gradually I became aware of the old island here that flowered once for Dutch sailors' eyes—a fresh, green breast of the new world. Its vanished trees, the trees that had made way for Gatsby's house, had once pandered[32] in whispers to the last and greatest of all human dreams; for a transitory enchanted moment man must have held his breath in the presence of this continent, compelled into an aesthetic[33] contemplation[34] he neither understood nor desired, face to face for the last time in history with something commensurate to his capacity for wonder.

And as I sat there brooding[35] on the old, unknown world, I thought of Gatsby's wonder when he first picked out the green light at the end of Daisy's dock. He had come a long way to this blue lawn, and his dream must have seemed so close that he could hardly fail to grasp it. He did not know that it was already behind him, somewhere back in that vast obscurity beyond the city, where the dark fields of the republic rolled on under the night.

[31] *inessential*: i.e., unsubstantial; shadowy, ghostly.

[32] *pandered*: to indulge another's desires, especially one's fancies.

[33] *aesthetic*: artistic; the skill of creating great art.

[34] *contemplation*: to behold something intensely and thoughtfully. In Catholicism, contemplation is the highest type of prayer; e.g., in Adoration, one contemplates the Lord in watchful silence: "He gazes at me; I gaze at him", as many saints have written.

[35] *brooding*: "to meditate moodily, or with strong feeling" (*OED*).

Gatsby believed in the green light, the orgastic[36] future that year by year recedes before us. It eluded us then, but that's no matter—tomorrow we will run faster, stretch out our arms farther. . . . And one fine morning——

So we beat on, boats against the current, borne[37] back ceaselessly into the past.

[36] *orgastic*: resembling the intensity and consummation of sexual intercourse that, properly ordered and unimpeded, allows the possibility of new life.

[37] *borne*: carried while supported. The play on "born", especially with "orgastic" above, leaves the reader contemplating Gatz's birth of Gatsby, who was born and borne into the past.

Contemporary Criticism

What Is *The Great Gatsby* Really About?

James Como
York College (CUNY)

A consensus (always dangerous, by the way) on *The Great Gatsby* is that its subject is the peculiarly male American drive to gain status and material wealth, and to get the girl—*and* the consequences of that pursuit. Certainly, in Fitzgerald's masterwork there is much window dressing pointing to amorous loss, and to the realization that getting stuff does not make for enduring happiness, and to one's origin being one's destiny (thus inviting theatrical efforts to "rise above" and, eventually, exposure, if only to one's self). Together these certainly make for a complex character, as well as for an astute (if simplistic) cultural commentary. But they are not—consensus to the contrary—what *The Great Gatsby*, or Jay Gatsby, is about.

Rather, these are elements in what C.S. Lewis in his *Pilgrim's Regress* has called "the dialectic of desire", a testing of this and that object of longing—sex, fame, high self-regard, social acceptance, creature comfort—until one realizes, by the process of elimination, that, in fact, these are not the genuine objects of desire at all, that our longing, somehow sweet, even if painful, persists no matter the winning of some prize.

Why is that? Lewis wondered. Because, he concludes, the object of our deepest desire is not of this world—nor was Gatsby's. Those large billboard optometrist eyes are watching from above, disinterestedly, to see if Gatsby will *get* it, that is, will discover in himself his *genuine* object of desire.

Of course, he does not. He is murdered; his dialectic aborted. Fitzgerald leaves his reader believing that his book is about the perils of one's reach exceeding one's grasp, and there is nothing false and much useful in knowing of such perils, and of their varying manifestations. Such a postmortem, especially when elegantly and movingly arrayed, is compelling.

But it is incomplete. At the end of the day, Fitzgerald had more in his soul than even he realized. He seems to have believed that psycho-social dysfunction is the *affliction*, whereas it is actually a *symptom*—of no less than despair, the absence of hope. *The Great Gatsby* certainly is a cautionary tale, but a caution against what?

We gaze at that green light at the end of the pier, not as a self-fulfilling sacrament but as a road sign pointing to our true home: "For Thou hast made us for Thyself and our hearts are restless till they rest in Thee", writes Saint Augustine[1]—Thee, the genuine object of our desire. *That* is what *The Great Gatsby* is really about. Not only the reader but sometimes the writer, too, is the last, if ever, to know.

Or did Fitzgerald, knowing that only a *strenuous* effort of mind, heart, and soul to discover a monumental truth is rewarding and lasting, simply not want to hit us over the head with his idea? Even Jesus kept some secrets. Here, though, I write of the book, not its author.

What needs clarification first is this word, "about", which is so misleading. I have already used it five times, taking for granted that we all know what it means. But I ask, Does it mean the plain *sense* of the matter? That painting shows us an apple—simple as that. The painting is about an apple. Or does the painter reveal some freshness of *feeling* in the shine of the fruit, a ripeness spreading to all creation? Or does the artist hold us, the viewers, in such disregard as to insult us with a representation so simplistic as to display a *tone*, an attitude, of contempt? Or, finally, is there some intention on the part of the painter to comment on, say, Original Sin?

Sense (the obvious subject), *feeling* (the artist's attitude toward that subject), *tone* (the artist's attitude toward the

[1] Augustine, *Confessions of Saint Augustine* 1, 1, 5, trans. F. J. Sheed (New York: Sheed and Ward, 1943).

audience), and *intention* (the artist's overall purpose) are the four types of meaning described so long ago by the great literary theorist and critic I. A. Richards in his landmark *Practical Criticism*,[2] now (regrettably) forgotten, as is often the case with old books. But not in *this* case. I suggest we ask of *The Great Gatsby*, What do we discern as its four types of meaning? What does the author make it to be "about"?

And so we shall, but first more about "about", beyond the author (whom I have already suggested cannot be trusted in the first place to completely understand his own material). Often, we identify the *theme* of a work, its sort of one-sentence proposition. The girl in the *Girl with the Pearl Earring* (in Vermeer's famous painting) emanates more beauty than she realizes. There is a theme. Or, we have no business removing a giant ape from his natural habitat, let alone arousing in him an alien passion (*King Kong*). Or, faced with dreadful spiritual and moral alternatives, we must eventually make a decision, no matter the cost (*Hamlet*). Does a theme overlap with any of Richards' four types? Probably not, though it comes closest to the fourth, *intention*.

The lesson here, I think, is to specify what your particular "about" is about, which I have almost—but not exactly—done. I have claimed our book is about unfulfilled longing, unfulfilled because its object is not of this world. Would that be its *theme*? Possibly, but if so it is, as I have suggested, buried. That is, it is one thing not to want to hit your reader over the head with your theme but quite another to hide it under layers of distractions. So, then, is it the author's *intention*?

I take Fitzgerald's sense to be plain: acquisitive, social-climbing, romantic ambition—all gone awry. But what of his attitude toward that, toward his hero? It seems sympathetic, making the outcome tragic, not merely sad. After all, is not Nick's narration just a bit judgmental—Nick, whose self-interest taints him with a whiff of hypocrisy? And as for us,

[2] I. A. Richards, *Practical Criticism: A Study of Literary Judgment* (New York: Harcourt, Brace, 1929).

his reader, Fitzgerald (by way of the narrator) seems to make us complicit in the judgment, so that, yes, we are unsettled: Gatsby deserved better—if only he had known it.

So where does all this *longing* come in? As a buried theme? An overly disguised intention? Perhaps as a subconscious intention? Maybe, ultimately, as an artistic failure: if no one, or very few, discern it, or work their way through the "dialectic", and fail to see a universal aspect of spiritual life (let alone an application to oneself)—then how can it be otherwise, no matter the intrinsic beauty of its construction, depictions, and stylistic allure (all of which are true of the book)?

The answer may lie with a writer even older, much older, than I. A. Richards—namely, Dante Alighieri, the poet who gave us *The Divine Comedy* (and much else), perhaps the greatest poem ever written. In the very early fourteenth century, in his *Convivio*, he offered this four-level model of literary interpretation, and with it we move to the work, leaving its author behind.

First is the *literal* level, what is actually depicted, the obvious action. Second is *the allegorical* level, what that action represents beneath the surface (King Kong as the native exploited by the colonizer, for example). Next is the *moral* level, the ethical truths applicable to the reader. And finally is the most difficult to understand: the *anagogical level*, the spiritual meaning of the text, including the complicity, and fate, of the reader.

These two patterns—Richards' and Dante's—can be very useful. For example, we could regard Richards' four types as an x-axis, with Dante's as a y-axis, and so plot a literary work on such a graph. But who would want to do *that*? Instead, we can place one pattern on top of the other and see where they coincide. Well, except for the first levels, *sense* and *literal*, they seem not to. What works more effectively, I think, is to take Richards' as a horizontal pattern, with Dante's *moral* and *anagogical* branching beyond Richards' *intention*.

That is, whereas Richards focuses on the author, Dante focuses on the work, and since our title deals, not with Fitzgerald (remember we are not asking, What did Fitzgerald intend?), but with the book, we must go with Dante. After all, authors have often told us that they do not know everything, or even best, about the art they produce (as I suggested above). Thus, *The Great Gatsby* is fundamentally about—that is, its subject is—the *moral* and *anagogical*. And that implicates *you*, the reader.

Here we arrive at a section of our process that usually comes at or near the beginning of a literary analysis, a summary of the book in question. However, I thought it best to arrange some thoughts before that, the better to behold the object of our interpretation. On the assumption that anyone reading this has read *The Great Gatsby*, this will be brief, citing mere touchstones.

Nick, the narrator, tells the tale, so the whole is a sort of memoir. He knows Daisy, who is married to Tom Buchanan, from the past and will visit her as he learns about bond-dealing in New York. The Buchanans are not only rich but "upper crust", so to speak. As it happens Tom is having an affair with Myrtle, the wife of a garage owner, George. And then there is Gatsby himself, who has been, and remains, soulfully in love with the presumably unattainable Daisy. He and the Buchanans live, respectively, in East Egg and West Egg on Long Island in homes separated both by a bay and social standing. And there, in West Egg, at the end of a pier, is the green light that enchants Gatsby and holds his gaze from afar.

Gatsby is ostentatiously and mysteriously rich (but certainly not upper crust), and though throwing lavish parties rarely appears at them. The principals travel between Long Island and Manhattan both by train and, on a side road, by car. On that road one will pass Myrtle's husband's garage (in the Valley of Ashes) and also a looming billboard advertising an optometrist; it features two large eyes that look down at the passersby.

Gatsby and Daisy do have their tryst, but she will not leave her meal ticket Tom; she has no romance in her, which she makes clear during a confrontation in Manhattan, when Tom tells Daisy that Gatsby is nothing more than a bootlegging gangster. Tom allows Daisy to drive Gatsby back to Long Island. During that trip Daisy runs into and kills Myrtle near her husband's garage. Gatsby, however, nobly takes the blame, and Myrtle's husband, having been lied to by Tom about Myrtle being Gatsby's lover, shoots and kills Gatsby. Only his father, one Gatz, shows up at the funeral. Nick goes home, back West, disgusted. And the green light shines on.

This stenographic sketch of the story does no justice to its telling. The opulent melancholy, emotional portraiture, stylistic evocations of contrasts (for example, between Gatsby and Daisy), layering of intensities (so that the reader foresees catastrophe: it can end no other way), and narrational filterings (Nick is not omniscient and has his own implicit point-of-view and interests)—these together, especially in a book so brief, make for a masterpiece, an elegant and dynamic economy that not only invites but compels the reader to find more than (as many critics have claimed) "the end of the American dream".

That may have been Fitzgerald's conscious intent, expressing a common post–World War I disillusionment. But Gatsby loves Daisy to the very end; in fact, he is self-sacrificial toward that end. The worldly Daisy, on the other hand, bereft of any romantic imagination, lives the good life, even as a killer without a conscience, though to what end we know not. Along the way we realize that George (Myrtle's husband) is a murderer, that Tom is a shallow, arrogant, cynical bully, and that Nick is an enabler who presumes to judge (implicitly) a tangled cacophony that he himself helped catalyze (and, by the way, sexually exploited oh-so-casually).

And Gatsby? Yes, he has an affair with a married woman, though one he loved unconditionally before she met her husband and to the moment of his death. We see him do no wrong, express no cynicism, practice no banal cruelty. Trapped by his past and (certainly) his upbringing, he shows one life, that of opulence, but internally lives another, that of transcendent devotion, perhaps believing that the first will win him the object of that devotion. Sure, he is wrong, but his spirit is more alive, more vital and worthy, than any other.

Would that Gatsby had lived and Fitzgerald written a sequel. If I were to write that book (*Gatsby Agonistes* perhaps?), I would show his struggle, out of his gangster life, out of all material motivation, and even out of his passion for Daisy, an unworthy passion given her unworthiness. Finally, he would become his authentic self, one united with the world lit by that light at the end of the pier.

Of course, he could not do this alone, or with psychotherapy, or with medication. Rather, he must fill the void as we all must, with divinity. Now, how does that manifest itself to him? Whom might he meet along the rough and rising road? Helpful to him would be the great spiritual writers such as Saint Bernard of Clairvaux (*The Twelve Steps of Humility and Pride*), Saint Bonaventure (*Journey of the Mind to God*), Walter Hilton (*The Scale of Perfection*), and *The Cloud of Unknowing* (anonymous).

Withal, we at least intuit the spiritual struggle and must decide either to engage it, or not. Perhaps not the business that Fitzgerald was consciously about, but it is, I believe—again, going beyond Richards and following Dante—what *The Great Gatsby* is, a sign, like that beckoning light.

The Michaelis Episode in F. Scott Fitzgerald's *The Great Gatsby*

Robert C. Evans
Auburn University at Montgomery

Maureen Corrigan's 2015 book *So We Read On: How* The Great Gatsby *Came to Be and Why It Endures* is one of the best and most accessible explanations of the continuing appeal of F. Scott Fitzgerald's classic American novel.[1] Corrigan herself has reread the book constantly throughout her life, and she and many others consider it to be one of the best works American literature has to offer. She recounts her progress from her first reading of the text at her Catholic high school (when she did not particularly like it) to her eventual obsession with it. That obsession has led her to study it intensely, celebrate it in presentations throughout the country, and try to explain why it is so much loved both by her and by so many other readers. At one point, near the end of her narrative, Corrigan describes returning to her old high school, in Queens, New York (not far from where the novel's plot is set). She returned there to see how the book was being taught and read decades after she herself was first exposed to it.

Back in Queens, Corrigan meets one of her old mentors, Mrs. Flood, who was a young teacher when Corrigan first met her but who later became a senior administrator at the school. Corrigan's affection for Mrs. Flood is obvious, but at one point her old teacher offers an interpretation of *The Great Gatsby* that Corrigan finds unpersuasive:

[1] Maureen Corrigan, *So We Read On: How* The Great Gatsby *Came to Be and Why It Endures* (New York: Little, Brown, 2015).

> "I always thought the novel was about the fact that Gatsby was looking for the wrong things to fill him up," [Mrs. Flood] says to me. "Am I wrong? What do you think? Gatsby wants money and clothes and Daisy, but if you're not fulfilled within yourself, you won't really be happy in the end." I hesitate. It's not that Mrs. Flood is off base, it's just that her reading seems to diminish the part of Gatsby that I love the most: his identity as a go-for-broke Promethean overreacher—for better or worse, an American. I don't even care much what he's striving for; it's that he throws his whole being into the effort.[2] (290–91)

Later, in a class taught by a teacher named Mr. Booth, Corrigan encounters students who seem to share Mrs. Flood's interpretation, even though nothing in her book suggests that any particular approach to the novel is pushed onto students at the school. She reports that during her visit to Mr. Booth's classroom,

> I hear more explicit strands of what I'm now thinking of as the Catholic reading of *Gatsby*. The kids mention Gatsby worshipping false gods and how he's restless because he's not content with himself as he is. I can see why, Catholicism aside, this reading would appeal to high-school students, especially those reared on the self-affirming PBS children's programming of the past forty years or so. "Love yourself." "Be yourself." "Be proud of who you are." Gatsby is none of this. He runs counter to those doctrines of self-esteem and, instead, reaches back to an older America—a Ben Franklin–Horatio Alger America—where striving was the reigning doctrine.[3] (295)

In both cases, then, Corrigan prefers her own interpretations to those offered by Mrs. Flood and the students. In contrast to Mrs. Flood, Corrigan offers the standard romantic reading of the book, one in which Gatsby seems admirable as a "go-for-broke Promethean overreacher—for better or worse,

[2] Ibid., pp. 290–91.
[3] Ibid., p. 295.

an American ... [who] throws his whole being into the effort"[4] to rewin Daisy's love. Then, perhaps a little uncharitably, Corrigan suggests that the students are naïve for thinking that Gatsby is flawed because he is "not content with himself".[5] This is the sort of reading (according to Corrigan, mentioned above) that would appeal to "high-school students, especially those reared on ... self-affirming PBS children's programming". Mrs. Flood, it appears, is a bit too straightlaced, while the students are a bit too egotistical and immature. Later, presumably, they will come to see that Gatsby is a man, like the man in the famous 1965 musical *Man of La Mancha*, who wins our respect because he dreams a presumably noble but ultimately impossible dream and even dies in its pursuit. This is Corrigan's reading.

But can anything be said for the insights of Mrs. Flood and the students?

George Wilson: I

In this essay, I want to draw attention to an episode in *The Great Gatsby* that tends to get very little attention—the episode in which a young Greek immigrant named Michaelis tries to comfort and console George Wilson when George's wife, Myrtle, is accidentally struck down and killed by a car being driven by Daisy Buchanan.[6] This accident happens while Jay Gatsby, Daisy's devoted suitor, occupies the passenger seat. George had recently begun to suspect that Myrtle has been having an affair with someone, not realizing that in fact her paramour has been Tom Buchanan, Daisy's husband. When Myrtle sees a car she thinks is being driven by Tom about to barrel past the gas station her husband owns, she rushes out to greet it, assuming Tom is driving. It hits her directly, killing

[4] Ibid., p. 291.

[5] Ibid., p. 295.

[6] F. Scott Fitzgerald, *The Great Gatsby*, ed. Stephen Mirarchi, Ignatius Critical Editions, ed. Joseph Pearce (San Francisco: Ignatius Press, 2025), pp. 149–53. All subsequent citations are from this edition and will be cited in the text.

her almost instantly and mangling her body in the process: Michaelis and another man notice "that her left breast was swinging loose like a flap, and there was no need to listen for the heart beneath" (see p. 132). Meanwhile, Daisy and Gatsby speed off. Neither of them seems greatly concerned with the death (and the heartbreak, in George's case) they have just caused. Gatsby is still intent on pursuing his romantic dream. Daisy does not seem to have even that excuse.

Carraway reports that the "young Greek, Michaelis, who ran the coffee joint beside the ashheaps", where Wilson's gas station is located, "was the principal witness at the inquest" (see p. 131). Carraway presumably attended that legal proceeding and paid close attention to everything Michaelis had to say. But as it turns out, Nick, Tom, and their friend Jordan Baker (in whom Nick is romantically interested) happened to be distantly following the car occupied by Daisy and Gatsby. The second car comes across the accident scene just after the police have arrived and after the police have begun interviewing Michaelis. Tom thus gets to see Myrtle's dead body, laid out in Wilson's garage, and he also gets to hear and witness Wilson's grief. So, too, does Nick. Tom even briefly tries to comfort Wilson before eventually leaving that job primarily to Michaelis. But the fact that Tom and Nick are present in the garage means that Nick is partly an eyewitness to some of the postaccident events, so that he can to some degree draw on his own memories.

The events leading up to Myrtle's death, and especially the events immediately following that death, are some of the most heart-wrenching in a book generally lacking much poignancy. George Wilson, in fact, emerges as one of the most emotionally "deep" characters in the entire novel. The grief he feels for Myrtle, combined with the pain he endures when he realizes that she has been cheating on him, makes it easy to feel sympathy for him in ways that are less true of most of the other characters, including Gatsby. Wilson's relative poverty, his hard work, his naïve devotion to Myrtle, and his dreams of living a life with a bit more financial freedom, all make him, in some ways, a much better and more realistic representative of the "American dream" than the somewhat shallow, if high-flying, Gatsby. Wilson comes across as a genuine human being, one to whom most of Fitzgerald's actual contemporaries would have been able to relate. He personifies some of the true virtues often associated with the promises and challenges of American citizenship. Unlike many of the other characters, he seems unselfish, responsible, trusting, and touched by the kind of realistic hope that can make Gatsby's lavish romanticism a bit hard to take seriously. George is not witty, clever, well-dressed, privileged, and (above all) rich, like most of the other characters—but then, of course, neither is Myrtle. But Myrtle aspires to live the high life and cheats on her husband to do so, and so her shallow values and crude superficiality help, ironically, to highlight the genuine common decency her husband epitomizes. If there is a genuinely tragic figure in *The Great Gatsby*, that figure may be George rather than the title character, the romantic overreacher. After all, many of George's very values (particularly his trust, his capacity for real affection, his sense of responsibility, and his loyalty) set him up for his fall.

George Wilson: II

In the hours before the fatal accident, Michaelis finds his neighbor George Wilson "sick in his office—really sick, pale as his own pale hair and shaking all over." Nick reports that "Michaelis advised him to go to bed, but Wilson refused, saying that he'd miss a lot of business if he did" (see p. 131). Wilson had already been sick earlier in the day, when Tom Buchanan and his fellow partiers (Nick and Jordan), on their way to Manhattan, had stopped by to purchase some gas. Tom, typically, had shown no genuine compassion for the ill mechanic but had instead belittled him for not filling Tom's tank quickly enough:

> "Let's have some gas!" cried Tom roughly. "What do you think we stopped for—to admire the view?"
>
> "I'm sick," said Wilson without moving. "Been sick all day."
>
> "What's the matter?"
>
> "I'm all run down."
>
> "Well, shall I help myself?" Tom demanded. "You sounded well enough on the phone."
>
> With an effort Wilson left the shade and support of the doorway and, breathing hard, unscrewed the cap of the tank. In the sunlight his face was green. (See p. 118.)

This passage seems worth quoting because it helps contrast Tom's self-centered boorishness with the later behavior of Michaelis. It also, incidentally, helps suggest the relative shallowness of Nick and Jordan, neither of whom expresses any concern for Wilson, neither of whom offers to pump the gas themselves, and neither of whom expresses any overt criticism of Tom, even though both of them know that Tom has been sleeping with Wilson's wife. In this scene as later, Wilson emerges as the one genuinely sympathetic figure, the one for whom most readers (if not Nick and the others) will feel the most pity. Wilson, we soon learn, feels "sick" mostly because he has recently realized that his wife has been cheating on him—cheating on him with the very man who is now berating him for not working hard enough (although Wilson has not yet figured that out).

After the accident, Tom does seem to feel some genuine pity for Wilson—presumably prompted, in part, by his grief over Myrtle's death and his guilt over the part he has played in her demise.

Michaelis: I

It is Michaelis, however, who seems to be the character most capable of genuine compassion in *The Great Gatsby*. When he finds Wilson still sick later in the day, Michaelis urges "his neighbor" (see p. 131) to get some sleep, but Wilson explains that he has Myrtle locked up in their apartment above the garage. He has discovered her unfaithfulness and plans to keep her locked up until they can leave together and head west for what George would consider greener pastures. Myrtle, of course, has no desire to leave the strange life she has made for herself in New York with Tom, even though Tom has already physically abused her and even though he treats her more as a harlot than as anyone he genuinely loves. Ironically, it is George who genuinely *does* seem to love Myrtle, but he is not rich enough and sophisticated enough to suit her tastes—tastes she shares with most of the book's other shallow characters.

Michaelis is at first astonished by the idea that George would imprison his wife. He and Wilson "had been *neighbors*" (emphasis added; the second recent use of that word) "for four years, and Wilson had never seemed faintly capable" (see p. 131) of such behavior. Michaelis does not seem to think of George as merely a fellow small businessman; instead, he seems to regard him as a genuine neighbor and even friend, someone whom Michaelis truly cares about. When Michaelis "naturally" (see p. 131) tries to discover what is troubling his friend, George at first refuses to tell him and even seems to suspect Michaelis of being Myrtle's secret lover. Michaelis, bothered by these apparent suspicions, suddenly sees "some workmen ... bound for his restaurant", and so Michaelis takes "the opportunity to get away [from George], *intending to come back later*" (see p. 131; emphasis added). Like George, Michaelis is a hard-working man who cannot afford, either financially or in terms of his own self-respect, to ignore his customers. But although Michaelis could now easily abandon George to his sickness and pain, he fully intends "to come back later", presumably to help his suffering neighbor as much as he can, despite George's offensive suspicions. Michaelis, increasingly, comes to resemble the kind of figure mostly missing in *The Great Gatsby*: the true friend, or at least the genuinely compassionate person.

It is Michaelis who later hears Myrtle screaming at George, Michaelis who sees her rush out at the oncoming car, Michaelis who sees her struck by the speeding vehicle, and Michaelis who is one of the first two men (along with the driver of another car) to reach Myrtle's body. When Tom, Nick, and Jordan arrive on the scene, Nick himself hears one of the most painful (in several senses of that word) sentences in the entire book when he hears Wilson repeatedly moaning, "Oh, my Ga-od! Oh, my Ga-od! Oh, Ga-od! Oh, my Ga-od!" (see p. 133). This grief-stricken cry is also one of the most significant sentences in the whole novel. I would suggest that it calls attention to a character who is mostly missing in *The Great Gatsby*. That character, of course, is God. He is missing in the sense that few of the book's characters seem to care about him or miss his presence in their lives. Indeed, his name is most often evoked when characters are merely exclaiming or actually cursing, as in phrases such as "God knows where" (p. 118), "a God damned lie" (see p. 126), "God!" (see p. 129), "the God damned coward!" (see p. 136), "Why, my God!" (see p. 166), and "By God it was awful" (see p. 170). The only character who seems to assume the actual *existence and importance* of God is Wilson, not only when he moans in the way already quoted but also when he refers to "God" several more times (once each on pages 149, 150, and 151 and three separate times on page 152). It is only Wilson who seems to take God seriously in what might otherwise be termed, in many ways, a literally godless or God-forsaken book.

Also absent in most of Fitzgerald's novel is any hint of real friendship. Admittedly, Nick and Gatsby ultimately do develop a kind of friendship, even though the text begins with Nick's confession that he often despised the title character. Gatsby, he says, initially "represented everything for which I have an unaffected scorn" (although he quickly concedes that "Gatsby turned out all right at the end" [see p. 4]). Much later, after Gatsby explains how and why he avoided stopping the speeding car to check on the now-dead Myrtle, Nick also says, "I disliked him so much by this time that I didn't find it necessary to tell him he was wrong" (see p. 137). Of course, by the *end* of the novel, Nick says Gatsby is "worth the whole damn bunch [of most of the rest of the characters] put together" (see p. 146).

In short, Nick's "friendship" with Gatsby is complex and conflicted, even as he recounts their relationship in retrospect. He still finds faults with Gatsby even after Gatsby is dead.

Similarly complex is Tom's attempt to show friendship to the grieving Wilson. Tom, when he arrives at the garage, does try to comfort Wilson a bit, telling him, with a "soothing gruffness", that he's "got to pull [himself] together." Then, when Wilson seems about to collapse, Tom actually holds "him upright" (see pp. 134–35). Tom-the-adulterer-with-Wilson's-wife even tells a policeman that he is Wilson's "friend" (see p. 135), and then later he even picks up Wilson "like a doll" and carries him "into the office, set[ting] him down in a chair" before returning to the garage (see p. 135). It is Tom, too, who actually urges other people to "come here [into the office] and sit with" Wilson, just as it is Tom whom Nick soon describes as having "tears ... overflowing down his face" (see pp. 135–36) as Tom, Nick, and Jordan drive off into the night and Tom presumably mourns Myrtle's death. In an example of what poet John Keats called "negative capability", Nick manages, at times, to make even Tom sound halfway decent. But Tom could never be anybody's idea of a true friend; he is much too self-centered to function with genuine concern for others.

Michaelis II

For all these reasons, it is Michaelis who offers the most extended demonstration of a simple, uncomplicated friendship in the entire text. It is Michaelis who turns out to be, perhaps, the most conspicuous, persistent, and admirable friend in *The Great Gatsby*, at least until Nick acts as a friend to Gatsby after Gatsby's death, when doing so can earn him nothing in return. Nick, presumably drawing on Michaelis's own testimony at the inquest, reports that in the hours after Myrtle's death,

> Michaelis and several other men were with [Wilson]; first, four or five men, later two or three men. Still later Michaelis had to ask the last stranger to wait there fifteen minutes longer,

> while he went back to his own place and made a pot of coffee. After that, he stayed there alone with Wilson until dawn. (See p. 149.)

The willingness of the strangers to stay with Wilson and try to comfort him is admirable; ironically, he seems to have a larger circle of people who genuinely care about him than does the wealthy Gatsby, who is surrounded, at his parties and elsewhere, by acquaintances, spongers, flatterers, and sycophants—all of whom abruptly desert him when he is no longer of any use to them. Of course, Wilson's comforters drift away as well, but their motives are purer than the motives of Gatsby's parasites, and the fact that they *do* drift away only helps call further attention to the dedication displayed by Michaelis, who returns with a gift that symbolizes the literal warmth of his feelings for his mourning "neighbor".

It is Michaelis who is present when Wilson, drained to some extent of his grief, begins to plot revenge. He wants to discover who was driving the car that struck and killed Myrtle, and he even says he has "a way of finding out" (see p. 149). He tells Michaelis that he had recently come to suspect Myrtle of infidelity, but "when he heard himself say this, he flinched and began to cry 'Oh, my God!' again in his groaning voice", leading Michaelis to make "a clumsy attempt to distract him" (see p. 149). Michaelis clearly wants to lessen Wilson's suffering. He asks Wilson how long he and Myrtle had been married, and when Wilson replies, "Twelve years", Michaelis probes a bit deeper: "'Ever had any children? Come on, George, sit still—I asked you a question. Did you ever have any children?" (see p. 149). Wilson does not answer this question directly, but the answer is obviously no. The fact that he is childless only emphasizes his isolation and also reveals that he has one less common reason to care about living—one less source of love for (and from) other persons. His extreme isolation (no other relatives seem to be in the picture) helps explain his eventual decision to commit suicide immediately after he kills Gatsby. Indeed, that decision in its own right suggests the depth of his suffering, and perhaps it also suggests his realization that he has just committed murder and thus deserves to be punished. In that way, Wilson once again displays a fundamental sense of morality that seems missing in most of the novel's "major" characters. Certainly Daisy seems hardly troubled by her role in Myrtle's death, and neither does Gatsby, for that matter. Both drive off, away from the accident scene, Daisy focusing (as Daisy usually does) on Daisy and Gatsby focusing (as he consistently does) on his obsession with Daisy, on "his identity as a go-for-broke Promethean overreacher".[7]

Wilson, meanwhile—and somewhat pathetically—seems less concerned with avenging himself than with avenging Myrtle's death. It is not so much that he wants to punish the man who committed adultery with his wife; instead, he wants to punish the man who (he thinks) *killed* his wife and then callously drove away. Michaelis, perhaps sensing that Wilson's thoughts are beginning to turn ugly, and definitely now realizing just how genuinely isolated his "neighbor" is, tries to think of some other people, besides himself, who might genuinely care about Wilson and who might, like Michaelis, try to help him:

> "Have you got a church you go to sometimes, George? Maybe even if you haven't been there for a long time? Maybe I could call up the church and get a priest to come over and he could talk to you, see?"
>
> "Don't belong to any."
>
> "You ought to have a church, George, for times like this. You must have gone to church once. Didn't you get married in a church? Listen, George, listen to me. Didn't you get married in a church?"
>
> "That was a long time ago." (See p. 150.)

Given his insistence on this point, Michaelis is probably himself a churchgoer, and, given the fact that he is Greek, he is almost certainly Orthodox. He does *not* speak of a minister

[7] Corrigan, *So We Read On*, pp. 290–91.

or pastor coming to help Wilson; he speaks specifically of a *priest*. And indeed, Michaelis himself in this episode is trying to act as a priest might act. He is trying to show compassion for Wilson, trying to help him, and trying to get him to focus on things larger than himself, whether it be God in particular or, more generally, on the fellowship and community that church can provide. It is interesting, in fact, that Michaelis does not ask Wilson whether Wilson *believes in God*, nor does he urge Wilson to pray. Instead, he asks whether Wilson attends a church and whether he has a priest (and, implicitly, a congregation) he can rely on. It is as if Fitzgerald, whose own commitment to Catholicism and Christianity were less strong when he wrote this novel than it had been in his youth (when he even considered becoming a priest),[8] wants to leave God, theology, and religious belief out of the picture, as if he wants to focus instead on churches as places where, if nothing else, friends gather and support one another.

George and Myrtle, it seems, "long ... ago" (see p. 150) used a church as many people tend to use them today: as places where public rituals (such as marriage) are performed, after which the church is then abandoned. George and Myrtle seem to have been living essentially secular lives for most of their marriage, and Myrtle, at least, seems not to have taken her marriage vows very seriously. Myrtle is one of the most self-centered and shallow characters in a book full of such people, including most of the main actors. George, in contrast, even if he is not a regular churchgoer, at the very least seems to have taken his wedding vows to heart: nothing suggests that he has cheated on Myrtle or would ever do so. In fact, it is precisely this aspect of George's character that makes Myrtle's infidelity so incredibly painful to him. It does not take long for most readers to realize just how empty-headed and frivolous Myrtle is—which, of course, makes George's assessment of her ("She's a deep one" [see p. 151]) all the more ironic. Far

[8] See Mary Jo Tate, *F. Scott Fitzgerald A to Z: The Essential Reference to His Life and Work* (New York: Facts on File, 1998), p. 146.

from being deep, except insofar as she skillfully hides her adultery (at least for a while), she lacks any sense of devotion to something greater than her own selfish and materialistic pleasures. Indeed, it seems safe to assume that she does not even really love *Tom*: she would probably desert him if a better (that is, better funded and perhaps more handsome) "catch" came along. But George is made of better stuff, and although Tom looks down on him and ridicules him, those facts alone make (or *should* make) George even more worthy of readers' respect.

It is part of the tragedy of George's life that he has no one to depend on except Myrtle—no children, no other obvious relatives, no wide circle of friends, no fellow congregants, no priest, not even any God. George, of course, does mention God repeatedly as he grieves, and later in his conversation with Michaelis he reveals that, in his last hours with Myrtle, he repeatedly warned her that God was aware of her infidelity:

> "God knows what you've been doing, everything you've been doing. You may fool me, but you can't fool God!"
>
> Standing behind him, Michaelis saw with a shock that he was looking at the eyes of Doctor T. J. Eckleburg [an advertisement on a nearby billboard], which had just emerged, pale and enormous, from the dissolving night.
>
> "God sees everything," repeated Wilson.
>
> "That's an advertisement," Michaelis assured him. Something made him turn away from the window and look back into the room. But Wilson stood there a long time, his face close to the window pane, nodding into the twilight. (See p. 152.)

Perhaps Wilson really *does* believe in God, or perhaps—like many of us—he thinks of God mostly when he is in need, when secular lifestyles and answers to questions and ostensible solutions to pain seem to have run out of steam. It has become conventional to suggest that if Fitzgerald himself believed in God, his use of the Eckleburg eyes (a recurring motif) in *The Great Gatsby* suggests that he was a deist, or perhaps merely an agnostic or even an atheist. In any case, if George Wilson *does* believe in God, he seeks no help from God. He does not head to a church to ask a priest for help; he does not seek consolation by joining a congregation; he does not even pray. Ironically, he ultimately does what most of the other characters in this novel do: he relies on himself, acts in isolation, makes his own decision without seeming to need others' advice or caring or love, and in the process creates a tragedy not only for another person but also for himself.

Michaelis III

Our last glimpse of Michaelis occurs in a paragraph describing events not long before Wilson commits murder and then suicide:

> By six o'clock Michaelis was worn out, and grateful for the sound of a car stopping outside. It was one of the watchers of the night before who had promised to come back, so he cooked breakfast for three, which he and the other man ate together. Wilson was quieter now, and Michaelis went home to sleep; when he awoke four hours later and *hurried back* to the garage, Wilson was gone. (See p. 152; emphasis added.)

This is an appropriate final view of a small but significant character. Although Michaelis is "worn out" after having spent the night consoling and counseling Wilson, he does not abandon those tasks or his friends. He stays until another thoughtful person—another "watcher"—shows up. Ironically, Wilson seems to have more people who actually care about him than Gatsby does. And Michaelis, at this point, does not simply go home and sleep; first, he cooks breakfast for everyone, and only then, assuming that the other "watcher" will stay with Wilson, does he go home for a bit of rest. But he does not rest long: in four hours he is prepared to return to duty, but at that point he discovers that both Wilson and the other "watcher" are gone. Fitzgerald leaves it to our own imaginations to decide what may have happened. Did the other "watcher" simply leave Wilson alone? If so, then such behavior would only highlight, through contrast, the steadfast devotion of Michaelis, who not only returns to Wilson's garage but actually "hurrie[s] back". Did Wilson quarrel with the other watcher, or simply storm away, leaving him with nothing else to do but leave? We cannot say for sure, but we do know that, compared to Gatsby's all-night watch at the Buchanans', which Nick terms a "vigil" (see p. 139), Michaelis' is rooted in self-offering and generosity, not self-absorption. And we *do* know for certain from this whole extended episode involving Michaelis that there seems to be at least one character in *The Great Gatsby* whom we can genuinely admire as a decent man, true friend, and (presumably) good Christian—someone who never himself speaks of God but someone who nonetheless acts according to Christian precepts.[9] In that respect, he is an utterly singular character in a novel mostly lacking in worthy role models.

In a book full of people who think of themselves first and others second (if at all), Michaelis can even appear to be the only truly and consistently admirable human being.

[9] For a brief discussion of Michaelis from a Christian perspective, see Alexander R. Tamke, "Michaelis in *The Great Gatsby*: St. Michael in the Valley of Ashes", *Fitzgerald Newsletter*, no. 40 (Winter 1968): 4–5. See also Robert Emmet Long, *The Achieving of* The Great Gatsby: *F. Scott Fitzgerald, 1920–1925* (Lewisburg, PA: Bucknell University Press, 1981), pp. 162–63.

The Romantic Consciousness in *The Great Gatsby*

Aaron Urbanczyk
Franciscan University of Steubenville

From a narrative and character perspective, *The Great Gatsby* and *Moby-Dick* have a suggestive commonality. Both classic American novels feature a first-person narrator who writes the history of his encounter with an individual who both fascinates him and has changed his life. Further, both narrators have certain things in common with the men at the center of their stories—Ahab and Jay Gatsby. At the very least, both Ishmael and Ahab share an obsession with whales, and one whale in particular. What traits do Nick Carraway and Jay Gatsby share? This question is too large to address definitively in this essay, but here I explore their common romantic temperaments. Gatsby's romantic *weltanschauung*[1] is constantly on display, but one might overlook the fact that Nick is Gatsby's equal in viewing the world through the lens of romanticism. Yet as romantics, they are not identical entirely. Nick's idealism is tempered—he has learned to compromise with the hard and immovable realities of life. Gatsby, tragically, cannot do so: as Nick describes Gatsby, he "dreamed [his dream] right through to the end"[2] and paid with his life for the purity of his romantic fidelity.

In what sense are Nick and Gatsby romantic figures? Here we do not use the term "romantic" to signify falling passionately in love; rather, the term references a broader, conceptual

[1] The German term *weltanshauung* signifies a type of broad or all-encompassing worldview, either for an individual or a group.

[2] F. Scott Fitzgerald, *The Great Gatsby*, ed. Stephen Mirarchi, Ignatius Critical Editions, ed. Joseph Pearce (San Francisco: Ignatius Press, 2025), p. 204. All subsequent citations are from this edition and will be cited in the text.

orientation of the self in the world. Romanticism as a philosophical and artistic movement emerged in Europe in the late 1700s and early 1800s,[3] one often described as a reaction against the neoclassical artistic views of the eighteenth century.[4] As a movement romanticism was broad, complex, and diverse, but the terms "romantic" and "romanticism" evoke certain characteristics in Western intellectual and cultural history. Romanticism is characterized by "emotional intensity, often taken to the extremes of rapture, nostalgia (for childhood or the past) ... melancholy, or sentimentality."[5] According to Keren Gorodeisky, "The romantic ideal ... [is that] aesthetics should permeate and shape human life", and "the creative imagination" is a central agent in achieving this ideal.[6] Critics of romanticism point to its "antirationalist and irrationalist" tendencies.[7] Further, the romantic imagination is deeply symbolic: the imagination generates symbols as part of the mythic worldview toward which the romantic aspires. We can thus generalize that a romantic—in this specific sense of the term—lives a profoundly interior life driven by aesthetically

[3] Figures associated with romanticism were various and diverse, spanning Europe, including such artists, poets, essays, and philosophers as Caspar David Friedrich, Friedrich Shlegel and August Wilhelm Shlegel, Freidrich W. J. Schelling, Novalis, the early Goethe, Victor Hugo, William Blake, Samuel Taylor Coleridge, William Wordsworth, Lord Byron, Percy Bysshe Shelley, and John Keats.

[4] Neoclassicism in art, literature, and architecture was a movement emphasizing classical models, formalized rules, symmetry, harmony, and a sense of restraint grounded in reason.

[5] Chris Baldick, "Romanticism", in *Oxford Concise Dictionary of Literary Definitions*, 2nd ed. (Oxford: Oxford University Press, 2004), p. 223.

[6] Keren Gorodeiskey, "19th Century Romantic Aesthetics", sections 1 and 2.1, in *Stanford Encyclopedia of Philosophy*, ed. Edward N. Zalta (Stanford University, Fall 2016 ed.), https://plato.stanford.edu/archives/fall2016/entries/aesthetics-19th-romantic/.

[7] Ibid., section 2.1. Gorodeiskey points out that some intellectual historians interpret romanticism's emphasis upon affectivity and imagination, and its implicit rejection of neoclassical rationalism, as giving it an "antirational or irrational" ethos. Gorodeiskey rejects the notion that the movement is inherently irrational or absurdist, pointing to the considerable tradition of criticism and theorizing that characterizes romantic writers and thinkers. In referencing the critique that romanticism is "antirational or irrational", she points out romanticism's tendency to subordinate the rational to individual imagination, creativity, desire, and autonomy. It is this latter sense that clearly applies to figures like Jay Gatsby.

charged ideals; for such a one the world is populated by symbols (largely of his own creation), beckoning him ever forward toward luminous, transcendent, absolutes. The romantic is also often obsessively nostalgic about the past, but the irrationalist tendency creates the perception that the past is malleable and open to alteration, even change. There is also a terrible paradox for the romantic regarding desire: attaining one's ideal precipitates crisis. The romantic consciousness lives in and for the unattainable absolute: the inability to possess the ideal is what energizes the individual to pursue it in an ever future-oriented fashion. Should the ideal be attained, reduced to the temporal and particular, the romantic runs the terrifying likelihood of destroying his ideal. The psychic dynamics of such a soul, which lives so strongly in the imaginative and the ideal, tend to make the romantic alienated, isolated, and lonely.

Fitgerald's Jay Gatsby is a pure romantic. Several of Fitzgerald's most striking passages capture Nick's magnificent articulation of, and insight into, Gatsby's romanticism. On the cusp of the narrative wherein Nick introduces himself and his book, he identifies Gatsby as a man with a "heightened sensitivity to the promises of life" (see p. 4), possessing a "romantic readiness which it is not likely I shall ever find again" (see p. 4). Fitzgerald operates much like Melville in the gradual nature of character disclosure: Jay Gatsby, just like Captain Ahab, is the subject of discussion, report, and rumor before he appears and speaks for himself. Once Nick and Gatsby strike up a relationship—one born of a sort of mutual affinity, utility, and neighborliness—Nick sees beyond the exaggerated narratives Gatsby initially provides about his background and into the recesses of Gatsby's colossal desires. The interior of Gatsby's soul is charged with a vital passion for his own ideals, and Nick tells the reader he doubts he will ever meet another man with such idealistic aspiration for the rewards life might provide him.[8]

[8] It is worth noting that, in this initial reference to Gatsby, Nick is both critical and complimentary. Nick finds elements of Gatsby completely contemptible, stating that Gatsby "represented everything for which I have an unaffected scorn" (see p. 4); yet he immediately follows this negative judgment with an admiring reflection upon Gatsby's "gift for hope" and "romantic readiness" (see p. 4).

The making of Jay Gatsby is an etiology[9] of romantic desire. The outsized ideals constructed by "James Gatz of North Dakota" (see p. 94) focus around two points: Dan Cody and his yacht, and falling in love with Daisy. Quite suggestively in chapter 6, just after the symmetrical middle of the novel (chapter 5), Nick inserts the backstory of how Gatz became Gatsby under the influence of Dan Cody. One could hardly find a more apt depiction of the romantic psyche than Nick's describing the young James Gatz:

> His heart was in a constant, turbulent riot. The most grotesque and fantastic conceits haunted him in his bed at night. A universe of ineffable gaudiness spun itself out in his brain while the clock ticked on the washstand and the moon soaked with wet light his tangled clothes upon the floor. Each night he added to the pattern of his fancies until drowsiness closed down upon some vivid scene with an oblivious embrace. For a while these reveries provided an outlet for his imagination; they were a satisfactory hint of the unreality of reality, a promise that the rock of the world was founded securely on a fairy's wing. (See p. 96.)

Gatz lived in and for his ideals, the absolutes that beckoned him forward toward "his future glory" (see p. 96). Once these ideals took definite form, they initially prove base and juvenile. They are constructed in the soul of a teenager on the fixtures of Dan Cody and his yacht, and these ideals remain immutably with Gatsby to the end. The yacht is a metonym, a stand-in for Cody's immeasurable wealth, and Gatsby is ravished by it: "To young Gatz, resting on his oars and looking up at the railed deck, the yacht represented all the beauty and glamour in the world" (see p. 97). The man behind the yacht, Gatsby's mentor whom he refers to as his "best friend" (see p. 90), is a hedonist who cruises the world in search of decadent indulgence. Nick describes Cody as "a gray, florid man

[9] "Etiology" is a term for discovering and describing the origin or causes of something (in its medical connotations the source of something pathological, like a disease or disorder).

with a hard, empty face—the pioneer debauchee, who during one phase of American life brought back to the Eastern seaboard the savage violence of the frontier brothel and saloon" (see pp. 97–98). Cody and his yacht coincide with the birth of Jay Gatsby—the man and the boat are part and parcel of the ideal to which Gatsby remained devoted:

> The truth was that Jay Gatsby of West Egg, Long Island, sprang from his Platonic conception of himself. He was a son of God—a phrase which, if it means anything, means just that—and he must be about His Father's business, the service of a vast, vulgar, and meretricious beauty. So he invented just the sort of Jay Gatsby that a seventeen-year-old boy would be likely to invent, and to this conception he was faithful to the end. (See p. 95.)

It is difficult to determine whether Daisy is an elevation, an ennobling of the "vast, vulgar, and meretricious beauty" to which Gatsby was devoted, or simply a crystallization of it. What is clear is that Daisy became the particularized site, the "incarnation" (see p. 107), of Gatsby's every desire. *The Great Gatsby* is populated by symbols—many derived from Gatsby's mythopoetic imagination which revolves around Daisy.[10] Gatsby's house, his car, his clothes, his parties—each serves the symbolic function of projecting Gatsby into Daisy's idealized sphere. The purest symbol Gatsby creates, in the romantic sense, is the green light at the end of Daisy's dock. It is the epitome of romantic symbol-making: its significance is absolute but purely private, and it shines only for Gatsby's own hugely vital interior life. Nick's initial perception of Gatsby, even before he ever speaks to him, is that of a solitary man gazing across the bay at night, adoring the symbol that points toward his highest ideal

[10] "Mythopoesis" is a term signifying the making of a myth (e.g., Gatsby's fertile imagination is mythopoetic insofar as through it he generates a mythic universe and narrative in which he forges and creates his persona). I here use the term symbol in its traditional literary sense: a symbol is a real object that is not only itself in the narrative (e.g., a car, a light, or a house) but also something that signifies a higher, transcendent reality. Fitzgerald is masterful in his use of symbols.

(the green light): "Content to be alone ... [Gatsby] stretched out his arms toward the dark water in a curious way, and ... I could have sworn he was trembling" (see pp. 21–22).

It is an arguable point whether a truly romantic consciousness is doomed to disappointment, tragedy, and catastrophe, but both literature and life make a strong case for it. *The Great Gatsby* illustrates the undoing and unsustainability of Jay Gatsby's ideals. Fitzgerald is a meticulous craftsman—he places the beginning of the end of Gatsby in the middle of the novel (chapter 5). Daisy and Gatsby reunite, and he recovers her affection. In classic romantic fashion, Gatsby's obtaining of Daisy's heart, after years of pursuing her as an ideal, is a crisis. Fitzgerald infuses this moment of victory with an aura of futility and disappointment. His elation in finding she still loves him immediately diffuses, and Gatsby finds himself disoriented:

> After his embarrassment and his unreasoning joy he was consumed with wonder at her presence. He had been full of the idea so long, dreamed it right through to the end, waited with his teeth set, so to speak, at an inconceivable pitch of intensity. Now, in the reaction, he was running down like an overwound clock. (See p. 108.)

Like all romantics, Gatsby is ill-prepared for the reality of Daisy; he was too long accustomed to her, and perhaps even preferred her, as an idea. His crisis is so acute it destroys Gatsby's most cherished symbol: the green light. With melancholy bordering on pain, Gatsby tells Daisy: "You always have a green light that burns all night at the end of your dock" (see p. 89). Nick interprets and intuits the psychic dilemma behind this seemingly innocuous observation:

> Possibly it had occurred to [Gatsby] that the colossal significance of that light had now vanished forever. Compared to the great distance that had separated him from Daisy it had seemed very near to her, almost touching her. It had seemed as close as a star to the moon. Now it was again a green light

on a dock. His count of enchanted objects had diminished by one. (See pp. 89–90.)

Nick develops this diagnostic insight in his reflection, near the end of chapter 5, upon the tragic effect of Gatsby's regaining Daisy's love:

> As I went over to say good-by I saw that the expression of bewilderment had come back into Gatsby's face, as though a faint doubt had occurred to him as to the quality of his present happiness. Almost five years! There must have been moments even that afternoon when Daisy tumbled short of his dreams—not through her own fault, but because of the colossal vitality of his illusion. It had gone beyond her, beyond everything. He had thrown himself into it with a creative passion, adding to it all the time, decking it out with every bright feather that drifted his way. No amount of fire or freshness can challenge what a man will store up in his ghostly heart. (See p. 92.)

The degree to which Gatsby's acquiring of Daisy is incompatible with his ideal of her is most apparent in Gatsby's perverse insistence that the past can be altered. Chapter 6 reveals a painful reality to Gatsby: Daisy does not enjoy his party because she is, by disposition and breeding, utterly separate from him. Despite her love for Gatsby, Daisy finds his party, his whole social milieu, distasteful, which he cannot fathom because in their youthful past they seemed so perfect for each other. Nick wisely attempts to counsel Gatsby to temper his expectations:

> "I wouldn't ask too much of her," I ventured. "You can't repeat the past."
>
> "Can't repeat the past?" he cried incredulously. "Why of course you can!" (See p. 106.)

Gatsby insists time is malleable—the idealized past can be recaptured and restored; it can be evoked to shed light and life. The romantic not only believes in a perfect time in the past but that such moments can be magically recaptured to transform the present. Gatsby's "colossal" (see p. 92) dreams are so powerful he believes they can even erase past realities that fail to harmonize with them. In chapter 7, at the Plaza Hotel, Gatsby insists Daisy tell Tom she never loved him: "Just tell him the truth—that you never loved him—and it's all wiped out forever" (see p. 126). While Daisy tries, she cannot bring herself to speak with such inauthenticity. Daisy mirrors Nick's own language in her response to his impossible demands: "'Oh, you want too much!' she cried to Gatsby. 'I love you now—isn't that enough? I can't help what's past.' She began to sob helplessly. 'I did love him once—but I loved you too'" (see p. 127). Shortly after this abortive attempt to rewrite the past, Gatsby loses Daisy permanently.

The Great Gatsby is a novel explicitly paralleling Nick Carraway to Jay Gatsby, and it is well to remember this paralleling is Nick's own doing (as he is both first-person narrator and author of this memoir). Nick's recounting of Gatsby's life is neither disinterested nor objective; thus, one might question what draws Nick to Gatsby. Nick has a deep, vital romanticism, but unlike Gatsby's, it is tempered by compromise with life's sterner realities.

Nick's romanticism is displayed in some of the novel's most lyrical passages. Nick, like Gatsby, has a "heightened sensitivity to the promises of life", a "romantic readiness" (see p. 4) of his own. For Nick this sensitivity is frequently associated with New York City. In chapter 2, as Nick describes the cramped, stifling party in Tom and Myrtle's apartment, he describes his longing to escape into the city:

> I wanted to get out and walk eastward toward the Park through the soft twilight, but each time I tried to go I became entangled in some wild, strident argument which pulled me back, as if with ropes, into my chair. Yet high over the city our line of yellow windows must have contributed their share of human secrecy to the casual watcher in the darkening streets, and I was him too, looking up and wondering. I was within and without,

> simultaneously enchanted and repelled by the inexhaustible variety of life. (See p. 35.)

In Nick's romantic imagination, the city is a wonderful and mysterious place. New York represents the "inexhaustible variety of life", tantalizingly concealed behind countless rows of yellow windows, each full of promise to Nick's imagination. Near the end of chapter 3, Nick provides a romantic meditation upon the allure of New York, and how it fuels his interior life:

> I began to like New York, the racy, adventurous feel of it at night, and the satisfaction that the constant flicker of men and women and machines gives to the restless eye. I liked to walk up Fifth Avenue and pick out romantic women from the crowd and imagine that in a few minutes I was going to enter into their lives, and no one would ever know or disapprove. Sometimes, in my mind, I followed them to their apartments on the corners of hidden streets, and they turned and smiled back at me before they faded through a door into warm darkness. At the enchanted metropolitan twilight I felt a haunting loneliness sometimes, and felt it in others—poor young clerks who loitered in front of windows waiting until it was time for a solitary restaurant dinner—young clerks in the dusk, wasting the most poignant moments of night and life.
>
> Again at eight o'clock, when the dark lanes of the Forties were five deep with throbbing taxicabs, bound for the theatre district, I felt a sinking in my heart. Forms leaned together in the taxis as they waited, and voices sang, and there was laughter from unheard jokes, and lighted cigarettes outlined unintelligible gestures inside. Imagining that I, too, was hurrying toward gayety and sharing their intimate excitement, I wished them well. (See p. 55.)

New York for Nick is scarcely less powerful than Daisy was to Gatsby. The city promises excitement, romance, and fulfillment, all just out of reach for Nick, always beckoning him forward. This ideal of New York leaves Nick with a sense of melancholy akin to Gatsby's aloof vigils over his parties or midnight meditations upon Daisy's green light. In chapter 4,

Nick describes New York from the perspective of crossing the Queensboro Bridge: "The city seen from the Queensboro Bridge is always the city seen for the first time, in its first wild promise of all the mystery and the beauty in the world.... 'Anything can happen now that we've slid over this bridge,' I thought; 'anything at all ...'" (see pp. 65–66). New York is an absolute, an ideal of exhilarating, pure promise for Nick.

Nick has an uncanny ability to narrate not only the events of Gatsby's life but also Gatsby's interior, psychic journey. Nick intuitively understands the romantic consciousness and how it operates and is uniquely qualified to detail Gatsby's journey from obscurity, to falling under the spell of Dan Cody and his wealth, to falling in love with Daisy. For example, from a narrative point of view, consider this exquisite passage from chapter 8, wherein Nick recounts Gatsby's growing obsession with Daisy and all she represented:

> He went to her house, at first with other officers from Camp Taylor, then alone. It amazed him—he had never been in such a beautiful house before. But what gave it an air of breathless intensity was that Daisy lived there—it was as casual a thing to her as his tent out at camp was to him. There was a ripe mystery about it, a hint of bedrooms up-stairs more beautiful and cool than other bedrooms, of gay and radiant activities taking place through its corridors, and of romances that were not musty and laid away already in lavender but fresh and breathing and redolent of this year's shining motor-cars and of dances whose flowers were scarcely withered....
>
> He found that he had committed himself to the following of a grail. He knew that Daisy was extraordinary, but he didn't realize just how extraordinary a "nice" girl could be. She vanished into her rich house, into her rich, full life, leaving Gatsby—nothing. He felt married to her, that was all. (See pp. 141–42.)

It is unlikely Jay Gatsby used phrases like "an air of breathless intensity" or "breathing and redolent of this year's shining motor-cars" to describe his experiences to Nick. Nick is a fellow romantic, whose imagination and sympathies are perfectly in tune with Gatsby's. Nick applies his literary and stylistic mastery to articulate the cadences and evolutions of Gatsby's romantic desires.

Yet wide though the comparison is between Gatsby and Nick, there is a considerable contrast between them. Nick Carraway has learned to compromise and negotiate with a world that is stratified, immovable, and unsentimental. Gatsby cannot accept a world where a green light is just a green light, or Daisy is a frail woman with divided loyalties. Nick, in chapter 8, reflects upon Gatsby's horror at finding a world not populated by ideals, symbols, and dreams, but of mere materiality:

> He must have looked up at an unfamiliar sky through frightening leaves and shivered as he found what a grotesque thing a rose is and how raw the sunlight was upon the scarcely created grass. A new world, material without being real, where poor ghosts, breathing dreams like air, drifted fortuitously about. (See p. 153.)

This passage details how Nick imagined Gatsby, nursing his shattered dreams, might have felt before George Wilson appeared and murdered him. It is the terrifying prospect of losing one's dreams and living in the world as it is, and not through the lens of one's desires. Nick is accustomed to living in such a world. As he introduces himself in chapter 1, he has no pretense about his uniqueness as an individual or as a member of his family. In unsentimental terms, he tells of his "grandfather's brother, who came here in fifty-one, sent a substitute to the Civil War, and started the wholesale hardware business that my father carries on today" (see pp. 4–5). No monied or storied aristocrats of ancient prestige, the Carraways rose to wealth and prominence in the old American way of rising up from the proletariat and experiencing good fortune in the burgeoning free market. Though Nick has attended an elite preparatory school in the East, then Yale, and though his family is now of considerable means, Nick, unlike Gatsby, accepts the realities of his past as they are.

Nick and Gatsby also differ regarding the women in their lives, and the significance attached to these women. Daisy is a pure ideal to Gatsby, who cannot easily abide reduction to human terms. Nick, on the other hand, laments that he has no such ideal; rather, he has Jordan Baker. In a passage from the end of chapter 4, Nick observes:

> Unlike Gatsby and Tom Buchanan, I had no girl whose disembodied face floated along the dark cornices and blinding signs, and so I drew up the girl beside me, tightening my arms. Her wan, scornful mouth smiled, and so I drew her up again closer, this time to my face. (See p. 77.)

Nick has a variety of feminine interests mentioned in the novel, though Jordan is primary during his time in the East. Nick seems incapable of idealizing the feminine as Gatsby does; he is attuned to women as they are, not as he might imagine them. Nick consistently describes Jordan in non-romanticized language: she is dishonest, snobbish, shamelessly prone to gossip and eavesdropping, and competitive to the point of cheating. He even describes her as a "clean, hard, limited person, who dealt in universal skepticism" (see p. 76), and a woman "too wise ever to carry well-forgotten dreams from age to age" (see p. 130). Nick pursues a woman who is hardly ideal, or even a candidate for being an ideal; he desires her for her imperfection, her flaws. He finds comfort in a woman who is what she is, and not what he might dream her to be.

Perhaps the greatest difference between Nick and Gatsby lies in Nick's sense of the passage of time and his own mortality. Gatsby pathetically clings to his dream of possessing Daisy long after it eludes his grasp. As tensions boil between Gatsby, Daisy, and Tom at the Plaza Hotel, Nick comes to the startling realization that it is his birthday. This occasions a sober reflection upon the passage of time:

> I was thirty. Before me stretched the portentous, menacing road of a new decade.... Thirty—the promise of a decade of loneliness, a thinning list of single men to know, a thinning brief-case of enthusiasm, thinning hair. (See p. 130.)

This somber reflection upon lost youth—lost ideals, possibilities, potential—becomes linked in Nick's mind to mortality. As he drives away from the calamities surrounding Gatsby, Daisy, and Tom, Nick the "birthday boy", accompanied by Jordan, meditates upon the finality of death: "So we drove on toward death through the cooling twilight" (see p. 131). Nick lives without illusion—people age; they change; their dreams are not always realized; and time requires a rendezvous with death.

Nick, though romantic in temperament, has reconciled himself to a world that woefully falls below his ideals. Nick realizes that the East is not all he thought it would be, and he abandons its allure. He deliberately avoids making any woman his pure ideal and persists into mid-life without a "disembodied face" (see p. 77) to call his own. He returns to his Midwest—the reality of his family and his socio-economic place in his home region. He is also painfully aware that he is aging, lonely, and still searching for a broader purpose for his life. Perhaps the greatest contrast between Nick and Gatsby, as two souls with deeply romantic tendencies, is that Nick survives. His ideals, significant as they are to him, do not destroy him. Nick consents to the non-romantic compromise with time, human imperfection, and ultimately mortality.

CONTRIBUTORS

James Como is professor emeritus of rhetoric and public communication at York College of the City University of New York. He writes cultural and literary journalism as well as short stories and poetry, and he enjoys travel with Alexandra, his wife of fifty-six years. He has written on such figures as Borges, Thornton Wilder, de las Casas, and Sigrid Undset, as well as on Peru, the Middle Ages, Chaucer, and Shakespeare. A founding member (1969) of the New York C. S. Lewis Society, his recent books are *C. S. Lewis: A Very Short Introduction* (Oxford University Press, 2019) and *Mystical Perelandra: My Lifelong Reading of C. S. Lewis and His Favorite Book* (Winged Lion Press, 2022).

Robert C. Evans is I. B. Young Professor of English (emeritus) at Auburn University at Montgomery (AUM). He earned his Ph.D. from Princeton University in 1984. In 1982, he began teaching at AUM, where he was named Distinguished Research Professor, Distinguished Teaching Professor, and University Alumni Professor. External awards included fellowships from the American Council of Learned Societies, the American Philosophical Society, the National Endowment for the Humanities, the UCLA Center for Medieval and Renaissance Studies, and the Folger, Huntington, and Newberry Libraries. He is the author or editor of roughly ninety books and of more than six hundred essays, online and in print.

Stephen Mirarchi is associate professor and chair of the English Department at Benedictine College in Atchison, Kansas. He received his Ph.D. in English and American Literature from Brandeis University. He is the editor of five annotated volumes of the works of Myles Connolly, including *Mr. Blue*. He has also published scholarly articles on Raymond Carver, Louise Glück, Robert Pinsky, Edgar Allan Poe, and William Gilmore Simms, as well as a host of popular articles on Catholicism and literature. Most recently he authored the entry for Robert Pinsky in the *Oxford Bibliographies in American Literature*.

Joseph Pearce is the acclaimed author of numerous literary studies, including *Literary Converts*, *The Quest for Shakespeare*, and *Shakespeare on Love*, as well as popular biographies of Oscar Wilde, J. R. R. Tolkien, C. S. Lewis, G. K. Chesterton, and Aleksandr Solzhenitsyn. He is the general editor of the Ignatius Critical Editions series.

Aaron Urbanczyk is a professor of English at Franciscan University of Steubenville. His teaching and research interests include American literature, literary theory and criticism, Dante, Shakespeare, and ancient Greek literature. His essays and reviews have appeared in *Religion & the Arts*, the *St. Austin Review*, *Modern Age*, *Humanitas*, *Essays in Arts & Sciences*, *Papers on Language & Literature*, the *Journal for Cultural & Religious Theory*, *Perspectives in Religious Studies*, *The Fellowship of Catholic Scholars Quarterly*, and the Ignatius Critical Editions of *Frankenstein*, *The Scarlet Letter*, and *Adventures of Huckleberry Finn*.